# The
# SABLE
# CLOAK

*Also by Gail Milissa Grant*

NONFICTION

*At the Elbows of my Elders: One Family's Journey Toward Civil Rights*

# The
# SABLE
# CLOAK

## GAIL MILISSA GRANT

GRAND
CENTRAL

New York   Boston

Copyright © 2025 by The Grant Living Trust

Cover design by Shreya Gupta
Cover images: dress © Richard Jenkins; face from Stocksy; background by Alamy; border by Shutterstock
Cover copyright © 2025 by Hachette Book Group, Inc.

Grand Central Publishing
Hachette Book Group
1290 Avenue of the Americas, New York, NY 10104
grandcentralpublishing.com
@grandcentralpub

First Edition: February 2025

Grand Central Publishing is a division of Hachette Book Group, Inc. The Grand Central Publishing name and logo is a registered trademark of Hachette Book Group, Inc.

The publisher is not responsible for websites (or their content) that are not owned by the publisher.

The Hachette Speakers Bureau provides a wide range of authors for speaking events. To find out more, go to hachettespeakersbureau.com or email HachetteSpeakers@hbgusa.com.

Grand Central Publishing books may be purchased in bulk for business, educational, or promotional use. For information, please contact your local bookseller or the Hachette Book Group Special Markets Department at special.markets@hbgusa.com.

Print book interior design by Taylor Navis

Library of Congress Cataloging-in-Publication Data

Names: Grant, Gail Milissa.
Title: The sable cloak / Gail Milissa Grant.
Description: First edition. | New York : GCP, 2025.
Identifiers: LCCN 2024038845 | ISBN 9781538742006 (hardback) |
    ISBN 9781538742020 (ebook)
Subjects: LCSH: African Americans—Missouri—Saint Louis—Fiction. |
    African American families—Missouri—Saint Louis—Fiction. | Saint Louis (Mo.)
    —Race relations—History—20th century—Fiction. | LCGFT: Historical fiction. | Novels.
Classification: LCC PS3607.R36289 S23 2025 | DDC 813/.6—dc23/eng/20240830
LC record available at https://lccn.loc.gov/2024038845

ISBN: 9781538742006 (hardcover), 9781538742020 (ebook)

Printed in the United States of America

LSC

Printing 1, 2024

*For my brother, David*

*Prologue*

# THE GHOUL ARRIVES

*Greenston, South Carolina, 1934*

B ig Will Anderson rarely attended funeral services, preferring to stay outside in the cemetery with the gravediggers. Towering over six and a half feet, with a muscle-bound frame and a chest as large and taut as a quarter cask, he could have dug the hole himself with a half dozen heaves of dirt. But he left that chore to the other men, and instead scooped up handfuls of the South Carolina, late-summer soil and dropped them next to where the preacher would stand. The mica-laden dirt sparkled in his palms. *Just don't seem right that ya feel so good and ya look so pretty today.*

Just before noon, the funeral cortege emerged from the church and made its way to the adjacent boneyard. Big Will fixed his gaze on Mrs. Thornton who, supported on each side by her brother and sister, walked behind the small casket that contained her son's corpse. When it started to drizzle, she lifted her chin, letting the falling droplets mingle with her tears, then pulled her veil down and cast her eyes at the ground.

1

The mourners surrounded her and exclaimed. By the time the worshippers assembled at the gravesite for the final blessing, the sun had returned. Big Will retreated to the back and interlaced his oversize fingers in prayer. After the reverend spoke his last words, Big Will watched members of the congregation stoop, one by one, pick up bits of the earth he had placed there, and toss them on top of the coffin to pay their final respects.

John, Big Will's father, approached him as soon as all had finished the ritual.

"C'mon, now. Get yo'self somethin' to eat with the others."

"My innards doin' flip-flops right now, Pa. Don't feel like goin' to the repast."

"Since when ain't ya had a hunger, Son?"

Big Will hung his head so far down that it reached the top of his father's.

"Ya know why," he whispered in his ear. "I don't think I can do this."

John took his son by the shoulders and made him stand up tall.

"Ya gotta. All of Sunset's been in the covenant since Samuel Miller's daddy started this thing. You done turned eighteen, so it's yo' time now."

Big Will's broad shoulders caved in around him and his shoes seemed to sink into the soil.

"I gotta take me a walk."

"Go on. But get back here in time. Samuel and the others'll be waitin' for ya when the sun sets."

"Yessuh."

Big Will turned on his heel and trudged to the nearest bald cypress grove. Those trees were just about the only living things that surpassed him in height, strength, and weight, and he would seek them out whenever he needed solace and protection. He found the largest one and hugged its trunk for longer than usual. He then turned around, leaned his massive back against it, and tilted his face upward, savoring the sunshine as it danced over his eyelids and spread across his face.

"Ah," he sighed and breathed in and out... slow, deep breaths, "won't ya just let me bury myself inside ya?" he pleaded. His tears fell quietly at first but then grew into a weeping and wailing so deafening that the woods grew still, as if all its critters had stopped moving in deference to him. The breezes even died down and the leaves ceased their fluttering.

When he'd wrung the last tear from his body, Big Will gathered his wits about him and pondered his fate. He had become the newest member of the vigilante group that patrolled Sunset when he turned eighteen last month. The whole community knew whenever the composition of the posse changed: when a new man was inducted, the longest serving one was released from duty. Always twelve in number they were, plus Samuel as their self-appointed sheriff. They were held in high regard since they kept the peace in Sunset. If some small-time thug acted up, they would set him straight with a good licking. Repeated stealing would get a hand broken, and rape, attempted or otherwise, got a thorough beating below the belt. Big Will shuddered when he thought of how they dealt with murder.

Women would smile at members of the posse with admiration, and the men would tip their hats or step aside to let them pass unencumbered. Big Will cared nothing for the respect or honor that came with this service because of the violence it required. Unless a man was too small or sickly, he had to serve, and Big Will couldn't lay claim to either one or the other.

He finally headed back to the church house and ducked behind the building, spying his father with Samuel and two members of his posse assembled along one side of the open grave. The gravediggers, poised to fill the hole, stood motionless opposite them. *Maybe they gonna just let that boy rest*, he thought.

"We'll take care of this," Samuel declared. "Y'all skedaddle. But leave yo' shovels." Once the gravediggers disappeared into the falling night, Samuel ordered his men to haul up the coffin.

Big Will had been there the evening that Maurice Jones, all liquored up and driving like the devil, swerved onto the sidewalk and took the life of Timmie Thornton. He, Mrs. Thornton, and Timmie had been sauntering to Wednesday evening church service. On such a steamy night, they didn't care if they were late. *If only I'd stopped that boy from walkin' next to the road but the chile wouldn't pay me no mind. Wanted to be a gentleman and protect his mama just like his daddy used to.*

One of the men opened the coffin and lifted the remains. The group examined the corpse.

"They fixed him up real nice over at Ol' Man Jeter's parlor," John said.

"Where's yo' son?" Samuel asked.

Big Will stepped forward. "I'm here, suh."

"Y'all take Timmie to the car," John said. "Big Will'll put the coffin back and we'll fill this hole up straight away. Join ya at yo' place in no time."

"Awright but don't dawdle," Samuel instructed them. "Mrs. Thornton already gave us the go-ahead. Said his spirit's gone, so she don't care what we do with the rest of him. We all want this over and done with."

Two of Samuel's men carried the body to the truck and then all three of them left.

Big Will slid into the hollow, dragged the empty coffin down, and then climbed out.

"Six years a long time, Papa."

"That's the time ya gotta serve. They took it from the Good Book. Six stands for man's weakness and the power of Satan. Every man's been pinched by both."

"But what if I gotta take him into the woods my first time pullin' the straw?"

"Ya won't have to pull the next time."

"But the time after that?"

John nodded.

They finished packing the dirt down and John took his son by the arm and steered him toward Samuel's house.

When the shuttered house was within sight, John dropped his hand and stood still. "Gotta leave ya here, Son."

"Can't ya wait outside for me? Find out if I gotta…"

"Ya know the rules. I ain't part of this now. Can't know anything more'n I already do." John hugged his son and meandered off.

Big Will walked to the front door and reached for the knob, but his sweaty hand slid off before he could turn it. He reached for it again and the door seemed to fling itself wide open.

"C'mon in," Samuel said. Big Will crossed the threshold. He looked around the room at the other men and they stared back at him. In their midst sat Maurice in his underwear, gagged and tied to a rocking chair. Timmie's body lay on the sofa girdled in white sheets with only his head visible, like an immense papoose.

Every time Maurice whimpered, one of Samuel's men would pound his foot on the rocker so hard the chair almost toppled forward.

"Ya keep moanin' and I'll start punchin' ya agin," Samuel told him. "I warned ya, ya bastard. Thought I smacked some sense into ya the last time ya went drivin' drunk around Sunset. Seems like ya didn't and now ya gonna pay!"

Big Will watched as Samuel broke off twelve straws from a broom, wishing he could vanish like smoke. Samuel then halved one of them and buried it with the rest. Big Will's hands started to tremble, so he clasped them behind his back. As the newest member, Big Will would pick last. He watched as each man drew a straw from Samuel's fist. When the eleventh man pulled the final long straw, Big Will's body began to shake. Samuel opened his palm and let the short one fall to the ground.

"Now, Big Will, take ahold of yo'self." Samuel surveyed the room to make sure all were listening, then turned back to Big Will. "My daddy got so doggone tired of how the white police did nothin' when one of our own did wrong here in Sunset that he took it upon hisself to deal with no 'counts like Maurice. He set this thing up and based it on what he heard *his* daddy say about how murder was handled where he came from in Africa. We're all in it now, no turnin' back."

"Yessuh, I understand."

"And the rest of ya?" Samuel glanced around the room at each man, and they all signaled their agreement.

"Well, then, get to work."

Big Will watched them begin their respective jobs: two untied

Maurice; another two grabbed him under his armpits and made him stand as he peed on himself; two more dragged a bin of sheets, ropes, and twine from a corner of the room; and two picked up the embalmed boy and flattened his remains against Maurice—face-to-face. Maurice jerked his head away, but the men secured the two heads to one another with the sheets and cord. Timmie's feet dangled above the ground so they laid Maurice on the floor with the boy strapped on top of him and tightened them together. Then they stuck a wad of cloth as big as a softball into Maurice's mouth.

"This one mug ya ain't gonna never forget while ya burnin' in hell," Samuel said.

The three remaining men placed the bundle in the back of Samuel's truck and threw a horse blanket over it. Samuel tossed the keys to Will.

When Big Will started the engine, Samuel reached through the open window and placed a hand on his shoulder.

"Only ya gonna know where ya dropped him. And each day that passes? Well, this burden ya carryin' tonight'll get lighter. This one's got no kin and fewer friends. Nobody cares if he lives or dies. And nobody else in town'll know which one of us took that piece of trash into the woods. We keep this under our hats."

Big Will gritted his teeth, gripped the wheel, and took off. He drove for miles along a rarely traveled road, tolerating Maurice's muffled blubbering in the back. He took out his handkerchief and wiped the sweat from his face. The bastard deserved this, he reminded himself, but why did he have to be the one? All he wanted was to roam the rolling hills of South Carolina, sniff the red clay, and fade into the thickets of bald cypress trees.

Before long, the road forked with the right prong leading to an unpaved lane just wide enough to accommodate Samuel's truck. He inched forward into the woods and the silence made Maurice's crying more pronounced. This time he wiped away the pooling tears in his eyes with the back of one hand.

When he felt sure he was deep enough in the woods so no one could see him, Big Will stopped the truck, and dragged the murderer and Timmie into the darkness until a red wolf howled in the distance. *This must be the place.* He dropped the end of the bundle. The sound of its fall and Maurice's harrowing groans bounced off the surrounding trees and boomeranged against Big Will's body. He stood there, stunned for a moment, picturing what the wild animals that prowled the backwoods would do to Maurice. He then ran back to the truck, covering his ears to block out Maurice's weeping.

Big Will plopped himself behind the wheel and cursed Samuel, his daddy, and any man who took part in this pact. *How could these God-fearing men do such things and make others do them as well?* The bundle may have been behind him, but Big Will quivered when he thought of what lay ahead. How could he go to church and hold his head up when the preacher exhorted the congregation to praise the Lord to the heights? How could he hold hands with the pretty little lady he yearned to meet one day and profess his forever love to?

His stomach began to curdle and his hands grew clammy, so he floored the gas pedal, feeling as though the earth might swallow him alive if he didn't speed away. *I just gotta get home. I just gotta get away from what I did.* Before he realized it, he had parked the truck at Samuel's and had left the key under the seat. He hurried to his house, tiptoed to his room, and collapsed onto his bed.

But sleep provided no solace. As he dreamed of being nestled in the groove of a cypress's bundled trunk, a voice screamed out. *KILLER! KILLER! KILLER!* He jerked his head up and swung it every which way in search of the screeching yell until he saw a ghostlike figure above him. It descended on him like a gossamer cloak. *KILLER! KILLER! KILLER!*, it ranted. He tried to rip it to shreds, but each time he reached for it, the translucent cloth evaporated in his hands. It then shrieked, punched his head with the force of a boxer, and disappeared. Big Will fell backward and slept no more that night. The next morning, he snuck away on an empty stomach without his father or two younger sisters knowing. He ambled toward downtown Sunset, wanting to feel grounded in this community and also hoping to fly away at the same time.

"Whoa there, Big Will. Looks like ya just seen a ghost," a shopkeeper shouted out as he prepared to open his shop.

Big Will pulled himself up short like a horse being reined in and studied his reflection in the storefront window. His deep reddish-brown complexion had lightened by two shades. He stuffed his hands in his pockets and decided to return home. Then he felt a tug on his shirttail, pivoted, and saw the sardonic phantom.

For the next two weeks, the ghost was an almost constant companion. During the day it trailed him, hammering him with obscenities. At night, it whispered in his ear, just loudly enough to disturb his sleep. All Big Will's praying and church-going and testifying couldn't make it go away. His stomach tolerated little food, and he grew gaunt and became exhausted. Never one for much talk, he remained silent most of the day. The cajoling from his two sisters had no impact. His father, however, let him be.

One muggy morning, just before the temperatures bowed to autumn's clemency, John insisted that Big Will accompany him to the family's skimpy plot of land where they eked out a living, planting and picking greens and tubers.

"First harvest comin' up soon. Lotta work in front of us," John said. They started to walk among the rows of greens and summer squash and potatoes.

"Papa, I dunno if I can."

"What? Ya don't wanna pick crops? It always makes ya so happy. Thought this'd bring ya back to us."

Big Will stopped.

"Papa, I gotta tell ya somethin'." He gulped. "I'm haunted."

"What ya mean, Son?"

Big Will explained.

"How long it's been on yo' tail?"

"Ever since that night, ya know, when—" Big Will gulped again. "Papa, I was the one. I picked the short stick...or it picked me."

"Sorry ya had to." John sighed and scratched his head. "Damn near a fortnight ago. What color is it?"

"Ain't got none. More filmy like."

"Does it keep ya from movin'?"

"No, just wears me down, all day, all night."

"At least the haint ain't ridin' ya. They paralyze ya. But some ghoul's got into yo' mind and it's messin' with ya, Son."

"But I see him, Papa, and hear him, and feel his breath sometimes," Big Will insisted.

"Ya can beat him, Son, but ya gotta leave town. Change the air around ya."

"But, Papa, where would I go?"

"We gonna let yo' cousin in the big house figure this one out."

"Ya think Nathan'll help me?" Big Will asked.

"Yo' mama, God rest her soul, was Nathan's aunt and blood's thicker than any stack of cash the Franklins got. They felt so bad when yo' mama died. Reached out to give me a boost many times, but I wouldn't take nothing. Nathan'll help us all right. Go on over there first thing after lunch tomorrow. Want ya to tell him yo'self. And ya can tell him all of it, ya hear?"

The next day Big Will polished his shoes and donned the suit he'd worn to his mother's funeral six years earlier.

"Where are ya, boy?" John called out.

Big Will left his cubbyhole of a bedroom and walked toward his father's voice. When John saw his son, he slapped both thighs.

"Sleeves and legs all short on ya, don't ya think?"

"I know, Papa, but..."

"Ya haven't put that on since..." John bit his lip. "Just get somethin' that fits." He attempted a smile.

Big Will changed into a pair of britches and a starched white shirt and set off toward the Franklin residence. It sat on the outskirts of Sunset, with acres of farmland surrounding it, and was grander than any house owned by colored people, and some whites, for that matter. Big Will and his family used to go there for eggnog at Christmas and he always felt like a bumpkin crossing the threshold, as he still did today. He took in the substantial front door before he raised the knocker and let it drop.

Clara, the housemaid, answered. "Why, Big Will! C'mon in here."

"Sorry I didn't let ya know I was comin'."

"What? Ya family. I'll go get Mr. Nathan." While he waited, Big Will noticed some specks of dirt on the top of his left shoe. He rubbed it on the back of his right pant leg until it shone again.

Everything in the reception hall looked the same as he remembered. The carpeted staircase rolled down from the second floor like an indigo sea, shimmering brass handrails containing it along the way. A colossal candelabra, outfitted with twelve white tapers, crowned the two-story foyer. Ten-foot-high pocket doors to his left and his right stood open, one revealing the parlor and the other the dining room.

Nathan came rushing from behind the stairway and hugged him.

"You're a sight, you are! What's kept you away from us?"

Big Will felt his face flush. "Cousin Nathan, y'all got so many nice things and we, well, we…" Big Will stepped off the massive plush throw rug.

"Don't talk such foolishness. Never could figure out why your daddy and mama stopped bringing you all here around Christmas. Guess they had their reasons. But you're always welcome. Now, tell me. How have you been? All grown-up."

Big Will paused and then blurted out, "I need somethin' from ya, Cousin."

Nathan guided him into the parlor and closed the doors. "Big Will, what is it? Have you put some girl in a family way? You know, not facing up to a situation…"

"Naw, Cousin Nathan, nothin' like that."

"Well, let's sit down and you'll tell me all about it."

They sat on facing settees. Big Will described how he had carried Timmie and Maurice into the woods and left them there to rot, and how, once at home that night, a transparent beast leapt from nowhere and had trailed him ever since. When he ended his story, Big Will turned away from his cousin's gaze.

"Look at me, boy. No shame here. Maybe I should be the one feeling guilty. Money got me out of having to pick a stick. Before Daddy passed, he made sure of that. Paid for some of the funerals. Or maybe that's why Samuel's got that fancy truck. I don't know."

"Papa thinks I need to get outta town. Says ya might find me a way."

Nathan stood, pulled a bottle of bourbon from the bar shelf, and poured himself a shot glass.

"You want a taste?" Nathan asked. Big Will shook his head. Nathan downed the liquor and sat next to his cousin. "I can help you all right, but I want you with family," Nathan started.

"Mama would like that."

"How long has she been gone?"

"Six years ago. Feels like yesterday."

Nathan patted Big Will's back and looked upward for a moment before he spoke.

"Mama and Papa both passed about a dozen years ago, but it still hurts like a fresh wound."

Big Will watched how his cousin's eyes started to mist over. Nathan refilled his glass and gulped it down as quickly as the first.

"Your daddy's a good man. Been raising you and your sisters all alone and doing a fine job of it."

Big Will wrinkled his brow. "Ya know 'bout us?"

"We keep tabs on all our kin. I've tried to help out your Pa whenever there was an early freeze or the crops came out spare. But he's a proud man and…"

"He sent me to ya."

"You see there? Only asking for our help when he can't do it himself. That's your Pa, all right. And I think I've got the answer." He shook his finger at Big Will. "My sister Sarah!"

"Ya really think she'll take me in?"

"Sarah's always had a soft spot for you, and her husband will do whatever she tells him." Nathan laughed.

"I heard she married herself some big-time undertaker up in St. Louis and…"

"Jordan's more than just that. They call him the Negro Mayor of St. Louis." Nathan walked over to the gleaming mahogany rolltop desk in the far corner of the room. He opened it, pulled out a pen and paper, and returned to Big Will.

"I'll send a telegram straightaway. We've been having telephone interruptions, but once they get this—"

"I won't be in the way, now will I?" Big Will interrupted.

"Don't talk such foolishness, Cousin. With all that house and the grounds they have, there's plenty of room, even for someone as big as you!"

Nathan sat down and began to write. "As I was saying, once this arrives, Jordan will find a way to get through to me, so I can explain."

"I can do whatever they need…the gardenin', drivin' the hearse, even housework. Just can't pull another straw."

"I understand. It's done." Nathan held up the paper and waved it in the air to help the ink dry faster. "I'll have Davis run this down to the telegraph office."

"There's one mo' thing."

"Tell me."

"Wanna leave straight away without Samuel and the others knowin'. Don't want anybody to think—"

"You're a coward?"

Big Will's chin dropped to his chest.

"This proves you're a man, Cousin. A kind, righteous, God-fearing man."

The following Monday, Big Will and his father walked down an unlit road at dusk. Big Will carried a suitcase and John had slung a weighty burlap sack over his back.

"Let's stop for a minute. I gotta give ya this now," John said.

He sat the bag down, opened it, and withdrew a small Mason jar, half full of water with seven silver dimes on the bottom.

"Keep this with ya from here on out. Wherever ya find yo'self. The water's thick with salt. And those seven dimes? Well, ya know seven is the holiest of numbers. This'll keep that ghost at bay. Don't let nobody touch it or try to wrest it from ya."

"Whatever ya say, Pa."

Big Will wanted no one to see him board a train in Greenston, so his father asked a friend, who lived outside Greenston and owned a wagon, to take his son to the next railroad stop. They walked in silence until John saw the man's house. He put down the sack again.

"Son, ya gonna be ridin' up front in this train. 'Bout the only time we get to do that. Jim Crow puts us in the back of the streetcar, the back of the bus, and backs us up against a wall any chance he can. But when it comes to trains, he carves out a special spot for us ahead of all the whites, right behind the coal pit, so we the ones who get coated in soot." He sniggered.

John stooped over, pulled out a lightweight blanket and a couple of towels, and handed them to Big Will.

"Use these to cover up. Keep as much of that filth off ya."

"Thanks, Pa. Ya thought of everythin'."

"I try, Son. We gotta take care of each other, take care of our own. If we don't, who's gonna?"

Big Will folded himself over and hugged his father.

"Go on, now. Mitch'll be ready for ya. I ain't good at good-byes, so I'll leave ya here."

John turned and walked away.

# PART ONE

# Chapter 1

# LITTLE SARAH DREAMS

*Greenston, South Carolina, 1911*

Little Sarah? Where in the devil are you?" Mattie called out as she searched for her younger sister in the Franklins' spacious parlor.

Sarah parted the brocade cloth that covered the wee teapoy where she hid, just enough for one of her eyes to peer out. She stifled a laugh as she watched Mattie scour the same obvious places: inside the maple wood trunk, behind the navy-blue drapes that hopscotched across one wall, and under the two matching settees. She waited until Mattie spread herself flat on the floor for a look under the low-slung cocktail table, then let out a squeal, burst forth from the deepest corner of the room, and ran toward her.

"Can I help you?" Sarah teased and offered her a hand.

Mattie jumped up and swatted at her with the kitchen towel she snatched from her apron pocket, but Sarah scooted away.

"You rascal, you. One day I'll beat you at your own game, Little Sarah."

Sarah turned toward her sister.

"Stop calling me that," Sarah demanded and put one fist on each hip.

"But you are a rascal. If the name fits…"

"No, not that. You know what I mean. I'm almost eight. I'm not little anymore."

"Mama is Big Sarah and you are Little Sarah and that's just the way it goes. We gotta know the difference between the two of you." She laughed.

"Well, I don't like it."

"But you are a little thing. About knee high to a grasshopper." Mattie giggled again as she reached to pinch her nose.

"No, I'm not," Sarah insisted and swung away again.

She hurried out of the parlor, crossed the grand foyer, and slammed the front door behind her. She sat on the top step of the expansive front porch and looked out over acre after acre of the Franklins' rich farmland. She squeezed her eyes shut to hold back the tears.

Her parents, Horace and Big Sarah, were tall and straight and towered over most of the colored in Greenston. Mattie, born four years before her, had shot up and already surpassed Anna, the first-born girl, in height. Yet Sarah remained petite for her age and her family never stopped mentioning her early delivery and how they had feared she wouldn't survive.

Her father had given his two older daughters their own teeny plots of land. She often watched them plunge their hands into the dirt, and lovingly drop seeds for collard and mustard greens. Whenever Sarah asked for some soil, her father would tell her:

*"Your delicate hands are better suited for needlepoint. Your brother*

*and sisters can learn how to feed us. You, my dear, can nourish us with beauty!"*

"Darlin'? What are you doing out here?"

Sarah looked up into her mother's soothing, doe-like eyes, and saw Davis, their driver, atop a buggy behind her. Clara, the housekeeper, smiled the little girl's way as she carried packages into the house.

"When did you get here, Mama?"

"Just now. You didn't notice me at all? Off daydreaming somewhere?"

"I don't know, Mama."

"I left you with Mattie. Has she been goading you again?"

Sarah said nothing as her mother lifted her chin.

"There's one way I know to turn the corners of your mouth up. Come with me." Big Sarah sat her daughter on the buggy's back seat and climbed up next to her.

"Davis, the emporium, please."

"Oh, Mama. Yes, let's go!" Sarah shouted and off they went to the family's store.

As they rode toward Sunset, the Negro part of Greenston, Sarah watched her mother acknowledge each Black passerby in some way: a bow of her head, a blown kiss, a wink, or a wave. Little Sarah copied each gesture. Her mother's demeanor changed, however, whenever a white person appeared, and instead she stared ahead or into her lap or leaned forward toward Davis to banter.

"Mama, why don't you say hello when you see white people?"

"My dear, all God's children are the same. But when some of them choose to act ugly, they should be ignored. That's all you need to know for now."

"You all treat me like I'm too young for everything." Sarah folded her arms in front of her chest.

Sarah unfolded her daughter's arms, took her hands, and looked into her eyes.

"Some white people think we aren't as good as they are. And when they treat us like nothing, they are actually showing us that they are the inferior ones. Always know that you are just as good as anyone, and be the best at whatever you choose to do. Never, never, settle for less. Understand?"

Little Sarah nodded. When they pulled up in front of a storefront with an outsized sign that read MADAME SARAH'S EMPORIUM, Sarah patted down her hair and pinafore before scurrying inside. She and her mother walked up and down each aisle of merchandise.

"Good morning, Mrs. White," Big Sarah said as she passed one customer.

"Good morning, Mrs. White," Little Sarah repeated.

When her mother stopped to adjust an out-of-place item, Sarah hunted for one to rearrange as well. When she stooped to inspect if the floors under the clothes racks had been properly dusted, Sarah did the same. They then stopped in the middle of the cavernous main room at the checkout counter where Mrs. Wilson controlled the cash box when Big Sarah was absent from the store.

While the two women talked, Sarah slipped off to the far wall where bolts of cloth slept on shelving, awaiting a seamstress to awaken them. She gravitated, as she always did, to the silks and velvets, fingering the ones she could reach. When she was sure there was no one in sight, she unwrapped the end of a striped eggshell-yellow-and-empire-blue fabric and rolled it around her torso.

"And where might you be going all dressed up?"

Sarah knew her mother's voice and the feel of her hand resting on her shoulder. She swiveled around.

"Oh, Mama. Don't be mad at me, please. I just wanted to know what it was like to be—"

"All grown-up? And off to a ball somewhere?"

"Oh yes, Mama. Yes!"

"You will, my dear. One day."

"But not the ones here. Bigger ones."

"My darlin', you have such dreams. I'll pray that they come your way. But first, let's rearrange this." Big Sarah smoothed out the cloth and rewound it.

"Mama? Can I go outside now, *please*?"

"If you hadn't drifted off to the king's formal dance"—she laughed—"you'd have been there already. Of course, my dear. Run along."

Sarah headed out the back door toward the small shed attached to the emporium and, once inside, surveyed the numerous emptied boxes and crates. She went from one to the next, reading the return labels aloud. *Atlanta, New Orleans, New York City, St. Louis, Savannah.* She turned a carton upside down and sat on top. *I'll order buttons and beads and all sorts of things when I take over from Mama. And I'll go to all these places myself and choose each one, I will.*

Before long, Big Sarah joined her.

"Darlin', where did you imagine yourself today?"

"Everywhere!"

Big Sarah stretched out her arms and her daughter ran to her.

"After all your traveling around the country, you must be ready for a cool drink. How about that?"

Little Sarah nodded, and hand in hand they walked to the modest soda fountain toward the front of the store.

Over the next three years, Sarah observed her siblings grow up around her. Although she remained pint-sized, she garnered the most attention in her family because of her beguiling face: oval with prominent cheekbones; bottomless dimples that announced themselves almost before she grinned; hazel eyes that took on a purplish cast if she wore blue; and a creamy, flawless complexion that sprouted a few freckles in the sun.

Sarah tagged along with Mattie whenever her sister allowed it. One early summer day when Sarah couldn't find her in the house, she opened the front door to take a gander outside, and startled Mattie and Henry Cornwall, Mattie's beau, who stood hand in hand before her.

Exasperated Mattie said, "Run along, Sarah."

"But why?" Sarah asked.

"Papa's waiting for us."

"What for?"

"You'll find out soon enough."

Sarah stood her ground and saw how Henry adjusted his tie, straightened his cuffs, and dug the soles of his shoes, one after the other, into the doormat for one more swipe before entering.

"I told you to run along," Mattie reiterated.

By this time Henry had positioned himself in front of the hallstand's mirror and Sarah watched as he smoothed his hair and checked for any flecks of anything on his coat jacket.

"Henry, you look dapper," she said, then turned to her sister. "That's the right word, Mattie?"

"It certainly is, you rascal," Mattie responded, and they both laughed.

"Thank ya kindly, Sarah," Henry answered.

"All right, Mattie, I'll go now," Sarah conceded.

She walked outside and waited until the pocket doors to the parlor banged shut. Then she returned to the foyer and put her ear to the key opening. The inaudible conversation frustrated her and just as she decided to wander away, Mattie started to sob as loudly as she'd ever heard her. Sarah jumped back when Henry pushed the doors apart, shut them, and, almost tripping over his feet, headed out of the house without a word.

That evening, the Franklins gathered for supper in their well-appointed dining room. Mattie, eyes still crimson, moved food aimlessly around on her plate. After the rest had eaten in near silence, their father, Horace, cleared his throat.

"You all are awfully quiet this evening," he remarked and looked around the table. "Maybe you already know what happened here today."

"Some white slickster trying to steal land from us again?" Nathan chuckled and Anna laughed along with him.

"If it were only that easy, my son. I've easily dealt with those scoundrels. But this is an affair of the heart," Horace emphasized. "Henry Cornwall came to ask for your sister's hand in marriage." Horace turned his eyes to Mattie and addressed her with a firm voice. "And we won't have it!"

Mattie rose from her seat, shouting back defiantly, "But, Papa, what about what I want?"

"First of all, Mathilda, you sit down and listen to what I say."

Mattie settled back into her seat. Nathan and Anna sat silently, transfixed. Little Sarah grasped Mattie's hand under the table while Big Sarah stared straight ahead.

"Your mother and I like Henry. He's a decent boy. Since he set eyes on you the first day of kindergarten, the two of you have been inseparable. But marriage? That's for a lifetime. It means children, heirs…"

"My life will be over if I can't be with him," Mattie sobbed.

"Mattie." His voice softened. "Your life is just starting. You've got to finish school. We're fortunate to live in a place where there's one of the only high schools for colored people in South Carolina. We Franklins are all educated."

"I will finish school, Papa. Henry was asking for a betrothal, so he'll know that as soon as I finish, we can…"

"That's not the point, darlin'. It's Henry. He dropped out of high school and"—Horace hesitated—"he comes from different stock."

"No, he doesn't!" Mattie insisted. She let Sarah's hand go. "Your parents, Mama's parents, might have served the massa inside his house while Henry's kin worked the fields. But we were ALL slaves, Papa! And these acres of fertile land you got? If Massa Franklin hadn't fathered your father, and hadn't given him all this, we'd be sharecroppers just like Henry's people. And Mama's mama got her land for the same reason!"

"Now, Mattie, you pay attention to me. All you see, all we have, isn't just because of the bequest of some depraved slave masters. We Franklins expanded our holdings after emancipation through our labor! And the parcel your mama's folks got was the worst that their massa owned."

Mattie stayed quiet as her father continued.

"Yes, we knew how to set a table and polish silver. But our folks emptied more than their share of filthy bedpans as well," Horace said sharply. "Your mama didn't just establish our emporium on a humbug. She saved until she could. You're too young to appreciate what heritage means. How it must be preserved and nurtured and enriched. You see what's become of your mama's baby sister. She ran off with that John Anderson who has next to nothing to give her."

Mattie started to weep, and Little Sarah reached up and patted her sister's eyes with a linen napkin.

"Darlin', you just don't understand." Horace shook his head from side to side.

"All I understand is that I can't go on without him. Please let me be his wife. I can't live without him. I can't!"

Anna crouched down next to Mattie and hugged her as tightly as Sarah did from her other side.

"Please stop that sobbing," Horace said.

"I know what I want. I know what I'm doing. Papa, please."

"I cannot give you my permission."

"Then I'll run off and you'll never see me again. I will. I don't care." She tried to bolt from her sisters' grasp, but both of them held on to her. As they stroked her head, she quieted down.

Big Sarah tapped her glass. "This conversation is over for now," she said.

"But, Mama, what does that mean?" Mattie and Little Sarah both blurted out.

"You heard me," their mother replied.

Mattie immediately retreated to her bedroom and did not emerge for breakfast or lunch the next day. Little Sarah brought up a tray of food and implored Mattie to eat, but Mattie refused. She would speak to no one.

After lunch, Little Sarah spied her parents entering the parlor. They locked the doors behind them and remained there until dinner.

The entire family was called to the table, including Mattie, who came reluctantly, still determined not to talk nor eat. After everyone sat, Horace tapped his glass.

"Your mama reminded me that human kindness will often accept what common sense denies. With that in mind, your mother and I consent to Mattie's engagement to Henry," he announced.

Little Sarah clapped her hands and hugged Mattie, whose mouth had dropped open.

"I knew you would say yes!" Little Sarah shouted. "Oh, thank you so much."

"You're not the one who's getting married, my dear," her mother kidded.

"I know, but it means so much to her, and she means so much to me, and I just want everyone to be happy! You wouldn't break Mattie's heart. You couldn't!"

Big Sarah now stood up and looked at Mattie.

"But our approval carries conditions. First of all, Mathilda Franklin, you will finish high school."

"Of course, Mama. You know that," Mattie declared and broke out into a confident smile.

"And Anna? You will chaperone Mattie and Henry whenever they are together."

"But, Mama, what about when Northrup comes to visit me? He doesn't get much time off from his work as a Pullman porter," Anna answered.

"Your fiancé will be glad to help you out with this, and get to know your sister and her intended better now, won't he? And once you marry him and move to Atlanta, your sister, Sarah, will assume this duty."

"Furthermore," Horace interjected, "I expect Henry to put aside as much money as he can during these next two years. I want to see periodic accountings of his savings."

"Oh, Papa. Yes. Yes. Yes. Henry can sprout beans out of rocks and he's also a smithy now. He'll do whatever you say. I'm so grateful," Mattie cried.

"I'm so happy for you, my Mattie, that I could cry, too," Little Sarah said.

She then led her sister to her parents and motioned for Nathan and Anna to join them in a family hug.

## Chapter 2

# JORDAN BECOMES A MAN

St. Louis, Missouri, 1914

Jordan Winfred Sable prided himself on his ability to rule any steed. His daddy, Jesse, worked for a white man who owned a small stock farm just outside St. Louis, and Jordan had spent every Saturday there since he was five years old. He began by currying the horses' bellies and wound up atop even the most rambunctious stallion in record time.

"Don't ya never come up behind one of them critters," Jesse repeatedly schooled him. "Or ya could get the kick of a lifetime and wind up dead. And don't show no fear, even if one of them starts buckin' and neighin' like he's plumb crazy. And keep yo' word with them. No backin' and forthin'. Ya gotta take control, ya understand me?"

"Kinda like with people, right?" Jordan would always reply.

"How'd ya get so smart?"

"By watching you."

\* \* \*

One late October day when Jordan was just shy of sixteen, he and his father stood in the stalls together, pitching hay and sweeping up the remnants.

"This place would fall apart without you, Papa," Jordan said, and threw down his broom. "You're the one who makes sure there's enough food for the cattle and horses, but never *too* much, so none of it's wasted. You always know when a cow's gonna calve or a filly's gonna foal. You know more and do more than anybody around here. Including that no-account owner."

"Hush, Son. Don't want Mr. Hart or nobody else to hear ya." Jesse glanced around the shed.

"Why do you make him think he knows everything?" Jordan approached his father and stared him in the eyes.

"'Cause I want to keep my job. We need the money. Wanna be able to give yo' mama and sister a few nice things. Ya smart. Want ya to go to college. Puttin' some money away for that, too."

"You don't need to, especially if it means kowtowing to some good-for-nothing…"

"I told ya to hush now. These walls got ears."

Jesse picked up Jordan's broom and handed it to him, but his son refused to take it.

"I still don't see it like that."

"While ya under **my** roof, ya *gonna* see it my way, boy! And you won't defy me. Now take this!" He rammed the broom into Jordan's chest. "The best way to make it in this world is to watch me. See how I treat white folks. When ya finish school, look for a decent white man to work for. That'll feed yo' family and keep a roof over ya, ya hear?"

A yell from the main house interrupted them.

"*Jesse!*" his boss hollered. "*Get up here!*"

Jesse scurried out of the barn and up the hill, with Jordan close behind, but stopped abruptly and clutched his chest.

"Papa, you okay?"

"Just a little heartburn, I reckon. Don't like the boss's tone. We gotta go."

"Papa, take it easy. We'll get there soon enough." Jordan took his father by the arm and helped him finish the walk.

"What kinda nigger mess have ya made?" Joe Hart hollered as soon as they arrived in his office.

"Mr. Hart, suh, I dunno what ya mean." Jesse looked bewildered.

Hart sat at his desk, rifling through papers. "Ya been fiddlin' with the inventory numbers. What do ya take me for?"

"But, Mr. Hart, just double-checkin' everythin' like ya told me to." Jesse massaged his chest as he spoke, and Jordan held on to his other arm.

"I don't care what I told ya. Ya not supposed to *change* anything."

"Whatever ya say."

"Now, go on and get outta here." Hart looked down at his desk as he snarled. "Rake up some leaves. Do something ya know how to do." He then raised his head. "And keep that big, fat, black, ugly nose of yours outta my books from now on."

"Yes, Boss."

Jordan's eyes stung from holding on to his tears.

"Why do you let him talk to you like that?" Jordan blurted the moment they got outside.

"And I told ya that ya gotta know how to handle white folks. They hold the key. Ya gonna get yo' education and…"

"Not if I have to get it this way." Jordan stormed off. He avoided his father for the rest of the day and sat as far away from him as possible as they rode back to town in the truck with the field hands.

That Monday after school, Jordan visited Marvin Mann, the local blacksmith, to ask for a job. Mr. Mann agreed to pay him to pick up horses and buggies every Saturday and deliver them back to their owners once the work was done.

"I work for anybody who can pay," Mr. Mann informed him. "And ya gonna see that most of my customers are white." He grinned.

When Jordan returned home, he informed his mother.

"Mama, don't want to get Papa riled up, so can you *please* wait to tell him until after I leave on Saturday morning?" he implored, then watched her answer in the form of folded arms and a nod.

The first day on the job, Jordan arose before dawn. He stuck his head out the window, smelled snow in the air, and prepared his attire accordingly: flannel long johns, winter wool trousers, shirt and overcoat, and well-worn snow boots. He dressed quietly, grabbed the railing, and felt his way down the staircase, leaving the lights out. He located the sandwich he had prepared the night before, tucked out of sight in the refrigerator, gobbled it down, and left through the back door. He pulled his leather gloves from his coat pocket and headed toward the smithy.

"Ah," he said, sighing. *I've done it! Broken free from having to tolerate my father's bowing and scraping and from that loathsome*

33

*white man*, he thought. He walked around in the darkness until Mr. Mann arrived.

Jordan worried about his father's reaction to his newfound job. Oddly enough, it never came.

One Saturday evening in early December, Jordan found his mother in the kitchen fixing ham and cheese sandwiches and preparing winter squash soup.

"Was just about to call for ya," she said as she poured the sizzling liquid into a tall thermos and stuffed the thick-crusted sandwiches into an oversize brown paper bag.

"What for, Mama?"

"Ya goin' to the stock farm."

"Aw, Mama. I hate that place. And I don't work there anymore."

"Ya ain't tellin' me nothing I don't already know. Broke your papa's heart, even though he never said a word to you. But tonight, ya takin' this food to him. Says Deb's about to foal and he's not leavin' her. Made enough for ya both."

"Whatever you say."

"Now, that's what I wanna hear comin' outta yo' mouth. Good thing Mr. Mann told ya to keep that horse and buggy 'til Monday. Go on now and don't give yo' daddy no guff. Keep him warm out there." She placed all the food inside a basket, covered it with a flannel blanket, and handed it over to him.

When Jordan arrived at the farm, he heard his father and Ossie, the full-time stable boy, talking in Deb's stall.

"Why ya stayin' here tonight? It's gonna freeze and she ain't due for more'n a month," Jordan overheard Ossie say. He peeked into the stall.

"Not so sure she's got that long. She's already bagged up." Jesse pointed to the mare's fast-descending udder. "And she's got titties bigger than both my thumbs put together."

"Ya know as well as me that means she got at least another month."

"Not all the time," Jesse answered. "Not all the time."

"But she ain't rattled a bit. She might as well be out grazin'." Ossie patted Deb and she paid him no mind.

"Go onto yo' bunk if ya want, but I'm stayin' right here."

Ossie opened the stall door to leave and Jordan brushed past him.

"Son, why ya out here in all this cold?" Jesse asked.

"Came to bring you something from Mama…and to stay here with you."

"That's good of ya, but ya didn't have to."

"Yes, Papa, I did. Here, eat," he said and gave his father the basket. "I'll be right back." Jordan left the stall looking for more horse blankets as cover for the night. He found an extra two and returned to his father.

"These should keep us alive until daybreak," Jordan remarked.

When they finished eating, they secreted themselves right outside Deb's stall so as not to disturb her. They nodded off quickly, but Deb's raucous pawing at the ground and furious pacing awakened them almost as suddenly. Then she started to grunt.

"I knew I was right to stay with her," Jesse said.

They tiptoed into her stall as her water broke. Jesse grinned broadly at his son as he patted her buttocks and she laid down.

"I love this part. Ya gonna see a miracle, Son. First the tip of a hoof comes out, then one foot right behind the other, then the nose, and then the shoulders. This foal is gonna slide right past me like a sailboat with a windstorm at its back. Get ready!"

Deb started to push and when the first foot appeared, Jesse gasped and shouted out.

"Lordy, the sole's turned upwards and it's the hind foot!"

"What's wrong?" Jordan asked.

"No time to explain." Jesse ran to the spigot and scrubbed his hands and arms up to the elbows. He lay down next to the mare.

"Deb, sugar," he whispered, "first, I gotta turn yo' young'un right side up and then I'm pullin' this critter outta ya backwards fast as I can. Ya don't need to do nothin'. Just lie there."

Jordan watched as his father used all his strength to pull the filly from her mother's hindquarters, careful not to damage either the animal or the umbilical cord. The newborn kicked her two hind legs right through the placental sac and up against the center of Jesse's chest as she slid out. Jesse fell back into the hay, sweating profusely. He grabbed his rib cage and panted.

Jordan rushed to him. "Papa?"

"Help me stand up," he wheezed. With Jordan's aid, he stood, but the pain got up with him and felled him to the ground.

Just then, Ossie entered the stall, rubbing his eyes. "Ya all right?"

"Don't talk, Papa," Jordan told his father.

"No. No. I gotta tell Ossie what happened. That filly's got an attitude and a temper, too. Came out backwards with a wallop." He attempted to laugh.

"Ya don't look so good. Think ya need a doctor," Ossie added.

"No, I don't!" Jesse countered.

"Well, I'm ringin' the bell. Ya know the boss always wants to know when he's got a new one in his fold."

Jordan wrapped both horse blankets around his father and pulled him close as they heard the cowbell break the winter night's silence.

"We have to get you to a doctor." Jordan tried to stand his father up, but Jesse's legs crumbled beneath him.

Before long, Joe Hart burst into the stall and snarled, "Why the hell ya rung that bell?"

When no one responded, he glanced around and saw Jesse on the ground with Jordan, and Ossie next to them. And then he spied the foal.

"Well, I'll be. She's a looker, ain't she?" Hart exclaimed.

"I think ol' Jesse's dying, suh," Ossie said.

"What are ya talkin' about? And Jordan, what the hell are ya doin' here?"

Jordan glared up at the man and said nothing.

Ossie continued, "That filly kicked him in the chest and—"

"Feisty, is she? I like that. That'll be her name. But spirited or not, no little newborn can kill a grown man. Don't be a fool." The boss man walked closer to Jesse and looked him over.

"Ya look sick all right, but if ya dyin', ya ain't dyin' here. Take the car and drive him home now. Then come right on back."

Ossie and Jordan lifted Jessie and carried him outside.

"I'll go get Dr. Cole and meet you at the house," Jordan said before he mounted the buggy and darted off.

He and Dr. Ethan Cole arrived before Ossie and Jesse. Jordan burst into the parlor screaming for his mother while the doctor tried to calm him. He began to pace until Myrtle appeared at the top of the staircase.

"For God's sake, Jordan. What's gotten into ya? And why aren't ya at the farm with yo' pa? Dr. Cole? What are ya doin' here?" Myrtle's questions tumbled out. Soon her daughter, Jessica, appeared next to her.

Jordan heard footsteps on the porch and ran to open the door. Myrtle and Jessica hustled down the stairs as they both rushed to join him.

"Oh dear God!" Myrtle gasped when she saw her husband cradled in Ossie's arms. Ossie laid Jesse on the sofa and Myrtle leaned over her husband. "Jesse, darlin'?" She touched his forehead and turned to her daughter. "Jessica, boil some water. Get some towels. He's sweatin' somethin' fierce and cold as ice all at once."

"Myrtle, if you'll permit me?" Dr. Cole interjected.

She stood back and said nothing. After the physician examined Jesse, he said, "His heart's given out."

"Well, let's get him to the hospital," Jordan insisted.

"You want to take him to what passes for a medical facility for colored in this town? He'd end up with pneumonia or meningitis or Lord knows what, the way they stack patients one on top of the other."

Jordan's jaw tightened. "Is he just gonna die like this?"

"Son?" Jesse stirred and whispered, "I might not be ready to go, but sometimes we ain't got a say. But ya gotta be ready to start. Come closer."

Jordan knelt down beside his father. "I was wrong." Barely audible, Jesse continued, "Stand up for yo'self and don't take no crap off them ofays. Do it for me, yo' family, and the race."

Jordan looked his father in the eyes and nodded.

"And Miss Jessica?" Jesse's voice rebounding as his daughter knelt next to her brother. "Menfolk can be tricky. Ya gotta be able to stand on yo' own and make some money, too." She rubbed her hand against her father's cheek, and he turned his head and kissed it. Jesse then looked up at his wife.

"Mother? Ya know all 'bout me. My heart's all used up now but it's still yours."

"Husband, ya just takin' a little nap right now. We gonna help ya rest."

She nestled herself between her children, laid her hands on Jesse's chest, and told Jordan and Jessica to do the same. Myrtle began.

"*The Lord is my shepherd; I shall not want.*" Myrtle stopped and brushed a tear from her eye.

"Go on, Mother," Jesse whispered. "Ya know this is my favorite psalm. And ya say it so good."

"*He maketh me to lie down in green pastures; he leadeth me beside the still waters. He restoreth my soul; he leadeth me in the paths of righteousness for his name's sake. Yea, though I walk through the valley of the shadow of death . . .*" Myrtle paused again and held her breath.

"Mama?" Jordan asked and put his arm around her shoulder. "I'll get the Bible and read it if you want."

"Oh, please."

When Jordan turned to stand, Dr. Cole handed him the family Bible, opened to the twenty-third psalm. Jordan began.

"I will fear no evil; for thou art with me; thy rod and thy staff they comfort me. Thou preparest a table before me in the presence of mine enemies: thou anointest my head with oil; my cup runneth over. Surely goodness and mercy shall follow me all the days of my life . . ."

Myrtle covered the passage with one hand and finished.

"And you, my dear, sweet husband and father of our children, will dwell in the house of the Lord forever."

With those closing words, Jesse expired.

Jordan grew into his manhood the day of his father's funeral. He stood taller, seemingly, by one or two inches and appeared at least two years older. As he walked his mother and sister down the aisle, he pressed their waists so closely to him that the three of them appeared as one. He remained outwardly stolid as the preacher extolled Jesse's virtues: his devotion to family, his work ethic, his love of God, and his determination to provide a more well-to-do life for his children. Jordan's innards, however, roiled and he took in small sips of air to temper them throughout the service. But nothing worked and his guts churned all day and all night. In bed, he punched his pillow, pulled his knees to his chest, buried his head between them, and cried for hours. At daybreak when his tears dried, he made a decision. He had to assume the reins of his family and he needed a full-time job.

That morning, Jordan listened to his mother's pleas for him to finish high school. *Ya already skipped two grades and ya gonna graduate this spring. Yo' daddy squirreled away enough for ya first year of college.* He paid close attention to her every word and, for the first time in his life, disobeyed and withdrew from the Samson Secondary School for the Colored.

The day after, Jordan left their house for city hall on foot. He easily surpassed the streetcars as they strained forward on iced rails and the mounting snowfall. Once he arrived, he found the

POSITIONS AVAILABLE board outside the hiring office and pulled an announcement for a garbage collector. He walked in and slid the notice across the counter toward a middle-aged white clerk.

"I want this. Says here that the ability to drive a horse wagon is a requirement. Been around horses all my life," he said, as he looked the clerk dead in the eye.

The man backed away from him, fidgeted for a moment, and then reached under the counter.

"Fill out this form," he said falteringly, and pushed a form toward him. "Somebody will contact you."

Jordan completed the application while the clerk squirmed even more and shuffled through papers.

"Here it is," he said, and put his forefinger on top of the paper and pushed it toward the clerk. "I'm waiting right here to talk to that somebody."

"This will take a while. You better go on your way now."

"Got nowhere to be."

"These things take time. Now go on."

"I'm going on, all right. Over there." Jordan pointed to an empty bench that faced the counter. He walked over, then sat down, crossed his legs, and spread out his arms. After an hour, Jordan got up and approached the clerk.

"Has Mr. Somebody seen my application?"

"No, not yet," the clerk mumbled.

Jordan returned to his seat but got up each hour and did the same thing until another white man appeared shortly before 4:00 p.m.

"You Mr. Somebody?" Jordan asked as he walked toward him.

"Sign here. You can start on Monday," the man said without taking his eyes off the paper he handed to Jordan.

*White folks may think they got power, but I got balls,* he thought as he wrote out his name.

Jordan blossomed in his new job. The lessons his father had taught him when they worked together on the stock farm served him well. Seemingly impervious to the blasts of frigid air that hit him each morning, he unbuttoned his coat at times and even tucked his cap inside his belt. He took instant control of the horses that winter, maneuvering them down ice-laden alleys and daring them to move when he jumped off the wagon to collect St. Louis's coal dust-covered debris. Cloaked in the knowledge that the Sable household would remain well heated and the icebox well supplied thanks to him, he was unstoppable.

During that summer, he went shirtless, and his rippling muscles and gingerbread complexion transfixed onlookers.

"Mister Jordan," a young boy shouted out. "Make the horses fly. *Please!*"

Jordan smiled down at the child from atop his wagon.

"Can't do a gallop here in the city, but just watch this!"

With a snap of his whip on high, the mares trotted to the end of the alley and stopped on a dime. Jordan's lash never grazed them. He determined their actions by the way he made it sing, along with a tilt or a tug of the reins.

The boy squealed as he caught up to the wagon.

"Like that, did you?" Jordan asked.

"Sure did!"

"You run along now and play with your friends but remember to practice some reading before you go to bed. I got to get back to work. Trash waits for no man." He laughed out the last words, turned the wagon around, and continued down the alley.

Jordan groomed his horses and kept his records better than anyone else. He even managed to scrub off the stench from his wagon at the end of each week. Toward the end of autumn, his boss called him to his office with a proposition.

"Want you to train the new boys."

"Why's that?" Jordan asked.

"You're doing a good job, that's why."

"Only a *good* job? Good's a passing grade. Why would you want somebody to train other somebodies with only a passing grade?"

"*Very* good, that's what you are. Is that what you want to hear? You want the job or not?"

"What's the pay?"

"Extra buck each month."

"What are you gonna call me?" Jordan snorted.

"Head garbage boy. You'll be in charge of all of them."

Jordan glared down at his boss. "That's all you got?"

"C'mon, Jordan, it's decent."

"*Decent* would be a proper title. Might as well be naming me head nigger *boy* in charge of all the other nigger boys."

Without another word, he left and went to stroke all the horses goodbye. He headed straight to the railroad employment office and applied for a job on the trains.

"We're still looking for Pullman car porters. Best position on the railroad for the likes of you," the hiring agent said.

"Where do I sign?" Jordan answered.

"Well, George, put your X right here."

"Name's Jordan and I can write it out."

"George. Jordan. They sound pretty much the same to me. But your name's George now like all the rest of the porters. Ol' Man George Pullman liked it that way."

"Well, you're wrong about my name, wrong about how I sign it, and wrong about me wanting this job."

"Pullman pays more than all the rest of the work we got here put together. Plenty of other colored boys would jump at the chance."

"Well, let *them* have it. No amount of money's gonna rob me of the name my mama and papa gave me," Jordan said and flipped the paper over. "What else you got?"

"You can clean up the trains in the station between runs."

"What's that called?"

"Railway car cleaner."

"I'll take it. And I got experience. Been cleaning up the city's trash for a year."

Jordan continued to work seven days a week—six for the railroad and every Saturday evening and Sunday for the smithy, Marvin Mann. As a result, his mother and sister wanted for nothing. New shoes, dresses, even proper raincoats and boots for the coming spring.

Mr. Mann worked every day as well and Jordan marveled at his ability with a hammer. Mann had the hardest anvil, the hottest forge, and the strongest arm in town. He never lacked clients, but Jordan couldn't figure out how he and his wife lived so high on the hog. They had no children to care for, but no amount of pounding could account for the two-story house they lived in and the rental property they owned. They even had an automobile.

"Mr. Mann, you sure make a good living and got a lot of nice things to show for it," Jordan remarked late one Sunday afternoon.

"Ya wonderin' why and how, are ya?"

"Well, yeah, but I don't want to pry."

"That's awright. Been waitin' to school ya, I have." Mann dunked his red-hot hammer into the bucket of water by his side, shook off his padded gloves, and let them drop to the floor.

"Why don't ya come home with me for dinner. I wanna tell ya somethin'." Marvin walked toward Jordan as he spoke, staring intently.

"I'd be pleased, honored, in fact," Jordan replied.

They closed the shop together and Marvin ushered Jordan outside, bolting the entrance behind him.

"Jordan," he started as they strolled. "I want ya to know that all my clients like ya a lot."

"Thank you for telling me that."

"And I've seen how ya treat the whites. Professional and respectful but not *too* respectful."

"What do you mean?" Jordan scratched his head.

"C'mon, son. Ya know. Ya don't make them feel any better than anybody else, like some Black folk do."

"Well, they aren't," Jordan affirmed.

"Exactly. Ya got character. Hard to find."

"Thank you, Mr. Mann."

"Ya can call me Marvin now, okay?"

Jordan smiled and they continued in silence. Once inside the house, Jordan took in the parlor and admired the luxurious velvet cloth that upholstered the sofas and chairs. He sidestepped the posh throw rugs, not wanting to muss them up.

"Joyful, baby. We got company," Marvin called out to his wife.

She soon arrived and Marvin introduced her to Jordan.

"I'm hopin' Jordan here's gonna be helpin' me with more than the buggies, darlin'." He winked her way.

"Glad to hear it. Ya work too hard. I'll put on another plate."

"Thank you, ma'am. It's a pleasure to be in your home." Jordan bowed ever so slightly.

"Got manners, too," she added.

Before long, they all sat in the dining room where Jordan almost inhaled Joyful's pot roast, intoxicated by the aroma and the tenderness of the meat.

When Marvin finished, he swiped the linen napkin across his mouth, slapped it down on the table, and stood up.

"Time to go to work," he declared.

Jordan thanked Joyful for her hospitality and trailed his boss out the door. They went to the smithy and entered the back office.

"Sit down here, boy, and just watch." Marvin pointed to the seat on his left, and the two of them sat behind a broad table. Before long, a Black man walked in without knocking.

"Butler, good to see ya," Marvin greeted him and stood, as did Jordan.

"This here's Jordan. My right-hand man. Or in this case, my left-hand man," he chuckled. "Ya can say what ya want."

"Havin' a real hard time right in through here, Marvin," Butler began. "The winter took a toll and they about to evict me and my family."

"Why'd ya wait so long to come on over here?"

"Tried to fix it myself. Ya been so good to me. Didn't want to stretch my luck."

"Luck don't figure in this. Ya keep doin' what we agreed to and ya don't ever have to worry 'bout nothin'."

"Ya know I'm good for that."

Marvin opened the desk drawer, pulled out a two-dollar banknote and handed it over.

"And I'll take care of the bill collector. Ya won't be movin'."

The two men shook hands, Marvin patted him on the back, and escorted him to the door.

Jordan watched in silence as the rest of the evening proceeded, more or less, in the same fashion. Man after man, some more threadbare than others, came and went after outlining what troubled them: not enough money to pay for a child's medicine, not enough coal to warm the flat, too many impending evictions.

After the last man departed, Marvin locked his office door.

"Ya understand what goes on here now?"

"You fix stuff and not just buggy wheels. But where does the money come from?"

"I deliver numbers. And I'm not talkin' about runnin' them. I leave that to the small-time hoods."

"What kinda numbers?"

"Poll numbers, son. I supply what those lyin', thievin' white Republican politicians don't know how to get. Negroes still tied to the Grand Ol' Party because of Abraham Lincoln, but what have we got for it? Second-rate schools, poor health care, dark streets after the sun goes down. But at least they will *pay* for votes. Plenty for me and more than enough to pass on to my people who keep them in office."

"Did my papa ever come to you?"

"Never. Bless his soul. He handled everything for yo' family.

But he knew what I did. Never had to ask him for his vote. He always toed the line, he did. Smart man, yo' daddy."

Jordan pulled himself up from the table, turned away from Marvin, and looked toward the floor. "He worked so hard for us that it killed him."

Marvin walked around the desk and approached Jordan. He waited until Jordan finished wiping his eyes and then began. "Ya wanna piece of this? I could use ya. Ya got a fine mind. Ya talk real educated like. And ya don't seem to fear nothin'."

"Reckon I learned that from being in charge of horses. My daddy taught me that."

"Horses is one thing. Not fearing men, especially white ones, another. Ya got character. Somethin' that can't be bought or sold. I can teach ya how to use it and get yo'self somethin' out of it, too. Come with me." Mann led Jordan to another room even deeper in his shop.

"Help me move this buggy wheel." Together they lifted it from the hooks and rested it against the wall.

"Now, turn yo' back," Marvin said. Jordan did and heard the clicking of a dial. He then felt a pat on his back and faced his boss. Marvin's fists each held a banded bunch of dollar bills.

"I'm ready to learn whatever you can teach me," Jordan remarked while eyeing the money.

"Ya gonna start as a block worker. Ya need to know more about every one of yo' neighbors than they do about they own selves. And then ya come tell me and I'll make it right," Marvin said as he held up the money. "But through *you*, ya understand?"

"But, Mr. Mann, you're the one who's taking care of them, not me."

"And they know that. They ain't simpletons. But they gonna know from here on out that they gotta go through ya. Ya gonna learn from the bottom up, bind people to ya and before ya know it, ya gonna be runnin' more than just yo' block."

"What's that?"

"The precinct…the whole ward one day and more. Ya gonna see. I'm gettin' tired of this business and my arm could give out any day."

"Don't know how to thank you."

"Don't have to 'cause I know ya gonna do a good job. I got instincts about people. Ya bigger than riding buggies back and forth to my shop. Wanna turn this over to ya, but ya gotta prove yo'self with the people first."

"I'll do whatever you say."

"Oh! And another thing. Start puttin' aside the extra cash ya gonna be gettin' for this work. Buy some extra property as soon as ya can. Nothin' like bricks and mortar to build a future *and* a fortune on."

"Yessir."

## Chapter 3

# MATTIE LOVES HENRY

*Greenston, South Carolina, 1916*

The day after Mattie graduated from Stellar High School for Colored Youth, she married Henry in a ceremony that united the two sides of Greenston's colored quarter. Henry's folks were dressed as best as they could, and Mattie insisted her relatives leave their fancy duds in their closets.

After the nuptials, Horace Franklin proposed a toast.

"To Mathilda, the most determined of my children," he said, then harrumphed. "And to Henry, a hard-working young man, I deed the southwest parcel of our holdings and the house that sits on it. May it bring you much pleasure and plenty of produce."

"Papa, you're the best daddy in this whole world." Mattie ran to her father and hugged him. Henry trailed her and shook Horace's hand.

"Don't know quite how to thank ya, suh."

"I think you do," Horace answered. "Keep her happy. And

remember, human kindness will often accept what common sense denies. I followed that adage this time."

After a month of wedding nights in their new home, Mattie blushed every time Henry admired her.

"Ya just bustin' out all over. Seems like yo' titties got bigger and yo' hips wider. And girl, I just love that fresh swivel in yo' step."

"You put it there." Mattie felt her nipples harden.

"And ya put me in a way every time I look at ya. Knowin' that ya all mine. Gonna have to wear my smithy apron whenever somebody else is around," he said, laughing.

"Which crops should we plant, sugar?"

"I think greens, that's what I think," Henry answered.

"Yes, yes. I want all the collards and turnips and mustards we can handle," she squealed. "And ours will be the best! We'll sell them at the market and help feed our neighbors. And no devil cotton. Our people had to pick it, but we don't!"

"I love ya, Mattie. Ya the one that's smart."

"And I love you," she declared. "We can borrow a horse from Papa. I mean, if you think…"

"Only if we pay him for usin' it."

"Whatever you say, husband."

"We got all summer to get ready. Can start in early fall. All three of 'em in the ground. We'll have somethin' to sell by the beaver moon."

"I can get some of my cousins to help and we'll pay them with meals and pocket change, if that's all right."

"Like I said, Mattie. Ya so smart."

\*    \*    \*

One morning in early August, Mattie awoke at daybreak while Henry lay still beside her. She felt warmth between her legs but not the type of heat when nature calls. Now she felt wet and smelled blood wafting up from between her legs. She slid herself closer to the edge of the bed to reach for the bedpan and it rattled when she touched it. Henry stirred.

"Mattie?"

She started to weep.

"What is it, baby?" He hugged her from behind and saw the blood creeping across their white sheets.

"I've lost it," she whimpered.

"What ya sayin', darlin'?" Henry rushed around to her side of the bed.

"I wasn't sure, so I didn't tell you. And now there's nothing to say."

"Oh, my Mattie," he shouted and held on to her. "Let me get some water, towels. Just lay there. Don't move."

"But the blood. I don't want you to get…"

Henry shushed her with his index finger, took the bedpan, filled it, and cleaned her.

After her miscarriage, Mattie complied when Henry insisted that she confine her activities to cooking and sewing. One afternoon, she sat down in the kitchen as he instructed her.

"I went to yo' folks' emporium and look what I got." Henry pulled out a crate from the bottom of a cupboard and emptied it, one piece of brand-spanking-new cookware at a time. She clapped her hands when he revealed the last piece: a fifteen-inch-wide used cast-iron skillet that made his muscles ripple as he placed it atop the stove. "Yo' mama even pitched this in from her pantry."

"Mama loves that pan almost as much as she loves me," Mattie said as she admired it. She turned her gaze toward Henry. "But not as much as I love being with you. I want to do everything with you. Can't stand being more than ten feet away from you."

"Ya can see me all day long. C'mon." He led her to the back porch that looked out onto their fields where he unveiled a handmade rocker with a thickly padded seat.

Mattie started to cry as Henry lifted her and sat her in the chair.

During their first year together, they prospered, harvesting almost more produce than they could sell. Furthermore, Henry supplemented their income by working as hard as two smithies for other families. In late June 1917, shortly after Henry turned twenty-one, a letter arrived.

"Only for a time, my darlin'," he promised her after they read the military draft notice.

"Only for a time," she repeated.

To quell the longing for her husband's deft touch and manhood, Mattie abandoned her rocker and worked harder than the day laborers and kin who helped her. By the end of each day, she could only think of falling into bed and dreaming of him.

Henry wrote letter after letter. They all started with "To my onliest love, Mattie" and ended with "Til death do us part, your onliest, Henry."

Mattie's falling tears smeared some of the words as she read how hard he worked as a stevedore on the shores of a place called Brest in western France, and how much guff he took from the white soldiers. *Never been treated this bad. Whites almost never stepped foot in Sunset, so I never had much to do with them. But here! Servin' my country and bein' kicked around and worse by lazy no-count crackers.*

She tucked each note inside a pouch she'd fashioned from her wedding veil and hung it on their bedpost. It grew fuller and fuller month after month for over a year until the one scheduled for the first week of December, just after the armistice, didn't arrive.

Mattie walked to her parents' house in search of her mother, Big Sarah.

"Mama, I haven't heard from Henry. You don't think that…"

"Of course, nothing's wrong, Daughter. They come straight away to tell the family. Do it even for colored. They have to. The war just ended. He's probably sailing back to you right now and will be walking through your door in no time."

"But what if he got lost? What if they forgot all about him?"

"I'll have your papa look into it. Don't you worry about a thing."

After several days, Big Sarah visited her daughter and allayed her fears. Henry, along with his unit, had been demobilized and would soon be honorably discharged.

"Dear, why not stay with us until Henry gets here? You're in this house all alone."

"My home isn't with you anymore, Mama. I've got to be here when he walks through the door."

Mattie celebrated the holiday parties with her kin in the big house but slept in her bed every night. Before she turned in, she'd bundle up in a woolen sweater, jumper, and coat, wrap a blanket around herself, and sit in her rocking chair. She gazed into the darkness and envisioned the next crop with Henry at the helm, tilling the soil and then thinning the seedlings when and where necessary. *I can already see all those shades of green: mustards got a tinge of yellow; collards are kind of, I don't know, dull, like they need a good dusting; and turnips? Now that's a true green for you.* She scooted to one side of the chair so as to finger some of the needlepoint she'd embroidered on the cloth that she had stretched over the padded seat. The full line read *Mattie loves Henry and Henry loves Mattie.* A sweet sentiment, she thought, yet she couldn't shake off the reason for the rocker.

"You're still a bit young to hold on to a child," she remembered her doctor saying. "You and Henry? Just be careful and wait your time."

*And when he returns, and I know he's coming back to me, it'll be our time. I feel it in my bones.*

Another month passed and late one afternoon, while she swept the back porch, Mattie heard the front door open. She jumped up, then tiptoed through the kitchen with her broom at the ready. No one entered her house without knocking, even though she never used the latch.

A tall, rawboned frame of a man stood in the doorway. He was backlit from the sun's tilted rays, so she couldn't make out his face.

"Who are you?" she asked.

55

"Don't know yo' own husband?" He dropped his bags.

"It's you, Henry!" she shouted. She ran and squeezed him tightly but pulled back when he barely returned her embrace.

"Henry?" She stared up at him, noticing his sunken eyes and how his walnut-colored skin had turned ashen. To fend off a chill that swallowed her, she drew her shawl around her shoulders and then cleared her throat.

"I'm so happy you're here, my husband. I prayed every day and night you'd come back to me in one piece. And just look at you. All tall and handsome." She attempted a smile.

Henry took a deep breath to speak. "And I'm so—" He choked on his words, covered his face with his hands, and started to bawl.

"Oh, my darlin'." Mattie grabbed him, but he nudged her away. She'd never seen Henry cry. Maternal love swirled through her body, and she yearned to cradle him. "Baby—" she began.

"Shut up!" he snapped and pulled out a handkerchief to wipe his face.

His tone startled her, and she stood as still as a stone.

"Mattie, I'm sorry. I don't mean to talk like that, but ya just don't know. Ya just don't."

She reached out for him, and he allowed her to hold him. "You're my husband. I want to tend to you, care for you, heal whatever wounds you got."

"Ya can't. Nobody can." He pulled away from her.

"No need for another word. Let me fix you something to eat. But first, I'll heat some water. You know how much I love to bathe you."

"No, no. Ya can't touch me. I'll do it my own self."

"But Henry…"

"Ya heard me, gal. NO!" he shouted and walked up the stairs.

Henry didn't have a moody bone in his body before he left. *The blasted war's done this to him.* Mattie walked to the kitchen, warmed up the leftover pot roast, along with some boiled potatoes, and took a plate up to him. She found him in his long johns staring out the window, as the sun faded over their fields. He jumped when she entered the room.

"Don't ya ever sneak up on me like that, ya hear?"

"Darlin', I didn't..."

"Oh yes, ya did," he snarled.

"Please eat something." She cleared her dressing table, put the tray down, and pulled out the bench for him. He lumbered toward it and sat. Mattie stood behind him and watched his reflection in the mirror as he ate. She remembered what delight he had taken in her cooking and how he'd savor each bite, complimenting her, and patting his stomach at the end of every meal. Now he moved the food back and forth on his plate, as if fearful of touching it. Then he stabbed a piece of meat and shoved it in his mouth.

"Is something wrong with the food, Henry?"

"I'm eatin', ain't I?"

Mattie covered her mouth to stifle a whimper.

"Oh, Mattie." He turned around and looked up at her. "Don't pay me no mind. I don't know what I'm sayin' or doin'."

"Henry? What's this?" she shrieked, as she ringed his throat with her finger, tracing a thick keloid from just below his Adam's apple to the back of his neck. "What happened to you over there?"

"NO!" he screamed, jumped to his feet, and slapped her. "Don't touch me." He pulled at the roots of his hair with both hands. Then he came at Mattie and plunged his forefinger and thumb into the sides of her neck.

"Not one mo' peep outta ya!" he yelled and squeezed her throat. Mattie froze. He leaned over, sucked the breath out of her mouth, and bit down on her lower lip. She yelped and jerked backward. Grabbing a handful of her hair with his other hand, he yanked her head farther back.

"What'd I say? Another sound and I'll choke ya even more."

He threw her down on the hardwood floor next to their bed and jumped on top of her. He ripped at her panties. Mattie lay motionless and focused on the bag of letters, silently reciting the words he had written as the darkness surrounded them, and as her husband, who had turned into a growling fiend, pumped his rage into her.

"Hen—" she started when he had finished.

"Damn ya! I told ya to shut up! Ya talkin' so loud." He flung himself on top of the bed and passed out.

Mattie dragged herself across the floor toward the bathroom. She picked up the stiffest wash rag on the shelf and scrubbed her body until her skin burned. She threw on a bathrobe, went to the back porch, and sat in her rocking chair.

"I'll just concentrate on my greens for now. We'll go back to planting together and he'll come to his senses. I know he will. He's got to. The war's done this to him. He'll come back to me just like before," she said to herself. Moving forward and backward, she soon fell asleep.

At daybreak, Henry appeared next to her.

"Mattie?" he whispered. "Darlin'? Wake up. I gotta talk to ya."

Mattie opened her eyes, grabbed her robe, and wrapped it more tightly around her.

"No, no. I won't do nothin'. I'm so, so sorry." He knelt down beside her. "Will ya forgive me? Ya gotta. I don't know what I'll do if ya don't." Tears welled in his eyes, and he laid his head in her lap.

"Henry?" She looked down at the wound on his neck. "This scar. Who did this to you?"

"I'm not talkin' 'bout it, ya hear. I can't."

"But I want to help you get better. I have to know," she insisted.

"Shut up!" Henry reared up, twisted her hand away from his throat, and hauled off and smacked her.

"And you just stop it!" she cried out.

"Oh, I'm so sorry. Please forgive me, Mattie. It won't happen again. I swear to ya." He started to sob again, nuzzled his face in between her thighs, and they wept together.

This seesaw way of life continued for weeks. Mattie began tiptoeing around the house, never knowing when Henry would abuse her or beg her forgiveness. Eventually, word got out of his return, but Mattie kept her family away. Henry was recovering. Henry was mending. Henry wasn't ready to see anyone. She came up with one excuse after the other while she gathered her crew to do the planting.

Then Mattie missed her period, and she knew. So did Henry.

## Chapter 4

# JORDAN TAKES ON
# THE WORLD

*St. Louis, Missouri, 1917*

Tending to his neighbors' woes came as naturally to Jordan as driving a team of horses. The more he got to know them, the more soft-heartedness he had for them. They felt it and became beholden to him in no time. He clasped the matrons' hands as they sobbed out their troubles, and if grown men hesitated to ask for help, Jordan coaxed them to talk. He became expert at sniffing out their troubles, sometimes before they even realized them. With Mann's till, he fixed them straight away. Meanwhile he kept his full-time job cleaning toilets, scrubbing floors, and turning blue-black when he swept out the train's cab. No work was too messy and he did it with no fuss until he accidentally bumped into one of his few white coworkers at the payroll office that summer.

"Dammit," the man grumbled as he looked at his paycheck.

"Was supposed to get a raise but it's still this measly eighty bucks, just like last month."

"What did you say, there?" Jordan asked him. "How much are you making?"

"Eighty, like everybody else."

"Don't you mean sixty-five?" Jordan asked as he stared down at his own.

"I said what I said. Take a look."

After the next month's wages were handed out, Jordan gathered ten of his Black coworkers at his mother's house.

"If you and I do the same work, we ought to get the same pay, right?" he said.

"Course, Jordan. Ya right," they all chimed in.

"Well, that's not happening. White men are getting a full fifteen dollars more a month than us."

"That's a lot and it ain't right," one of them said.

"Well then, we ought to do something about this, don't you think?" Jordan continued.

"Sure 'nuff," one said.

"I looked into what we can do. I wrote to the president of the biggest union in America and he wrote back that we only need ten men to start a union." Jordan eyeballed every man in the room. "By my count, I got them right here. So, what about it?" No one spoke.

"I said, **So, what about it?**" Jordan's voice boomed this time and he pounded his fist on the table.

"Who ya think ya yellin' at?" Black Jack, a string bean of a man, almost screamed out. "We all got more years than ya, more work under our belts, and got more to lose. We got families!"

Jordan hesitated for an instant and questioned himself; he was, after all, only eighteen years old. But he felt an energy, wisdom, and rectitude beat from within. He stuck out his chest and charged back at them.

"Well, tell me what your years of experience and working for nigger wages have brought you, and I'll shut up!" he demanded to know.

"Well, I hear that they firin' anybody who even thinks 'bout joinin' a union," Black Jack continued.

The group began to grumble.

"If you can't see the wisdom in this, then you're a fool. Sticking together, sticking up for one another, sticking it out. That's the only way to get our due," Jordan said.

"But they axin' white folks who join up, too," another man piped in.

"Listen up," one man said. "We work *more*'n they do. When the trains come in late, it's us who get stuck workin' 'til all hours. And they all go on home."

"Now you're talking," Jordan said. "We can fix that, too. You ever heard of a strike? We can sit down until the work's spread out more even."

"Ya the fool, Jordan. And a young one at that. Wise up!" Black Jack said as he and three other men headed for the door.

"Y'all can go," Jordan shouted after them. "But remember. We always got room for you. And you'll be back. I know it."

Over the next weeks, Jordan gathered men until he convinced ten to join him. He petitioned the American Federation of Labor for membership, received a charter, and Railway Coach Cleaners Union No. 19376 was born. Colored men filled the ranks from wherever there was a train station in Missouri. Almost overnight, the union grew into the hundreds with Jordan at its helm. The first order of business? Equal pay.

Jordan's puffed-up chest, however, deflated the day he came home from work and found his mother crying enough tears to flood the banks of the Mississippi.

"Mama?"

"Jordan," she sobbed. "They came over and threatened to hurt ya. Told me to talk some sense into ya. Stop all this union work. Oh, Son. Ya gotta quit."

Jordan's nostrils flared like a bull's as he pulled his mother to him and stroked her hair.

"Hush, now. It's gonna be all right."

"Just promise me ya gonna stop. *Please.*"

"It's gonna be fine."

"Darlin'," she sobbed. "Yo' daddy's gone. I can't lose the only other man I got."

"Nothing's gonna happen to me but woe betide whoever came over here today, messing with you. What did they look like?"

"Three of them came in here and the one who did all the talkin' had a big ol' flesh mole on his chin. That's all I remember."

"I'll fix it. Don't you worry about a thing."


That night Jordan gathered the most active cadre of the union at Fine's Laundry. Its proprietor, a Jewish man who supported their movement, had given Jordan a key to the shop if they ever needed to meet in secret. Behind drawn curtains in a candlelit room, they huddled around the pressing machine.

"I want to get sacked for union activity and quick," Jordan told them. "They came to my house and scared the daylights out of my mama. They're *paying* for that visit."

"Do whatever ya gotta and I'll organize enough men for a quorum by tomorrow night," Jones Battle, the union's second-in-command, answered.

The next day Jordan called in sick and then took a soapbox to the front of the station and mounted it.

"If you want to get paid like the white boys, better join the Railway Coach Cleaners Union, Number 19376," he shouted at every colored man who passed by. To those who stopped, he handed out applications. To those who didn't, he harassed.

"Still want to work for nigger pay? You know how much less you're making because your skin's black?"

By sundown, he was sacked for insubordination and that night the union members voted to stay home the next day. The day after that, Jordan was back on the payroll and discussing salary equity with management. And the day after that, Black Jack and the three other men pounded on Jordan's door.

"All aboard?" he asked them.

Word of Jordan's triumph lit up his entire ward like fireflies on a sultry summer night. He set up shop on his front porch, proud to let all his neighbors witness the reams of people who now came from the whole precinct to congratulate him and get assistance. Before long, just as Marvin had predicted, Jordan had the entire ward in his hip pocket.

"I knew it!" Marvin said one day when Jordan showed up to report on his week.

"What's that?"

"Ya makin' an impact, boy. The precinct captains can't register new voters fast enough."

"Glad to hear it. Mighty glad I'm working out for you."

"Never worried about that, boy."


The union's membership also benefited from Jordan's brash bucking of the system, and by late 1917, it mushroomed to well over one thousand men from every railroad stop throughout the state. Less than a year later, however, the landscape changed.

Jordan first read warnings about the Spanish flu invading St. Louis in the newspaper in late September 1918. Almost immediately thereafter, he noticed a steady uptick in the number of no-shows in the railroad station's workforce, Black and white. A hush fell across the country as the disease devastated cities and their health departments attempted to cope.

The Black community now clamored for something else during his meetings with them.

"We need caskets, Jordan! Our funeral parlors are all out."

"My brother died and they put him in a mass grave."

Mass graves? The thought of his brethren buried on top of one another unnerved him. Ordinarily, Jordan dutifully reported to his boss every other week, but once he sensed the enormity of the ward's problem, he darted to the shop immediately only to find a mammoth lock on the door. An envelope with his name on it was stuck to the door.

*This blasted thing got a hold of me. Don't come see me. Wait 'til I'm gone and talk to Joyful. She's got everythin' for ya. I love ya like the son I never had. Goodbye, Marvin*

Jordan dashed over to Marvin's house and pummeled the door. "It's me! I've got to see you, Marvin!" he shouted and kept banging.

"Jordan, stop it! Ya know ya can't come in here," Joyful screamed back at him from inside.

"Don't mean to disrespect you but I'm not leaving."

Joyful let him in and he swept past her and headed upstairs toward the bedroom.

"At least put these on," she said, pulling on his sleeve. She handed him a gauze mask and some gloves. "And don't touch anything. I'll open the door."

Jordan held back a gasp when he saw Marvin. He'd heard that the flu had turned white folks blue, but nothing prepared him for the hue of his boss's skin. Milk chocolate had turned to a muddy, moss green.

"I told ya not to come," Marvin rasped.

"Sorry, but I couldn't obey that order. Besides, this is just a temporary setback."

"Never heard ya say somethin' foolish 'til now. Ya know damn well where I'm headed. Ya in command now. Sooner than I thought, but that's life. Or in this case, death." He tried to smile. "I changed the combination on the safe to your union's number. 19376. That's right, ain't it?"

"Yeah, that's it, but—" Jordan began.

"No buts, Jordan. Joyful got her share already. Ya take the rest and keep buildin' up the numbers when this thing's over."

"You're not going anywhere, Boss," Jordan lied.

"Ya know better than that. Go on, now. Get outta here before it grabs ahold a ya, too."

Jordan shifted from one foot to the other.

"I said get outta here."

"I'm leaving, but I'm not saying goodbye. I'll see you later, chief."

"Yeah, we all gonna wind up in the same place sooner or later."

The next morning, a young boy pounded on Jordan's door.

"Mrs. Mann sent me to come get you right away," the boy said.

Jordan threw on his overcoat, handed the child some coins, and rushed to the Manns' residence. As he approached the house, he saw Joyful, draped in black, staring out the living room window.

Jordan twisted the front door handle and found it unlocked.

"Miss Joyful?" he whispered as he walked toward her. She didn't move, so he raised his tone a bit and she turned to face him.

"He left us in the middle of the night. Much as I wanted to sleep with him, he wouldn't hear of it. I didn't care if it latched on to me. Just needed to be near him. His death rattle woke me from the other bedroom. It was so loud." Joyful hung her head and Jordan put his arms around her.

"I'm so, so sorry," he said.

She, however, abruptly wiped away her tears and turned steely.

"There'll be plenty of time for mournin', Jordan. I've been standin' here all night, and I'm at my wit's end. No coffins, no shrouds, no nothin' for a proper burial for colored in St. Louis and all over the state, I hear tell. Once I let anyone know, they gonna scoop him outta here and put him in a mass grave if we don't do somethin'."

"All right if I leave you for a bit? I think I've got an answer."

"I knew ya would."

"Keep all the doors locked. I'll be back."

Jordan went to Marvin's shop and pried a folding top from the one buggy that remained. He baled the leather, secured it with the lash of a whip, and lugged it back to the house.

"At least he'll be protected," Jordan said as he spread out the leather next to Marvin's bed. Joyful disappeared and returned with hand-embroidered linen sheets.

"We used these on special days. I want them next to his body for all eternity so his skin'll touch where ours was together."

With their gloves in place, they placed Marvin's corpse on top of the bedding and leather, rolled it around him, and secured it with the whip and belts.

After dark, Jordan dug a hole at the back of the shop and placed Marvin's remains in it. He held Joyful by the hand as she sang:

*I'm pressing on the upward way,*
*new heights I'm gaining every day.*

She sobbed her way through the rest of the spiritual, then turned toward Jordan.

"Can ya say somethin'? I'm better at singin' than preachin' but, Jordan, I know ya got the gift. I just know ya do."

Jordan looked down and moved his head from side to side as if searching the ground for words, then fixed his gaze on one spot. He recalled his mother's strength when she recited the twenty-third psalm as his father passed. *No way I can remember all that.* He took a deep breath and raised his head until he saw the sky above.

"Lord, take the soul of this decent man, Marvin Mann, and raise it to the heights of heaven. Wrap it in Your bosom. Warm it in Your shining light and give it everlasting life. Yes, Lord, plant his soul on higher ground. Amen."

"Thank ya, Jordan," Joyful said.

"Not much. All I could muster."

"Just the right touch."

Unlike the bodies that lined hospital corridors, Marvin received the semblance of a funeral that night. Jordan filled the hole and left Joyful sitting next to the grave by candlelight. He went to the shop, opened the safe, and emptied it. Divvying up the money into two packets, he put one in an envelope marked "my people" and the other he labeled "my casket-making business," and shoved it inside his jacket. *Marvin, I'm gonna make sure that not one of our people will ever have to go under like you did.*

By the start of 1919, with the flu subsided, Jordan and his men went about rebuilding the union's membership. The plague had put its claws into young adults and the middle-aged but didn't touch youngsters or the elderly, so they went after high school boys across the state. Over that year, the union numbers rebounded. The following January, Jordan relinquished the top position to his deputy, Jones Battle, and got himself elected as the union's business manager. Awash in money from all the new recruits, he handled the books and created his own method of allocating the funds throughout the year. *Two for the union and one for caskets and its maker.*

"I'm through," he told Jones one day. "Get yourself another accountant."

"Never thought you'd stay this long," Jones told him. "Doin' Marvin's work full-time now, are ya?"

"You'll find out soon enough."

Marvin's shop became Jordan's base. He contacted every well-heeled Negro in the city and set up a meeting there.

"We need to make sure that none of us ever has to suffer the kind of humiliation we did when that damn disease hit us. We need to make caskets, I tell you, and plenty of them. We can serve our needs here and all across the state. It's gold just waiting to be mined. Are you with me?" He took off his Stetson, upturned it on the table in front of him, pulled a rubber-banded wad of dollar bills from his inside coat pocket, and tossed it into the hat. "Not asking you to do anything I'm not doing myself."

"Amen" rang out from all the men.

"It took my brother," one of them mused, followed by a litany of similar laments.

Dr. Ethan Cole stood. "Jordan, no need convincing me. I was with you when your father passed, saw how you rose to that occasion, how you cared for your family. And now you want to tend to your community. As a physician, I saw the toll this damned thing took on our community and witnessed how our bodies, *colored bodies*, were treated, or rather *mistreated*. That damned health commissioner said this flu didn't affect us as much, so the authorities tended to their own at our expense. Come on, everybody, cough it up." He walked to the front of the room, counted out twenty dollars, and added them to the sum inside the hat. One by one, the rest trailed Ethan and contributed what they could.

"You won't be sorry; I swear to you. And I'll repay you all with interest, you'll see," Jordan said at the end.

"Whose interest?" one of them joked.

"Ten cents on the dollar's interest? How's that sound?" he answered.

"You heard him," Ethan responded. "We've got his word on this."

Jordan and Joyful assessed the front of Marvin's smithy as two workmen atop ladders affixed a sign: SABLE'S CASKET COMPANY.

"This is what he'd want," Joyful said and squeezed Jordan's forearm. "Marvin never was one for stayin' in the past. He'd want ya to move forward. Give this place a new name."

"Glad you approve. Still keeping Marvin's old office in the back for, well, you know for what. But I am moving ahead all right. We'll be making wooden caskets as well as stainless steel. If that foolproof material was good enough for World War I, it's good enough for us Negroes."

"Jordan, ya a man of the future. Marvin always said that."

"He did?"

"That and more."

"Makes me feel real good, Joyful, knowing what he thought about me. I want to show you my next step. Gotta minute?"

"For ya, of course."

They walked to his mother's house and he flung open the front door.

"Welcome to the Jordan W. Sable Funeral Parlor and Mortuary Home," he announced with a sweep of his arm.

"My, my," Joyful remarked as she saw heaps of cloth spread across freshly upholstered sofas and rows of folding chairs filling the room. Myrtle and Jessica sat at tables in the middle of it all, stopped sewing, and looked up from their machines.

"We're having quite a time here, Joyful," Myrtle said, and lifted the hem of a lilac shroud. "Jessica's hands are better 'n mine so she's workin' on the drapes. Too heavy for me."

"Ya like them, Miss Joyful? They're velvet, see?" Jessica asked.

"Just like I said, my, my."

"By the time we finish with this place, I'll hang my own shingle outside and our funeral parlor will be the best in town," Jordan added.

"I really can't say much other than *my, my*. Y'all's quite a family."

*Chapter 5*

# MATTIE'S BROKEN HEART

*Greenston, South Carolina, 1919*

Mattie stared at herself in the hallstand's mirror at her parents' house while she cradled her abdomen. Her body had healed quickly from the last row she'd ever have with Henry and the only remnant of that beating was the faintly chartreuse-colored skin encircling her right eye. She plucked a straw summer hat off its hook, tipped its wide brim to hide the bruise, and rolled down the veil as far as it would go. Little Sarah and their big brother, Nathan, stood on either side of her. She patted her white cotton dress and fingered some of the embroidered spring flowers scattered on the bodice. She knew she wasn't pretty like her sisters. *You're a handsome girl*, her father always remarked. But she also knew that her bearing, the way she held her head with her chin thrust forward, her broad straight shoulders, and the sunshine in her eyes made heads swivel when she passed. Her decision to leave Henry and begin a new life in Atlanta with Anna and Northrup made her raise her head even higher than usual.

Horace and Big Sarah soon joined their children, and Mattie turned toward them.

"Please don't say anything more. We've been over this. I never should have married him. You've repeated it time and again. Please, just let me go in peace."

Her mother enveloped Mattie in her arms and then stood back and looked at her children.

"Your father and I just want what's best for you. You made a mistake, Mattie. We all do in life and now it's time to put this behind you."

"The war was a mistake, Mama!" Mattie countered. "Henry left here a sweet man and returned an evil one. You both know that."

"Yes, my dear. Indeed, he did, but…" Big Sarah stopped mid-sentence and looked at Horace.

"You are doing the right thing. Moving on with your life. Going to Atlanta to become a teacher and all," Horace said. "I think you're wrong to let that scoundrel have the property that I gave you, but there's nothing I can do about that."

"I can't ever go there again. It will only remind me of what happened out there. Let him rot to death on it. I don't care." Mattie stared at them in silence.

"Clara!" Big Sarah called out.

The housekeeper soon descended the staircase carrying a dark brown duster coat that she handed to Big Sarah.

"This will keep a good amount of the coal dust and smut off you in that filthy Jim Crow car up front, and you can wrap your mouth and nostrils with this. You'll be hot as the devil in this summer heat, but so it goes," Big Sarah said and pulled an over-size linen napkin from her pocket.

"Thank you, Mama. I *will* miss all of you so. You *do* know that, don't you?" Mattie almost whimpered, and Little Sarah quickly gathered them for a family embrace before they went to the train station.

Northrup picked Mattie up and the first thing he did was put her coat in the trunk.

"We'll dispose of that thing once we get home. It's full of Jim Crow's rubbish."

"North, I can't thank you enough for taking me in," Mattie said.

"Not another word, Sister. We're happy to have you. Anna stayed home because she's cooking up a storm. She has to welcome you the right way."

When Mattie crossed the threshold of her sister's modest bungalow, Anna rushed up to her and embraced her tightly, causing her hat to topple. Anna gasped when she saw the bruise.

"My darlin', darlin' little sister." Anna's eyes misted over as she tried to joke, looking up at Mattie, the tallest Franklin girl. "Come, let me take you to your room." They shuffled down a narrow hallway with Northrup behind them, carrying Mattie's luggage. "You've been on that train all day, so we'll leave you to freshen up."

Anna ushered Mattie into a tidy room on the left and quickly shut the door behind her. When Mattie sat on the twin bed, the starched linens crinkled and the milk-white petticoat lampshade on the nightstand seemed to dance. She noticed the basin and its matching jug of water on a stand, and the towels draped over a straight-backed rattan chair. She smiled when her eyes fell upon a bookcase with a few manuals from the Atlanta University Normal School. *Anna thought of everything.*

Mattie washed her face, adjusted her hair a bit, and returned to the front of the house where she found Anna and Northrup sitting at their food-laden dining room table. She didn't know where to look first: at the platter of golden fried chicken, or another holding ham hocks embraced by various greens, or a third with sweet potatoes peeking out from a blanket of melted marshmallows, or last, a mound of coleslaw that punched the air with its smell of fresh mayonnaise and apple cider vinegar.

"My word!" she gushed and closed her eyes as she inhaled all the smells.

"A feast fit for the queen you are, dear sister," Northrup blurted out.

"I can't thank you enough. Both of you," Mattie said.

"I told you, Sister, there's no need for that," Northup answered.

After the meal, they retired to the living room where a box of Whitman's Sampler chocolates sat on the cocktail table. As Mattie popped a morsel in her mouth and savored it, she assessed her new home. *So small. Our family home is four times as big. Wonder how Anna has adjusted? At least they don't have any children yet. Guess it's big enough for the two of them.* She also remembered the spacious farmhouse she'd shared with Henry, but did not linger there, turning her attention instead to how comfortable and cozy Anna had made her home. Tufted cushioned armchairs throughout, patterned throw rugs scattered around, and landscape paintings hanging on the walls. Sunlight illuminated a cut-glass vase that sat on a pedestal by the front window, and flimsy pastel drapes danced as the early summer wind blew through them. *This will be fine, just fine. I know it will. It has to.*

"Sister, you haven't missed one thing," Mattie mused.

"Now that we have you, we *are* complete," Anna added.

"But I must tell you just how much this means to me. Uncle Wesley figured out how to file for my divorce in Georgia since it's still illegal in South Carolina. My being here makes everything easier."

"Thank the Lord there's a lawyer in the family," Anna said with a chuckle.

"And thank the Lord Papa's got the money to pay for whatever it takes," Mattie added.

"Speaking of money, you know that where we live, Sweet Auburn, will soon be called the richest Negro neighborhood in America," Anna declared.

"No, Anna. *In the world*," Northrup corrected her.

"Yes, I know. It's famous all over the South," Mattie agreed.

"I'll take you to our store as soon as"—Anna patted her own right eye—"you've completely healed. Okay?"

"Oh yes, yes. I'd like that."

"It's smaller than the emporium at home, but not for long!"


Anna and Northrup's neighborhood was so quiet that all Mattie heard that night as she climbed into bed were the sounds of crickets and an occasional cat in heat. She drifted off to sleep and a dream swept over her like a bat's wing. *She was back in the rocker that Henry had fashioned for her, admiring their extensive vegetable field from the back porch of the farmhouse that her father had deeded to her and Henry as a wedding gift. She rocked herself to and fro until it stopped so abruptly that her head bumped against its back crest. Henry reached from behind, lifted her up by her neck, and shook her like a rag doll before dropping her down.*

*"I want some grub!" he screamed. "Get up and make me somethin' to eat!" Mattie scurried into the kitchen and pulled her immense cast-iron skillet from the cupboard. When Henry came charging at her, she lifted it above her head, but he twisted it from her hands before she could slam him.* Just as he aimed it at her waist, the frame froze in her mind, and she screamed out "NO" so loudly that she woke herself up and sat up straight.

Anna rushed into her room.

"Darlin', what is it?" Anna asked.

"He wanted to kill me," Mattie cried out. "But he just got my baby. I was pregnant, Anna. And he killed it!"

"I know. Mama told me."

"Did she tell you I might not be able to conceive again?"

"Yes, she did. But miracles happen every day."

Anna climbed into the narrow bed and cuddled Mattie until she went back to sleep.

After a week or so when the skin around her eye returned to normal, she and Anna headed straightaway toward Auburn Street, the Atlanta neighborhood's main thoroughfare. Mattie could barely catch her breath when she turned the corner and saw stores dotting the block in both directions. Streetcars, delivery trucks, jitney taxis, bicycles, and even a few cars packed the street.

"Well, I'll be. I've never seen so many vehicles in one place in all my life. And colored folk all behind the wheels," she remarked as they began to walk. They continued past a clothing store, a newsstand, a funeral parlor, an open-air food market, a bank, several beauty shops, an insurance company, and a few taverns. "And I never imagined there could be so many shops, and with colored working in all of them."

"They don't just work there. They *own* those businesses," Anna informed her. "Negroes used to have their stores downtown alongside white folks. Held their own against them, too—until that riot broke out in 1906. Some story about Black men going after white women set the whole thing off. So the businesses relocated here and turned this place into a Negro mecca. We keep our money and our real estate in the family, so to speak." Anna laughed.

"Just like we do in Sunset."

"Do tell."

The millinery window was jammed with a pastel rainbow of hats, one bigger than the next. Mattie's mouth dropped when she saw how many chairs filled Adam's Barbershop.

After another half block, Anna led Mattie into Annthrup's Emporium, which was housed in a one-story building with a narrow storefront. The two shopgirls jumped to attention when they saw Anna, who introduced her sister to them and gave her a tour of the store.

"Why, it's a miniature version of ours," Mattie remarked. "You've done us proud, Sister."

"I know it can't really compare, but just you wait. We're at the end of the street now, but one day, we'll get a spot smack-dab in the middle! All this walking, let's sit down for a spell."

They crossed the avenue and came upon Millie's Tea Room, located in a petite, three-story row house. Pots of pink and purple zinnias lined the staircase. Mattie noticed how the compact facade almost sparkled.

"Miss Millie rents out rooms overhead to make ends meet, but she's best known for her sweet cakes and mint and sassafras teas."

When they entered the narrow parlor, Mattie inhaled the aromas so deeply that she became lightheaded and broke out into a sweat.

"Anna? I need to sit down."

"Something wrong?" Anna pulled out a chair.

"No, no. Not at all. Everything's so right here. My heart's just bursting with happiness."


Mattie spent the remainder of the summer preparing to enter school and assisting her sister at the store. By September, she was ready to start studying.

"I'll keep helping out," she promised Anna the first morning she headed out to take the streetcar for school.

"Your studies are more important than anything now, but why don't you let me drive you?"

"I don't want to be a bother. And I like public transport."

"You know Mama and Papa wouldn't have let us step foot on it, even if they had streetcars in Greenston." They both laughed as Mattie kissed her sister and walked out the front door.

Mattie dove into her classes, loving every minute. On occasion, she worked afternoons at the emporium, but never missed completing her homework.

On the last day of exams before the Christmas holiday recess, Mrs. Lemmon, the school principal, asked Mattie to serve as proctor when one of the teachers fell ill. She was, by far, the star pupil at the school, so there was no need for her to take this test herself. Mattie demurred, not wanting to appear above her classmates, but the principal insisted.

So Mattie found herself sitting behind the front desk with her head bowed as the students entered the classroom. She listened as murmuring filled the room, but it subsided when she stood up. She looked over the students and clutched her throat when she saw a lone man in the last row.

"Please, stay in your places," she said as she headed for the door.

The man rose and followed after her. Mattie swished down the hall quickly, but Henry caught her swinging forearm and spun her around.

"Ya comin' home with me now," he stated.

Her eyes locked on the hand that held on to her. It was so thin that the knuckles stood out like burnt popcorn and the veins looked like a mass of tangled ropes. Then she saw not only unwavering intention in his eyes, but also unabated madness.

"Henry, dear, we'll go outside and talk about this. But first I have to let someone know that I can't stay. All right?" She spoke in a low, calm voice.

"Yeah, but I'm not lettin' ya go." Henry tightened his grip.

"Why, of course. Come with me."

Just then, a teacher appeared at the end of the hall. Mattie had wrestled her arm behind her to disguise Henry's clasp and walked toward her.

"Could you please supervise class five? I can't," she said, and pulled Henry toward the front door without waiting for a reply. Before Henry could say or do anything, Mattie had hustled them both outside and into the throng of passersby. She yanked her arm free.

"You do that again and I'll start such a ruckus that any one of these people will run screaming for the police. Now, what do you want?"

"I want what's mine. And ya mine, Mattie. All mine."

"Not anymore." She stood her ground and put her hands on her hips. "Now go on back to where you came from."

Henry moved closer to her, and Mattie took a step back and held on to her stomach as she assessed how he looked—his stained, threadbare overcoat; the stench wafting her way; his unshaven face; the dirt under his fingernails. Her once-upon-a-time, neat-as-a-cat Henry had disappeared inside cracked and swollen lips, the deep folds across his forehead, and the crow's feet that traveled into his hairline.

"You take another step and I'll start screaming like a banshee."

"Have it yo' way for now, but I'm takin' ya back with me...or else."

Henry stormed off and a shudder ran from Mattie's forehead to her tiptoes, but she also felt a resolve to stay put that hit her like a lightning bolt. No matter how mad he was, she no longer feared him. She went to Mrs. Lemmon's office and asked the secretary if she could use the telephone to call Anna at the emporium.

"Please send someone, anyone, to fetch me. I'll explain when you come home," she said, and hung up.

Mattie waited at the school's front entrance, and within a half hour, Anna pulled up. Mattie jumped into her car, panting as she described Henry's visit.

"He's looking to take me back with him or kill me trying."

"Oh, dear me. Mattie, you need to go stay somewhere else. Everybody in Sweet Auburn knows where we live and where the store is. Henry will find you easily enough."

Mattie cupped her face in her hands.

"I can't keep moving away from him."

"But you won't be leaving here. You can go to Northrup's sister on the other side of town. He'll be back from the road soon and we can all celebrate the holidays there...out of sight."

Mattie said nothing on the ride home and pondered what she should do.

"I'm not going anywhere," she told Anna when they got home.

"I don't think that's a wise decision."

"I said I am *not* going anywhere."

"But Henry hurt you more than once. I don't want that to happen..."

"And I'm telling you that I'm staying put. My will is stronger than his is now."


Mattie tossed and turned in bed that night. In this half-awake state, she saw Henry hovering over her.

*"Mattie, ya comin' home with me. I'm gonna have ya."*

He then banged his head on the ceiling so loudly that she shot upright just as the apparition faded. But the sound continued from outside her room. She threw on her robe and followed the noise down the corridor and up to the front door where Anna stood.

"Who's that pounding?" Anna shouted, but Mattie pushed her aside, slid back the peephole cover, and looked at the bloodshot eyeball that filled the lens. She jumped away from the door.

"It's him," she whispered.

"I know she's in there. Ya open up or I'm gonna kick it down," Henry slurred and then rammed his foot into the door.

"Stop it, Henry. She's not here!" Anna shouted.

"Oh yes, she is. I can smell her. I know my own wife."

"You better go on back to wherever you came from *and now*!"

"I can't live without her. I ain't goin' on all by myself. She's mine and I'm gonna have her."

"We don't have our posses here, but we've got police that take care of business, if you know what I mean. You best be on your way now," Anna answered.

"Awright, but I'm comin' back. I'm not goin' 'til I take her with me. Ya hear me?" He yelled out the last words.

Mattie and Anna heard him stumble across her porch and down the stairs.

"He's out of his mind," Mattie said.

"You need to leave here. Go to Ethel's like I said."

"If I leave, he wins. I won't let him dictate where I live, what I do."

Anna hugged her and led her to bed.

"Have it your way. But, darlin', all you have to do is study now. No working at the store. We won't let anything or anybody harm a single hair." Anna stroked her sister's face and kissed the side of her head.


The next evening Anna and Mattie ran to the front door when they heard a tap.

"Anna, I'm so sorry 'bout last night. Please forgive me, will ya?" Henry blubbered.

"She's not here, Henry. I told you that yesterday and I'm telling you again. Now go on!" Anna responded.

"Can't I just come in and leave some flowers for her?"

"She won't see them because she's not here, you understand? Now go on back to Greenston. There's nothing for you here."

"I'm gonna just put 'em down outside. Show 'em to Mattie, please," he whined. "And tell her I'm a changed man and I can't go on without her."

"All right. Leave them but go on now."

"Ya gonna tell her, right? That I'm sorry and ready to be a good husband agin and take care of her and be nice and gentle? Ya will, won't ya?"

"It's time for you to go, Henry."

"Ya was always my favorite, ya know that? Always so kind to me. Tell her. I know ya will."

"Good night, Henry."

"I can't leave 'til ya promise me. Will ya promise me? Please. Ya gonna tell her. I'm different now. I won't hurt her... ever. Will ya?"

"I will if you leave, and I mean now. North will be home from his run shortly and you don't want to tangle with him."

"Awright. I'm leavin', but I got yo' promise, right?"

"Yes, yes. Now go on."

Anna parted the front room's window drapes, and she and Mattie watched Henry walk away.

"He's walking like an old man, all stooped over with his hands in his pockets. He used to hold his head up, even when he got back from the war," Mattie said. They saw him sit down on the curb and bury his face in his hands.

Mattie closed the curtains. "I can't look anymore."

Before long, Northrup unlocked the front door and came inside.

"I saw Henry outside, talking to himself. Guess he left these for Mattie." Northrup threw a paltry bunch of hand-picked leaves and wildflowers on the hall table. "Thank goodness I'm off my runs through Christmas. Couldn't come at a better time."

Anna ran to hug her husband and they both pulled Mattie close to them.

"I just don't know what I'd do without the two of you," Mattie said.

The next night when the doorbell rang again, Mattie sat in the parlor, with curtains drawn, poring over her schoolwork. She stood and walked into the foyer.

"I bet it's that dang fool Henry," she heard Northrup say to Anna as they hurried from their bedroom. Anna stopped at the front hall closet and pulled out a baseball bat.

"Just in case you need some help," she said as she handed it to him.

When Northrup saw Mattie in the foyer, he motioned for her to go to her room.

Mattie shook her head no and didn't budge.

"Anna, would you talk some sense into your sister?" he whispered.

"I can't fight with her now. She's not going anywhere." Anna almost mouthed the words.

Northrup looked through the peephole.

"Henry, what do you want now?" Northrup called out through the door.

"Just got a letter for my Mattie. That's all. I'm leaving town now. I won't bother ya none, I swear 'fore God."

"You can leave it on the step."

"Can't I just see Anna's face? Won't be seeing my Mattie again. Just one last look at one of her sistahs?"

"Henry, you just need to go on," Northrup continued.

"The war did this to me. I went into hell and stayed there. I'm all scrambled up in my head. Just wanna say goodbye to one of her kin. I don't mean no harm. Can't think straight or even sideways."

Anna tugged at Northrup's shirt.

"Let him in," Anna told him. "We've got the bat."

Mattie walked into the darkened parlor. "He won't see me," she murmured to them.

Northrup opened the door. "You make one false move, and I will beat the hell out of you," Northrup threatened.

Henry walked in with his head bowed.

"No. No. Just got this letter for her." He passed it to Anna. "Can I just rest my eyes on ya for a minute since I'll never lay them on Mattie again. Ya look the most like her."

"You know that's a lie. I favor my mama and she looks just like Papa, but never mind. Go on, take one last look."

"Ya was my favorite. Always was real nice to me. Ya know that?"

"Yes, Henry, I know. You already told me."

"I did? When?" He wrinkled his brow. "Well, I'm sayin' it agin."

"All right. You can go on home now. You got one, thanks to my sister," Anna told him.

"No, I don't. I got no place to go. That damned boll weevil took it all." Henry fell into the chair in the front hall.

"You lost the land Papa gave you fooling with that devil crop? Mattie made you swear you'd never touch cotton. And you went ahead anyway."

"A white man made me an offer to grow it. Just wanted to ruin me and take my farm to plant tobacco."

"Well, you're a bigger fool than I thought," Northrup rang in.

"Mind if I use the toilet 'fore I leave? Gotta go something fierce." Henry started to cry and grabbed his crotch.

Mattie watched Northrup help him to his feet and prod him down the hallway with the baseball bat. Henry stumbled inside the bathroom, and she heard him turn the lock.

"Hurry up, you hear?" Northrup demanded.

"I will. I will."

Northrup leaned his ear against the door. The toilet flushed. Silence.

"I can't go on!" Henry screamed. The gunshot cracked like a tree trunk being split in two. Northrup dropped the bat and kicked open the door as Anna rushed up.

"Oh dear God! Anna, stay back," Northrup shouted.

Mattie ran down the corridor and pushed past them both.

She looked down at Henry's lifeless body, and one of his eyes, wide open and bloodshot, stared back at her. She turned away as blood swallowed the eyeball, but not before seeing pieces of squiggly gray matter splayed across the white-and-black tiled floor. She buried her face in Northrup's chest while Anna held on to her from behind and they moved away from the door, entwined like a three-cord twisted rope.

Anna spoke first. "Lost his mind and then shot it all out. Poor soul."

Their shock was interrupted by loud pounding and screaming outside, and the three of them turned toward the front door.

"The neighbors," Northrup said. "Must've heard the shot."

"Please tell them to go away. Not now. I don't want anyone in here," Anna said. Northrup walked to the door.

"I want to see the letter," Mattie said. "We need to know what he said before we call the police."

Anna thrust her hand into her housecoat pocket and pulled it out. Mattie read it aloud.

*Mattie—If it wasn't for ya and yo' blasted family. So siddity and uppity. High yella. Light, bright, almost white. Always thinkin' ya was better. I curse the day I met ya, curse the ground ya walk on. Hope ya and all the Franklins go to hell!*

Mattie walked to the kitchen and burned the note with one of the long wooden matches used to light the stove, watching it turn black in the sink. "Lord have mercy on his soul," she prayed out loud.

The local mortuary embalmed Henry's body within twenty-four hours and put it on the next train to Greenston. Northrup went to the station to tend to the formalities, leaving Anna with Mattie. When he returned, the women had not stirred from their spot.

"Mattie? Are you all right? You look so—"

"I'm just fine, Brother. I'm just fine."

"Well, you don't look it at all," he continued.

"I said that I am *fine*!"

"North, let us be for now," Anna said.

After Northrup left the parlor, Anna pulled her sister close to her. "Tell me, what are you feeling?"

"Don't feel much of anything. I can't grieve over a man I no longer knew."

"But you knew him once upon a time. The two of you have been in love since he spotted you on your first day of kiddie school."

"That was then, and this is now. I don't know the man who killed himself," Mattie declared.

"Dear little sister. You can do it now or you can do it later. But you will have to give into some sorrow one day."

Mattie shook her head. "I don't rightly see that day coming. Mama and Papa taught us to go on with life in the face of death. That we have bigger mountains to climb. Have to stick up for ourselves. Put white folks in *their* place so they don't put a crimp in ours. Remember?"

"I know. I know. But human kindness will often accept what common sense denies. Papa said that, too. You're a kind woman, Mattie. Under all your armor, there's a soft spot. And Henry still lives there."

*Chapter 6*

# JORDAN GETS KNOCKED DOWN

*St. Louis, Missouri, 1923*

By early 1923, Jordan had firm command over all the colored wards in the city. Even so, his sway wasn't powerful enough to get even one Negro elected to the municipal board. The Republicans, however, still had to receive Jordan's imprimatur to win almost any Black votes, and they needed them for an upcoming bond proposal for city capital improvements. Jordan accepted their request to meet with his usual stipulation: that they come to him.

When Myrtle walked into Jordan's office the night of the gathering, she looked around it and let out a hoot.

"Ya somethin', ya are."

"Why do you say that, Mama?" He smiled and leaned back in his tufted maroon leather chair.

"Ya make the city bosses come to yo' house in the dead of

night"—she laughed—"and then make sure they sit on the worst chairs we got. Take the cushions off and everything as well."

"I like to see them squirm. They never know what I'm gonna ask for or what they're gonna have to do."

Before long, the doorbell rang. Jordan had Douglas, his driver, answer it and escort five white men into his office. He stood and directed them to their seats, organized in a row facing his desk.

"Before any of you say one word or ask for anything, you're gonna listen to me." He moved to the front of his desk and half sat on it. "I know you want us to support your bond issue, right?"

"We sure do," one of the men said.

"Some say it's going to be for $87 million, which is the biggest the country's ever seen. I understand a lot of things about it. But what I really don't understand is why there's not a word about *improving* health care for Negroes in this town."

"There's a whole hospital for colored people downtown. The city made sure of that," another man said.

"Humph! Don't play me for a fool! That rattrap has sent more Black people to their graves than the Spanish flu did." Jordan glared at each man, one after the other. "I let my daddy die right here in this house rather than risk taking him to what you call a hospital for colored."

"Jordan, what do you want?" the same man asked.

"Well, if **you** want **us** to show up and vote for this thing to help Mayor Stinson look good…" He paused, looked upward, and then stared at them all again. "Let me see. A million's a nice round number. Yeah! A line item in that amount for the construction of a hospital for Negroes. Otherwise, we not only sit this one out but also the next municipal election when, I believe, you're all running to keep your seats."

The white men remained silent.

"Speak up now. I surely wouldn't want any of my men to have to pull on your collars or, better yet, your suspenders, if you know what I mean."

The men mumbled a bit, then nodded in agreement.

"*And* I want to see a draft of the language before it goes on the ballot. Want it buried somewhere in the middle, so most of the whites won't even know they voted for it. But we will," Jordan added. "And one last thing. I know these things take time. Building permits and bids and all that. In this case, however, I want the first shovel of ground turned for that hospital within a year from the vote. I'm sure as hell that the building with the mayor's name on it will be already up by then!"

The politicians all grumbled in agreement as Jordan shook hands with each of them. The following month, the line item passed with the resounding support of voters from both parties.

Over the next year, Jordan scouted out a larger and more upscale locale for his burgeoning funeral business. He found nothing big or grand enough in the Black parts of town, especially because none of the houses sat on much land. He wanted extra space for a garage to house more automobiles and to construct outbuildings, if need be.

One afternoon, as Jordan worked in his office, he heard Ethan calling out his name. He then burst through the door.

"I just bought a home west of Grand Avenue! One of those *big* houses." He stretched out his arms.

"How in the hell did you manage that? It's whites only. And mostly wealthy ones at that."

"A couple of white-looking Negro families managed to buy some property there. You know, the Fords and the Jeffersons?"

"Yes, I do. One's a schoolteacher and the other's a lawyer. As invisible as they come."

"Well, once they moved their belongings in, they threw a joint housewarming party and then *all* their colored friends started knocking on the door." Ethan nudged Jordan's stomach. "FOR SALE signs sprang up and prices fell. You need to take a look right away."

The moment Jordan laid eyes on a three-story, redbrick mansion on a half-acre of land, he fell in love with it and purchased it. He turned his former home and funeral parlor into a rooming house and bought the buildings on either side and did the same with them.

"Marvin encouraged me to buy property," he told his mother.

"But, Son, I'll have to—" Myrtle began.

"You won't have to lift a finger. I'll get someone to run them for us."


In early March of the following year, Jordan and his ward captains stood in the front row amid the city's luminaries to witness the first shovel of dirt be turned for the new hospital. Spring refused to arrive, so the ground was still as hard as peanut brittle, and it took the mayor and two of his aides to break through. Journalists scribbled away and photographers documented the event.

The day after, Jordan sat in his office rifling through the

newspapers and its coverage of the story. He heard footsteps and called out, "Who's there?"

A robust young white man walked in and took off a Legionnaires hat to reveal a close-cropped head of kinky hair. Jordan let out a belly laugh.

"Frenchie? I get such a kick seeing you in that hat, looking like you just walked out of the desert. That prop's about the only way to keep them from knowing you're not one of them."

"That's why I always leave it on."

"So, what's the latest, Frenchie? How's life as the mayor's chauffeur?"

"Stinson don't give half a damn about that hospital."

"And I don't give *half a damn* what he thinks just as long as he builds it."

"They ain't gonna do nothin' now. He got in the car with the building commissioner after the ceremony and told him to start diggin' out the basement and then stop."

"He said that, did he?"

"Yessir. Said he'd like to build it in the middle of the Mississippi, so it'd sink with half of St. Louis's colored inside. Also said that if he could start another flu, just in the colored wards, he'd be done with all of us. Then they all laughed."

"We'll see who laughs last."

"There's more, Boss." Frenchie took a deep breath. "They plannin' on doin' away with ya."

"Oh yeah?"

"We dropped off the commissioner and then picked up one of the mayor's henchmen, the one with a flesh mole on his chin the size of Chicago?"

"Oh yeah. I know him. Threatened my mama years ago."

"Yeah, well, he's the one who's gonna do it. They both went into somebody's house on the far north side, and I snuck up and listened. They got all riled up and were shoutin' by the end. I heard everythin', Boss. They wanna stop ya now before ya get too big for yo' britches."

"I'm already too big."

"Talked about how when ya chop off a chicken's head, the body runs around, flappin' its wings until it keels over."

"They think killing me will stop what I've started? But if these bastards think that they can take us down, they got another think coming. Keep your ears in the back seat."

Jordan handed Frenchie an envelope. "Ya know ya don't have to," Frenchie said.

"I know, but I also know you got a sick child at home, so take it."

"Thanks, Mr. Jordan."

After Frenchie left, Jordan poured himself a straight shot of bourbon and telephoned Ethan.

"I'm calling a meeting tonight for eight o'clock sharp. I want every precinct captain, ward chair, and block worker there. Be sure to tell all of them to keep a lid on it. My mama can't know anything about this, either. Best she stays in the dark for now. Call Ol' Man Fine, too. We'll use his store just like the old days. Come fetch me early so I can explain. Then we'll go together. Mama thinks I'm only up to good if I'm with you."

When Ethan arrived, Jordan took him into his office, shut the door, and told him the mayor's plan.

"If anything happens to me, you make sure our machine doesn't stop. I don't care how they threaten you or what they offer. You hear me?"

"But Jordan, without you, *there is no machine*," Ethan countered.

"And I'm telling you that there is. There *has* to be. Scramble around. Make them think it's gone off the rails but keep it on track."

"But—"

"I said, keep it on track. Now we've got some special elections in a few months. And tonight, I'm announcing that we're sitting them out. That bastard's cronies still may win—they know a thing or two about stuffing ballot boxes—but the Republicans will still see how strong we are at the polls." Jordan stood and walked out of his office with Ethan following.

The early spring evening remained stubbornly cold, and Jordan pulled his overcoat from a rack.

"This won't take long, Mama."

"As long as ya with Dr. Cole, take yo' time." Myrtle smiled as she waved them off from the front door.

They walked across the porch and down the steps toward Ethan's car. Jordan stopped to tie a shoelace.

"And another thing, Ethan," Jordan said as he started to stand up.

A gunshot interrupted the stillness. Jordan fell to the ground as a car pulled out of the alley facing them and swerved down the street. Ethan rolled him over, saw the wound in his throat, stuffed Jordan's lapel into it, and hollered out. A few neighbors came running, but none faster than Myrtle and Douglas.

"Remember we're sitting out," Jordan whispered. "Get me inside **now**." He spat out blood and fainted. Myrtle cradled Jordan's head as Douglas carried him inside and Ethan rushed to his car for his doctor's satchel.

\* \* \*

A crowd gathered at the front door, calling Jordan's name and straining to look into the parlor. After almost an hour, Ethan stepped out and wiped away a tear.

"He's gone. But he left some words for all of you. 'Continue my fight. Don't ever give up. Let those crackers know we mean business on Election Day. We're sitting this one out!' Are you in? For Jordan?" Ethan asked.

Amid the sound of women sobbing, shouts of approval rang out.

"We'll be bringing him out soon," Ethan continued, "taking him where nobody can find him, where no one can desecrate his final resting place. He wanted no funeral. No tears to be wasted. Turn your wailing into action. You hear him talking to you, don't you?"

"We do, we do," the crowd repeated.

Before long, the dead wagon rolled down the driveway with Douglas at the wheel. Myrtle, veiled and dressed in black, walked alongside it. He parked the vehicle in front of the house and the onlookers rushed toward it. Ethan opened the rear door and let them walk by in single file. Jordan's body lay on a stretcher, covered by a shroud up to his neck. Ethan closed the door, Myrtle got in next to Douglas, and they departed.

Neighbors trailed Ethan and the wagon until they got to the end of the street.

"That's it." Ethan held up his hand and started to wave good-bye. All took his lead as Douglas accelerated and disappeared down the street.

# Chapter 7

# JORDAN SKEDADDLES

*Greenston, South Carolina, 1924*

Jordan awoke to the sound of a horse neighing. He attempted to turn toward the noise but struggled; his head and neck seemed packed inside something soft and fluffy, but rigid at the same time. When he opened his mouth to speak, his mother, Myrtle, shushed him with her forefinger.

"Hold on. Ya can't talk for a while or move. Dr. Cole dug that bullet out yo' neck and stitched ya up, but it grazed yo' cords. Gotta let them heal and make sure ya don't tear anything open. This pillow round yo' neck gonna keep you still, so stop trying to budge." She patted him on the chest. "We passed by the farm while the help was sleepin' so nobody knows ya ain't dead. Got the horse truck and brought Bessie along 'cause I know she's yo' favorite mare."

He wrinkled his brow.

"Calm down. The Lord's gonna fight for ya. Just be still. We're on our way to warm weather, down-home cookin', and a place where nobody can hurt ya. Takin' ya to a farm outside Green-ston, South Carolina, where some of Dr. Cole's kin live. And with Douglas behind the wheel? It's as good as havin' St. Christopher carryin' ya."

"Hey, Boss!" Douglas shouted from the front of the truck.

"I can't stay long. Gotta go back and mourn ya, but Bessie's gonna keep ya company," Myrtle said, and then she and Douglas both laughed.

She bent over him and kissed his cheek.

"We hatched a plan. Dr. Cole and me. Ya dead but ya ain't"—she laughed—"and ya gonna return to St. Louis resurrected as soon ya heal. And take over yo' machine again."

Jordan grinned broadly and winked.

"Dr. Cole didn't have nothing in his case to ease yo' pain. But I brought somethin' else ya favor." Myrtle showed Jordan an unopened bottle of David Nicholson 1843 bourbon and a jar of honey. "Just squeeze my hand whenever ya can't take the pain."

Jordan gripped it.

"Ya rascal, ya." She chuckled. "Douglas, pull over. Ya gotta help me raise him up so I can pour some liquor, cradled in this here honey, down his throat."

After three days of almost nonstop driving, they reached Ethan's second cousin's home on expansive farmland. Jordan watched from inside the truck as a couple and three young girls burst out the front door.

The head of the family rushed up and opened the wagon's door.

"I'm Charles Cole," he announced. "Let me help get Mr. Jordan Sable out."

Jordan attempted to sit up straight and acknowledge his host, but only managed to wave. He watched his mother descend from the wagon and put her hands on her hips.

"No titles here. I'm Myrtle and my son's Jordan. We ain't real formal people. Thanks for helpin' us out."

Jordan tapped on the window with his hand and nodded in agreement.

"Our pleasure. Our pleasure, sure 'nuff," Charles said.

Charles's wife, Helen, approached and peered inside the trailer. "All due respect, ma'am. But I can't change my ways. He'll be Mr. Jordan here. No less."

"Suit yo'self."

The two women and the children trailed Charles and Douglas as they carried Jordan into the house and laid him on the sofa. He had finally accepted his lot and remained calm while Myrtle described how to care for her son once she left. He did begin to grunt when Helen said he'd be sleeping in their bedroom.

"What did I tell ya, boy? No noises! At least a month," Myrtle called out.

Jordan refrained from making a fuss when he saw his room, a spacious one filled with natural light. Once Charles and Douglas laid him on the four-poster bed that abutted the far wall and lined up with the window across from it, he started writing in the air.

"He needs a pencil and paper. Gotta say somethin'. That's my boss," Douglas explained.

Charles came back and handed the items to Jordan. "Whatever

ya want, just write it out. I don't read too good but my young-uns do," he said, laughing.

Douglas helped Jordan sit up as he wrote.

*Could you please move the bed closer to the window so I can get a better look at the fields and watch all the planting? Especially want to see how your horse plows the land. Bessie's never done this kind of work, but I wouldn't be surprised if she didn't catch on right away. Use her as you wish.*

"Mr. Jordan, suh. Bessie's just gonna wait for ya to ride her. I can tell what she's made for. She can graze all she wants 'til ya ready to take her out," Charles responded.

Myrtle arrived with Helen, cowbell in hand. She placed it on the night table next to the bed.

"Borrowed it from a neighbor. Just ring it if ya need somethin'," Helen told him.

Jordan smiled and nodded.

"Ya finally learnin', Son," Myrtle said.

The morning after his mother and Douglas left, Jordan opened his eyes at daybreak. He watched the South Carolina sun hail the farm: observed how, row by row, it revealed the lengthy mounds of dark soil, how it bathed the seedlings as they peeked up, and how it kissed each unfurling leaf. Each week brought a modicum of improvement. First Jordan could sit up straight in his bed, then he could stand next to it for a few minutes, then he could walk to the window and remain there for a half hour or so. He unwrapped his neck, impatient with the confinement, but remained silent until the requisite month passed and he could test his voice. Initially, his words sounded like a croak and then they grew crunchy. Finally they landed in the back of his throat and came out as a soft rasp. He became comfortable with this new tone, as it demanded even more attention than before. The Coles all shushed whenever he spoke so they could hear his every word.

He took a daily constitutional by walking through the Cole residence, investigating every nook and absorbing the love they'd put there. He soon learned why Charles's father had built their two-storied, clapboard farmhouse with three dormer gabled windows, like bugged-out eyes, on each face of the second floor.

"My daddy said, 'Any Klansman come to burn me down, wanna see 'em riding over on their horses.'"

The deeply shaded veranda that hugged the entire ground floor with a door on each side had a reason as well.

"'If we need to hightail it outta here, we got plenty a ways,'" Charles said, again quoting his father.

When he became strong enough, he would start his day by swathing one of Helen's white linen napkins around his neck and mounting Bessie bareback. The South Carolina sun beckoned to them both, and they would ride until 10:00 a.m., Bessie obeying every swivel of Jordan's hips. By then, he had wrestled with the recurrent nightmare of his near death and crushed it under the mare's hoofs.

After weeks of drinking liquids and eating anything that could be minced, Jordan felt ready for more hearty fare. Helen obliged and provided him with grits, soft-scrambled eggs, sassafras tea with tablespoons of honey, and homemade biscuits sopped in buttermilk. Soups of all varieties, shredded chicken and rice, meatloaf as soft as butter, and greens cooked to within an inch of their lives filled out the other meals.

Then the day came when Jordan harnessed Bessie to his host's one-hoss shay and decided to venture into town. He wanted to buy gifts for the entire Cole family and asked the oldest daughter, Martha, which store had the finest offerings.

"That'd be Madame Sarah's Emporium in Sunset," she explained.

"Sunset? Where's that?"

"It's the colored part of Greenston."

"Well, Madame Sarah's it'll be. Will you come with me? Don't want your folks to know about this, so we can just say that you'll be showing me around town and taking care of me today. Okay?"

"Oh yes, I'd like that."

Jordan almost tripped over his feet when he saw the array of goods inside the emporium, then stood tall and surveyed the main room. From stem to stern stood rows of clothing: girls' and women's on the left and boys' and men's on the right, with narrow corridors running through each section and a wide aisle separating the two. The side walls held every kind of item to outfit a kitchen, an office, a sewing room. Overhead fans whirred throughout the store. Jordan could barely make out what filled the far wall, so he strode there to find bolts of fabric, grouped by color, from top to bottom.

"Never expected to see all this in Greenston."

"Everything for farmin's outside," Martha added.

"Guess you don't need to go anywhere in this wide world for whatever you need, now do you?"

"Madame Sarah says we need only buy where we're welcome. None of those shops downtown let us try on anythin', let alone work there, so we don't go."

"Madame Sarah sounds like she's ahead of her time."

"Yeah, she is and the head of everythin' inside these walls."

"Help me now, Martha. I want to get you and your family exactly what you'd buy for yourselves. And make sure Madame Sarah stays in business!"

Martha suggested autumn frocks for her mother and sisters and a cardigan for her father.

"And a dress *and* a Sunday bonnet for you, Martha?" Jordan said as he plucked one off a shelf. "I want you to have something extra for all your help."

Martha blushed.

Jordan put the hat on Martha's head, gathered up the other presents, and glanced around the room until his eyes rested on a buxom, tightly corseted woman at the cash register. He strode up to her as she shuffled through receipts while keeping her eye on every cranny in the store.

"Madame Sarah, I presume—" he started.

"Never assume, never presume. I'm Mrs. Wilson," she answered.

"I beg your pardon, ma'am."

"Better beg hers." She pointed her nose toward the entrance. "She's the mistress."

Jordan turned and saw a slip of a young woman greeting customers. She seemed to dance from one person to another as they crossed the threshold, smiling at the men, kissing the women's cheeks, and hugging the elderly. Jordan's chin almost hit the ground, and if he'd been able to put her inside his pocket and whisk her off to St. Louis in that very moment, he would have. Jordan laid his wallet on the counter without taking his eyes off Sarah.

"Here, Mrs. Wilson, pull out whatever you need."

Entranced, he assessed every bit of Madame Sarah. Petite in stature with thick, wavy, chestnut-colored hair pinned on top of a perfectly oval face, almond-shaped eyes, buttermilk skin with a smattering of freckles, and wearing a fitted dress more yellow than a field of buttercups. *How in the hell could I have missed her when I came in? She's a tiny little thing, but she's got character and fortitude, and if need be, rigor. I can tell. I've never seen a prettier girl in my life.*

"Mr. Jordan," Martha said and yanked his sleeve. "We can go now. I took the liberty of emptyin' your billfold," she said, laughing.

Dumbstruck, Jordan walked past Sarah without uttering a word or casting a glance.

The moment Jordan's shoes touched the sidewalk, he stopped and began peppering Martha with questions.

"Tell me what I have to do. Should I bring her flowers? Candies? Order a dress from New York? Get to know her brothers? Does she have brothers? Call on her father? Mother? Grandma? I have to have her and I need your help!"

"Well, I declare. This is the most talkin' ya done since ya started talkin', Mr. Jordan. And ya practically pantin'." She laughed. "Just slow down."

"But I can't. When I see something I want, I go after it. Why is she called *Madame*? She's not married, is she? She can't be!"

"She's single, all right."

"I'll do anything."

"Talk to my mama when we get home. She can school ya."

When they arrived at the Coles', Jordan jumped off the shay and ran into the house, leaving Martha to tend to Bessie.

"Helen, Helen!" he called as loudly as he could. "Where are you?"

"What's all the ruckus, Mr. Jordan?"

"I just met the woman I'm going to marry."

"Would that be Miss Sarah?"

"How'd you know?"

"Get in line 'cause she's got more suitors than a men's store. Actually, she's practically a spinster at her age. Almost twenty-one." She laughed. "She's a picky one. Waiting for the right man, I hear tell."

"Well, that'll be me! No one else can have her. She's mine."

"Now, hold on to yo' britches."

"But I can't. I have to have her. Tell me everything about her."

"Well, where to start? She inherited the store from her folks. Her mama was named Sarah as well, so it's still called Madame Sarah's Emporium. She's got a brother and some cousins, just in case she needs help. Her two sisters left Greenston a few years back. But tough as she is, she handles it all herself."

"Just tell me what I have to do."

## Chapter 8

# SARAH CONQUERS JORDAN

*Greenston, South Carolina, 1924*

W hen the tall stranger strode right past her into the emporium, Sarah almost huffed out loud. He hadn't even acknowledged her, something that never happened whenever anyone laid eyes on her for the first time, especially a man. She calmed down somewhat when she saw how taken he appeared to be with her store. Sarah watched him from behind as he stopped in his tracks. He put his hands on his hips, and even rocked back and forth on his heels, as if he owned the place while he talked to Martha Cole. Once the two of them began picking up items, Sarah returned to her routine of welcoming customers in between strolling the aisles to keep the pickpockets at bay.

When they left the store, he still ignored her. *Is he blind or rude?* Sarah went to the display window and peered outside. He and Martha were parked on the sidewalk, talking up a storm. He even pointed at the entrance now and then. Sarah found herself transfixed until they walked away. *My, my. That is one good-looking somebody.*

The following Sunday, Sarah attended church service, and as usual, greeted members of the congregation and patted their children as she made her way down the aisle to the front pew. On her way out, she spied the stranger in the last row with the Coles. As she passed, he put on his hat and tipped its brim her way. By the time she reached the vestibule, she was fanning herself with her hankie, blaming it on the summer heat when Nathan, her older brother, asked why she was so visibly flushed.

"It's a little warm in here, that's all," she answered and sashayed off.

During the after-church social, Sarah held court in typical fashion, dallying and dismissing each of Sunset's eligible bachelors who approached her. The stranger hadn't arrived with the Coles and she glanced around the room in search of him to no avail.

The following week, the stranger popped in and out of the store and it was now she who disregarded him. And each time she did, she noticed how dejected he appeared. He would turn on his heel, drop his shoulders, and leave.

After several Sunday services, she saw him with Helen Cole, who walked toward her with the stranger at her heel.

"Darlin', I want to introduce Ethan's dear friend, Jordan Sable, from St. Louis," she started. "He's been stayin' with us and—"

"And just why has it taken you so long to bring this handsome man out in the open?" Sarah asked.

"Ya mean ya haven't seen him at the emporium?"

"No, I don't think so." She stared up at him. "No, no, not at all."

"Well, I've been in and out for a couple of weeks," Jordan countered.

"Is that so?" She stood back from him and looked him up and down.

"Next time, I'll say something to you. I mean, if you don't mind."

"Yes, you do that, you hear?" Sarah said.

"Oh, I hear you all right, and I'll be looking forward to speaking to you."

"And with that soft, raspy voice of yours, I'll be sure to remember you next time."

"I'll try to get ahold of my vocal chords," Jordan said as he cleared his throat.

"You'll do no such thing." She waved her forefinger back and forth at him. "I like the way it sounds. Distinctive. People will have to be quiet to hear you."

"Why, I am flattered that you would think that…"

"Not another word. Nice to meet you, Mr. Sable."

"Likewise," he said, and bowed slightly from the waist. "Looking forward."

"Why, Mr. Sable, you said that already."

"Just want you to know how much I mean it."

Sarah responded with a blush as fleeting as the flap of a hummingbird's wing, turned away, and walked off as she grinned all over herself.


On Monday afternoon, as Sarah mounted the staircase in her store, Jordan rushed up to her.

"Good day, Madame Franklin."

She turned toward him. "Why, how are you, Mr. Sable?"

"Much better now."

"Now, just why would that be?" she teased.

"Why, I hear that it's teatime here in Greenston, no? And I was hoping I could offer you—"

"A cool drink?"

"Yes, yes. Anything you would like," he almost pleaded.

"I'm so sorry, really I am, but I have to meet with some of my suppliers today. They are waiting for me upstairs, so I must run."

"Tomorrow, then?" he asked.

"Perhaps. I'm really not certain."

"Well, I hope so."

"Good day, Mr. Sable." Sarah turned and introduced a decisive sway to her hips as she walked up each step, feeling his eyes on her backside.

The heat awoke Sarah early the next morning. The late June temperature had skyrocketed overnight and by sunrise, Greenston was as hot as a bolt on the gates of hell. She figured that Jordan would still come to her shop and was determined to look as fresh as a sprig of Carolina jasmine in early spring. The housekeeper, Clara, and the driver, Davis, attempted to dissuade her from leaving the house. She ignored them both and ordered him to prepare the buggy.

As they rode toward the emporium, Sarah saw how the sun assaulted everything in sight, and how the few people foolish enough to be outside ambled along as if wading through molasses. She arrived before any of her employees, opened the windows, left most of the lights off, but turned on the overhead and table fans. Eventually, the help straggled in. She ignored their lateness and flitted around the store, rearranging bolts of cloth and straightening out the curio cabinet.

Suddenly the lights went out and the fans stopped whirring, extinguishing what little relief they provided. The last thing she remembered was darting toward the fuse box while holding her breath in confusion.

"Ooh," she murmured as soon as she regained consciousness. She lay with her eyes shut and continued to moan. She must have fainted among the clothing racks.

"Miss Franklin?"

When Sarah heard this, she fluttered her lids and relaxed. That was Jordan's voice. Was he holding her in his arms? She felt his perspiration commingling with hers and it excited her.

"Oh, please, please," he continued. "Please wake up. I don't know what will become of me if you don't. You've got to come back to me."

"Come back?" Sarah started.

"Yes, come to, I mean," he responded, stumbling over his words.

"Why, Miss Sarah!" Mrs. Wilson's voice now rang out from above them. "I'll get some water. Hold on to her, Mr. Sable. I'll be right back."

"Oh, I'm not going anywhere," he answered.

"My, my. What happened to me?" Sarah said with her eyes still closed.

"You fainted, I believe, from the heat."

"Mr. Sable. I heard you talking to me from far away. You said such things." She opened her eyes and gazed up at him.

"Here, let me tend to her." Mrs. Wilson returned with a glass of water and a wet towel.

Jordan held on for a moment and then relinquished her. He stood and stepped back.

"Byron! Bring me some cushions," Mrs. Wilson called out to the stock boy.

"Miss Sarah! Are you all right?" she asked as she stroked Sarah's face.

"Oh yes. I'm just fine," she answered as she looked at Jordan.


The heat remained so fierce that most shops, including Sarah's, only opened their doors and shutters as the sun began its descent. Nathan's wife took over for her while she was confined to her upstairs bedroom in order to regain her strength. After three days, with Clara by her side, she came downstairs and almost fainted again when she entered the parlor. Yellow flowers filled the room: hibiscus, daffodils, black-eyed Susans, and long-stemmed roses almost as tall as her.

"We ran out of vases, so I put the rest in the tub out back." Clara laughed.

"What? They're more of these?" Sarah said as she turned her head from side to side.

"He sure wants to make an impression. Brought them here himself," Clara added.

"He? You mean Jordan Sable?"

"Almost broke the buggy. Think he was hopin' to see ya, I do."

"Where's the note? There must be one."

"Of course." Clara picked up an envelope from the cocktail

table and handed it over, along with a sleek letter opener next to it.

Sarah slit it open to read.

*Dear Miss Franklin,*

*I only hope, better put, pray, that you have recovered fully.*

*I also hope that these flowers, which pale in comparison to the yellow dress you wore the first day I saw you, bring you comfort and joy during your convalescence, and that I might be allowed to call on you once you can receive visitors.*

*Anxiously awaiting your reply,*
*Jordan Sable*

Sarah let two days pass and then sent Davis with a response.

*Dear Mr. Sable,*

*Thank you ever so much for your help when I fainted in my store.*
*I hear you hand-delivered the flowers. How thoughtful.*
*They are lovely. I truly don't know how to thank you properly, but I would like to invite you for a cool drink at my house once the heat abates. Please let Davis know if that suits you.*

*Sarah Franklin*

The next afternoon, when the temperature had dropped by more than a few degrees, Sarah ventured outside for some air. She positioned herself on the cushioned porch swing and sipped on a tall glass of iced tea stuffed with sprigs of mint. After she finished her drink, she put it on the side table, tilted her head back against the fluffy headrest, and dozed off until she heard a horse's snort.

"Miss Franklin, I hope I didn't startle you," Jordan said as he tied Bessie to a hitching post. "Are you feeling better?" he asked as he approached her.

Still half dozing, she stared at him in silence.

"The weather abated a bit, as you said, so I took the liberty of coming without your—"

"Why yes. Do join me," she said slowly, and patted the seat next to her. "Would you care for some?" She lifted her tumbler.

"Oh yes, yes. I'd like that more than anything in the world."

"More than anything in the world? A little old glass of tea?"

"Yes, more than anything because I'll be drinking it with you."

"Clara," she called out, and the Franklins' housekeeper appeared. "A glass for the gentleman, please."

Jordan sat down and his large frame made the rocker toss so much that it pitched Sarah next to him. She pushed herself away, but not before lingering for a moment and glancing up at him. Then she started laughing.

"You should have seen your face, Mr. Sable. You looked as if you just went down with the *Titanic*." She kept on giggling.

His guilty expression softened into a plaintive one. "Well, I wouldn't want to ever do anything that might sink my chances of getting to know you better."

"What? This? A simple little bump. You'd have to do much more than that in order to—"

"You mean, you will permit me to get to know you better? Take you for a stroll? Anything, anything you'll allow."

"I think I'd like that," she answered, and began to cool herself with a fan she pulled from her dress pocket.

Clara arrived with the drink and a pitcher filled to its brim, then disappeared.

"Now, Mr. Sable..."

"Jordan. Would you please call me that?"

"If you like."

"Yes, I'd like that very much."

"Well then, Jordan, would you please tell me about yourself? I'm sure you know all about me and my people, the way folks talk around here. Such a small town, Greenston. And in Sunset."

"I don't need to know anything more than what I saw of you the first time I came into your store."

Sarah continued fanning herself.

"Jordan, will you rock us while you tell me about yourself?"

He pushed the floor with one foot, and they swayed back and forth and talked until the sun set and the tea ran out.

"I guess it's time for me to go. I hope I can see you again, Miss Franklin...soon." He stood and reached for her hand to help her rise.

"Oh no. That won't do. Not at all." She remained seated.

"What do you mean? I thought we were..." He gave her a puzzled look.

"Not unless you just call me Sarah." She batted her eyelashes.

She watched Jordan's face relax as his chest expanded.

"Oh yes, yes. I'll do anything you want."

"Anything? That's a tall order you've taken on for yourself, Jordan." She stood up.

"One thing I didn't mention about me. I don't much like to

repeat myself. My word is my word. But for you, yes, anything. Might I begin by taking you to lunch when you go back to the emporium?"

"Well, the first days may be a bit busy, but…" Sarah hesitated as she stared into Jordan's eyes. "But yes, I think I can make time for you. I'm going back the day after tomorrow, as a matter of fact."

"Until the day after tomorrow, then." He bent from his waist, raised her left hand, and kissed her ring finger.

After several weeks of meals at Sunset's lone luncheonette, and evening strolls, and bundles of flowers delivered to her home, Sarah invited Jordan for Saturday supper, where several of her relatives gathered for their weekly get-together. Before eating, they all congregated in the parlor.

"You're awfully quiet, Jordan," Nathan declared. "We won't bite, or maybe we will." He laughed.

"Now, darlin', you leave Jordan be. He's just shy, that's all." Sarah winked at Jordan.

"We're just small-town folk. Nothing to be afraid of," Nathan continued.

Jordan cleared his throat.

"No, I'm not cowed. Just impressed by your splendid family and the gracious hospitality of your sister. She's special and it's clear all of you are as well."

"Well, then, speak up! Impress us over supper!" Nathan exclaimed as he ushered everyone into the dining room.

Sarah listened as Jordan regaled the group with stories of St. Louis and its music. Two of the city's hit tunes, "Stackolee" and the "Saint Louis Blues," dominated the radio across the country, and he provided background information on each. He even knew W. C. Handy, the author of the latter, he told them. And now it was Sarah who could barely take her eyes off him.

After the group finished their cordials, Jordan said his good-byes and Sarah walked him to his buggy.

"Thank you so much for having me here today."

"My pleasure, Jordan. My pleasure indeed."

"You've got a mighty fine family and a beautiful house." He made a sweeping gesture across the facade as if presenting it to her.

"It's my home. My roots are here but…" She frowned and crossed her arms.

"But what, Sarah?"

"Oh, nothing. Just foolish thoughts, that's all." She scrutinized the house.

"Tell me, please. I want to know all about you. Foolish or not."

"I just always had a feeling. A hankering…" She laughed.

"For something else?" he added.

"For something different. Something bigger."

"Bigger than all this land your house sits on?"

"Large like the sky above us with all those stars." She threw her arms upward. "See"—she let them drift downward, then hugged herself and swayed a bit—"I told you it was silly."

"Not at all. You let me see some more of you. And I'd like to…"

"It's nothing really. Nothing. Just dreams. Thank you again for coming. I need to go back inside now. You charmed everyone."

"Well, I only care about my effect on one person here tonight." He pulled her close and kissed her.

"You've made an impression all right," she said as she backed away, straightened her dress, and looked over her shoulder to see if anyone had seen them from inside. And then she grinned at him.

"I'll be on my way, Sarah. Until tomorrow," he said as he mounted the buggy. "And the day after that and the day after that," he called out to her as he snapped the whip above his head and galloped off.

After another two weeks of nonstop courting, Sarah decided to keep Jordan at bay for a few days. She sat at home each night, contemplating her feelings for him and puckering her lips whenever she relived their first kiss. On the fourth night, she heard a knock on her bedroom door.

"Miss Sarah? Mr. Jordan's outside," Clara announced. "Said he's sorry he didn't call ahead. Said he's gotta see ya *now!*"

"I'll be down. Put him in the parlor, please," Sarah answered.

"He's carryin' a big something or other."

"Just put him where I said to."

Sarah pinned up her hair, powdered her face and underarms, and applied the loudest shade of red lipstick she had in her vanity. Then she sat in her armchair for almost a half an hour.

When she slid back the pocket doors to the parlor, Jordan jumped to his feet.

"I've got to tell you why I came over here without letting you know. Got a lot to say."

"Why, Jordan, I've never seen you in such a state. Whatever is the matter? And what in heaven's name is that?" Sarah pointed to a two-foot-tall mound that sat in the middle of the room, covered in a cotton throw with an iron handle peeking through the slot on top.

"Let me explain," he said as he led her to one of the settees and they both sat. "You see, I'm dead. No, I'm supposed to be, but I'm not."

"Clearly," she stated, laughing.

"The white boys in St. Louis tried to kill me and I let them think they did. Came down here to heal while my political machine went to work. Negroes sat out the last election and the Republicans felt our power. But now"—Jordan handed her a telegram—"this arrived today."

Sarah read it aloud.

```
RESURRECTION TIME HAS COME STOP WE
CRIPPLED THEM BUT MORE WORK TO DO STOP
MUST UNSEAT MAYOR STOP SENDING DOUGLAS
TO FETCH YOU STOP ETHAN
```

"So that means..." she started.

"That I have to leave," Jordan finished.

Sarah leaned back.

Jordan stood and went to the mysterious mound. He carried it to her, pulled off the cover to reveal a pair of mourning doves. The birds looked startled for an instant and then began to bill and coo. Jordan pointed to the envelope attached to the roost's door.

Sarah plucked it off, pulled out the note, and again read out loud.

*They mate for life. Will you be my wife?*

She got up and let her eyes trace the contours of Jordan's face. She then lost herself in each of his features…his scrumptious lips, his broad nose and pronounced cheekbones, his high forehead, and his square jaw.

"I know it's sudden, darlin'," Jordan noted. "And I know it's not the proper way. Not asking Nathan for your hand and all, but I can't go away from here without knowing that you'll be mine. Say yes. *Please.*"

Sarah put her hands on his waist and stood on her tiptoes to kiss him. Jordan wrapped his arms around her and lifted her up. They didn't let go of each other until they had to exhale.

"Is that a yes? Oh, *please*," he repeated as he put her down.

"It is," she murmured with a nod.

"You've made me happier than I can say. I'll have to leave when my driver gets here, but I'll come back to Greenston as soon as I can. As soon as you say. And I'll talk to your brother before I go. Ask all proper and—"

"You'll do no such thing," she interrupted. "You've seen how I handle my store. Well, I run my life the same. I'm glad you came straight to me."

"Yes, ma'am." He saluted her.

"And I want to do this my way as well."

"Any way you want."

"Clara?" she called out.


Sarah smiled when Davis led Reverend McKensie into her parlor an hour later.

"Sarah, what's this I hear? Davis tells me ya want to get married?" the reverend said.

"What?" Jordan gasped.

"Jordan, darlin', that doesn't suit you?"

"Why, of course. Of course. I just can't believe it."

With Davis and Clara as witnesses, they married on the spot.

"I'm doing this like a shotgun wedding and it's legal and all, but I still need you to do something, Jordan." The reverend asked for a pen and paper, sat down, and wrote. He handed both to Jordan. "Sign this."

Jordan looked at it and smiled. "I'm signing it and reading it out loud for the world to hear."

"*I, Jordan Winifred Sable, do solemnly swear to marry Sarah Virginia Franklin in church with all the proper documents signed inside a month from today.*" He looked up from the paper. "But no, this won't do." Jordan sat down and wrote some more.

"*And I promise I'll put a rock on her finger bigger than my Cadillac and give her a ceremony at Grace Baptist to beat the band. I'll send for all the Franklins. Each and every one of them.*" He then scribbled his name as fast as he could.

"Reverend McKensie, thank you so much for coming. It's late and your wife is missing you, I'm sure," Sarah said.

"A pleasure, little lady. Always happy to help the Franklins." The Reverend kissed Sarah's cheek, shook Jordan's hand, and left.

"The emporium, Sarah? What about *it*?" Jordan asked.

"Nathan's wife has wanted to take over all along. She'll be happy I'm gone. And I told you that I was yearning for something bigger, something outside of this town." She beamed at him. "You let me tend to my business."

"I know you will."

"Clara!" Sarah called out and the maid bounded in from the kitchen. "Please fix my husband a pot of tea and then join me in my bedroom." As Sarah walked up the stairs, she didn't turn around as she heard Jordan address Clara.

"Clara? You heard that? She called me her husband. We're really married. She's my wife."

Before long, Sarah appeared at the top of the staircase, draped in a shimmering night-robe.

"I'm waiting, my love," she said to him.


After five days, Jordan pulled up to Sarah's house in a black boxy wagon with a driver she assumed was Douglas behind the wheel. She stood on the front porch next to Nathan, Clara, and Davis with a trunk, a suitcase, and a pair of matching hatboxes lined up in a row behind them.

"Is this all you have, Sarah?" Jordan marveled as he mounted the stairs.

"Nathan will bring the rest to the wedding. He and his family are moving in here so they'll be glad to clean out this house." She laughed.

Jordan approached Nathan, hand extended. "Forgive me if I didn't come to you first."

"If you'd done that, she might have turned you down. Always been her own person, my baby sister. If you think she's headstrong, wait until you meet the other two." He looked toward Sarah. "But Sarah, this will always be your home and if, for any reason"—he eyed Jordan—"you need to come back…" He pulled her toward him and nuzzled her until she pulled away.

"I know, darlin'. I know," she answered.

"Welcome to the family, Jordan." Nathan shook his hand.

"Why, thank you. See you in St. Louis."

Sarah lifted her skirt a bit with one hand and threaded her other arm through Jordan's as they walked down the steps.

"So sorry that I'm not taking you home in style, but—"

"Hush," she whispered. "As long as I'm with you, it doesn't matter what we're in."

Sarah strode ahead of him with Davis carrying a footstool behind her. He put it down next to their means of transportation and she stepped into it as if it were a royal carriage. Jordan climbed in next to his wife and snuggled her. Douglas started the engine and let it idle while Clara and Davis loaded her luggage in the back.

"Ready for your new life, my dear, lovely bride?" Jordan asked.

"Yes, more than you know. I said my goodbyes yesterday and handed over all the keys and ledgers."

"Ya somethin' else, Mister Jordan, ya are," Douglas declared. "Rising from the dead with the prettiest girl south of the Mason-Dixon Line as yo' wife. Ya gonna shock the whole town, especially yo' mama."

"Prettiest girl anywhere, my man. But speaking of my mama. We'll stop in Nashville and send a telegram. Don't want her to faint when we get home."


"We're almost here," Jordan announced once they crossed into the Negro part of St. Louis.

"What? I've never seen so many stately homes in one place.

And colored own them?" Sarah asked as she took in as much as she could in the fading light.

"We sure do and ours is the biggest!"

As the dead wagon crept along, Sarah noticed that no one on the street paid much mind to it. *More remains. More flesh and skin and bones*, she heard people mumble.

They pulled up to the back of a house and Jordan hustled her inside. The only light came from atop a staircase and Sarah soon found herself in a kitchen on the second floor where two women jumped to their feet.

"Welcome to your home!" they shouted in unison and swallowed her in their embrace.

"Why, thank you," Sarah said when they let her go. "I'm so glad to meet you. To be here."

"But not as happy as I am." Jordan pulled her to him. "Mama, Jessica. I guess you know who you just hugged. And Sarah's heard all about you."

"No, Son, she hasn't, and ya haven't neither. We've got news of our own." Myrtle turned to her daughter. "Go on, tell him."

"You remember Johnny, don't you? The newspaperboy?"

Jordan nodded.

"Well, while you were down South, he started courting me and he wants to marry me."

"And you?" Jordan stared down at her.

"More than anything, but—"

"What?"

"He got a real job with *The Call* in Kansas City, so I'll be moving."

"Sister, I'll miss you but follow your heart."

"Just like I did," Sarah said, and gripped Jessica's hand.

"Children," Myrtle interrupted them. "They'll be plenty of time for celebratin'. It's time to eat!" She laughed out loud.

After dinner, Jordan led Sarah to their bedroom.

"Why, my goodness gracious!" she gasped.

Sarah didn't know where to look first. The immense canopied bed made of black walnut and festooned with white organza immediately captured her eye. But then she couldn't wait to explore the ivory-colored vanity that hugged the right wall of the room, brimming with tortoiseshell combs, and silver-backed hairbrushes, and faceted bottles and jars. She walked to it, fingered its scalloped edges, and sat down on the accompanying tufted ottoman chair. Two matching highboys stood against another wall, positioned on either side of a broad, mirrored chifforobe, with her luggage piled in front of it. Floor-to-ceiling white drapes covered the windows, and several frosted crystal lamps illuminated the varying grains of the polished walnut flooring. She closed her eyes and imagined scattering bowls of flowers throughout, but otherwise, she wouldn't alter anything.

"You like it, do you?" Jordan asked, breaking the silence.

"It's regal."

"Mama fixed it up for you. Anything you want to change, just..."

Sarah walked up to Jordan as he talked and buried herself in his chest.

"No, my darlin'," she told him.

\* \* \*

The next morning, Sarah jumped up with an eagerness to bedazzle her new town. She straightened their bed, made her toilet, and then opened the chifforobe where she'd hung the eye-popping yellow dress she was wearing when Jordan first entered her store. She pulled a hat that matched the frock from a hook and donned them both. Her heart pounded as she whisked down the corridor toward the kitchen and found Myrtle there.

"Come. It's already started." Myrtle took her hand and led Sarah back down the hallway to the main staircase.

"Oh dear. I'm late. You should've gotten me up," she said as they rushed down the steps.

"Jordan wouldn't hear of it. He wanted ya rested."

Sarah heard the tumult outside the house and gazed through one of the hallway windows. Hundreds of people, mostly Black, filled the front yard: journalists scribbling on pads, photographers snapping, women and men fanning themselves in the stubborn, late-summer heat. All his supporters hooted and clapped whenever Jordan paused.

"I took a punch, but I'm not out. I've come back swinging! The way I sound may have changed, but my voice hasn't. You can still hear it, can't you?" he asked. "And you'll keep hearing it as long as I live, which, as you can clearly see, will be longer than some thought. But remember: *YOU* did this. *YOU* showed those lying, thieving, useless thugs in the Grand Old Party just how powerful *YOU* are. *YOU* carried on when I couldn't. And another thing. *YOU* and I together are going to get a new hospital, city jobs, decent schools, and safer streets. And a new mayor! Hear that, Stinson? Because you know what, Your Honor? I'm considering moving across the aisle and bringing all the wards with me. I feel a change a coming. Hear that, Democrats?"

The crowd began to grumble.

Myrtle tapped on the window and Jordan turned and saw Sarah.

"Calm down. You'll see that I'm right. One step at a time. But hush now because it's time for the pièce de résistance. That's French, for the cat's meow." He guffawed. "Mrs. Sable?"

Sarah stepped onto the front porch as she felt a bevy of butterflies fill her stomach. She maintained her composure and strode toward Jordan, but she had doubts. Sunset, the place that she had dominated with aplomb, was just a speck of a neighborhood in comparison to St. Louis's colored part of town. Jordan had explained the political and social complexities of his domain. She now wondered if she could handle them, as she assessed the quieted crowd, and they, in turn, judged her. She looked downward, but Jordan tipped her chin up and pulled back the netting of her broad-brimmed hat for his world to see her. Met only by what seemed like an interminable whisper of a faint wind as it lapped the trees, tears pooled in Sarah's eyes. She gazed up at Jordan until a thunderous applause broke out.

## Chapter 9

# SARAH ASSUMES HER ROLE

*St. Louis, Missouri, 1924*

It didn't take long for the Black women's tongues to start wagging every which way after the brouhaha of Sarah's arrival subsided.

*Just who does she think she is, snatching up the most eligible man west of the Mississippi? Comes from some nowhere town the size of a matchbox. Heard her people have a confectionery! Imagine that! Selling penny candies and yard goods. She has no idea what kind of a world this is. She's gonna fall off that throne. Just wait and see.*

Soon enough, Sarah heard the snide remarks via her mother-in-law.

"I want ya to know what ya up against, Daughter," Myrtle warned her.

"Thank you, Mother. I have to admit that I *am* worried."

"Well, try not to be. Ya got more smarts and Southern charm than all those women put together."

As hard as she tried to heed Myrtle's advice, Sarah's anxiety increased as the wedding date approached. She had been at the top of Sunset's social hierarchy and now she had lost her footing. Maybe she shouldn't have been so quick to abandon her life and come here? Maybe she had bitten off more than she could chew? She counted the days to her nuptials, hoping that a magic wand would sweep away her doubts, once she said "I do."

True to his word, Jordan wed his stunning bride at Grace Baptist Memorial Church within a month of their arrival in St. Louis. Sarah had no role in the ceremony's planning or execution. Jordan turned all the details over to his staff because he wanted her rested and fresh, without a worry.

As she entered the church on Nathan's arm, the flower arrangements almost blinded her. Fulsome bouquets of yellow roses and white calla lilies with their piercing, saffron-hued stamens adorned each pew and filled the altar. She could only think back to the first dress Jordan had seen her in and knew he hadn't relinquished all the preparations to his employees. She held on to her brother more tightly as they proceeded down the aisle, a bit daunted by the lofty, vaulted church ceiling above her and the goggling guests on each side. But once Jordan took her hand and they said their vows, she felt an inner resolve well up inside her, knowing she could now handle whatever came her way.

The wedding reception was held in an office building owned and populated by an array of the city's Negro professional class, and businesses and institutions: doctors, lawyers, insurance companies, worker's unions, a bank, a newspaper, a pharmacy, and so on. A crowd of onlookers awaited them outside and cheered Jordan's name as Douglas opened the door of the Cadillac limousine and the couple stepped out. Sarah went straight up to the gawkers and began shaking their hands as if she knew each one. Some refused and instead bent over to kiss her white-gloved wrist. She turned toward her husband who stood on the sidewalk and relished how he beamed at her.

Sarah quietly motioned for Jordan to join her. In two giant steps, he caught up with her. They seduced the crowd together until they arrived at the entrance and Jordan led her to the elevator. The operator took them to the building's crowning glory—a penthouse ballroom, the only one for colored in town. As they crossed the threshold to an ovation, Sarah smiled at her husband while saying, "Who is that couple to our left?"

"Schoolteachers," he answered.

"Their names?" she asked through her grin.

"Belton."

Sarah led Jordan over to them. "Mr. and Mrs. Belton, I'm Sarah. So glad that you could come. My husband has told me of your fine work in the schools. It will be so wonderful when we can send our children to you. If you agree, that is?" Sarah looked up at Mr. Belton and slightly batted her lashes.

"Why yes, yes," Mr. Belton sputtered.

"And Mrs. Belton, I'm a newcomer here and you must let me know where you shop. You look lovely."

Mrs. Belton stood up straighter. "Oh yes, yes. I will."

"Excuse us now. We've got a reception to attend," she said, laughing.

Sarah continued in this fashion, flummoxing most into silence until she and Jordan reached the head table where Myrtle, Jessica, and Sarah's family sat.

Jordan brushed back the side of her veil. "You're even wilier than I thought," he said, and kissed her neck.

"No, sugar. It's called gumption. I married the biggest catch in town. Kill them with kindness or they may knife me in the back."

Jordan kissed her again, on the mouth this time, and a hush fell over the guests as they gazed at the couple.

The couple continued in bliss for weeks with abundant breakfasts in bed, long afternoons chatting, and passionate lovemaking through the night. Sarah was certain she had conceived in Greenston, but kept her pregnancy a secret from Jordan, wanting to surprise him over a candlelit dinner on the anniversary of two months of their first marriage. She miscarried the day before. When she told Jordan, her stoic response puzzled him.

"It's all right, darlin'," she said. "My mama lost a baby before I was born, and she always told me that it was God's way of making sure she got me. I know everything will turn out fine. I just know it will," she told him.

On the heels of her first loss came another. She tried to remain optimistic, but a gloom that matched the overcast skies and dreary winter weather soon overtook her. Each time Jordan tried to cheer her up with gifts of jewelry and dresses and handmade hats, she refused them.

"Take them all back. I don't deserve anything because I can't give you what you want from me," she'd repeat over and over again.

"Sarah, it doesn't matter. Really it doesn't. All I need is you."

\* \* \*

After a month of Sarah ensconced in their bedroom, one mid-morning Jordan suggested that, despite the chilly temperature, she dress for an outing.

"But darlin', I'm not up to it."

"All you have to do is sit. I'm taking you for a little ride. It's powerful cold outside, but the sun is shining. C'mon."

Emma, the housemaid, helped Sarah get ready and led her to the garage where Jordan's latest acquisition, a Buick Master Six, sat warmed up and humming. He had yet to arrive, but she soon felt his hands from behind as he draped something on top of her bulky loden-green coat.

Confused, she turned toward him, only to feel her chin brush against the fluffiest fur conceivable.

"What on earth…" she started.

"It's sable. Fitting, no? And I'm not taking it back," he declared.

Sarah stroked the coat which wasn't, after all, a coat, but rather a full-length cloak or a mantle or a cape or she didn't know what. It ended just above her ankles and its heft caused her to break into a sweat.

"It's too much, Jordan."

"You can slip out of that woolen coat when we're in the car. Let's go!" Jordan said and helped her into the front seat.

"Douglas isn't taking us?" she asked.

"No, no. Unless you're worried about my driving?" He laughed.

"I like this, husband. Just the two of us."

"Oh, I'm so happy that you're pleased to be alone with me," Jordan said while blushing.

"What? I want that more than anything. There are always so many people around us."

"Not *always*." He winked at her.

They headed out of town, due west, and as the winter sun struck her face through the windshield, Sarah's mood brightened. After almost an hour, they pulled up to a bolted wooden gate with six-foot-high fences extending from it in each direction. Jordan honked the horn and a field hand came running and let them in. They proceeded to the main building and were greeted by three more men. "What's all this, darlin'?"

"It's our stock farm."

"What? You never said anything."

"You won't take any of my presents, but I thought that just maybe you'd accept this as a true wedding gift. You and your kin are used to having land. This can't compare to all you have, but it brings in more income."

"Oh, darlin', you don't have to."

"I know, I know, Sarah, but this farm means a lot to me. My daddy taught me everything I know about horses out here. There was a no-account named Joe who made himself out to be the owner. Rankled my father every chance he got. Nearly bankrupted the place with all his stealing, but it came to light. Now it's ours. I mean, yours!"

Sarah threw her arms around Jordan and kissed him as the staff clapped.


They now made a habit of taking an excursion every week or so, on occasion with Sarah initiating their outings despite the frigid temperatures.

"Take me to see where the Mississippi and Missouri Rivers meet," she suggested one morning at breakfast. "Our South

Carolina rivers are so puny. I want to see one of the longest in the world for myself."

"It'll be freezing cold on the lookout point. Spring's a better time to go," Jordan suggested.

"I don't care. It'll be the two of us. Just the way I like it." Sarah then left the kitchen and came back with the fur cloak in her hands. "With this around my shoulders and you bear-hugging me!" She laughed as she swathed herself in the sable.

On another day she insisted that he take her through all the Negro neighborhoods, so she could get a feel for the breadth of his political turf.

"Some of it's a bit rough, sugar," he warned her.

"Never mind that. I want to know everything I can about you and what you control."

Sarah was startled as Jordan headed south.

"Why are we going where whites live?" she asked.

"You'll see soon enough."

He drove south on Grand Avenue, one of the longest transportation arteries of the city. They passed parks and shops and churches and homes and apartment buildings with nary a Black face to be seen, but plenty of white ones gawking and hissing at them. When the street had almost run its course, he turned east toward the river. Now all Sarah saw were colored folks, trudging along and bundled up in winter wear, but not too buried inside their overcoats to miss Jordan as he slowed the car and waved.

"Where are we?" she asked.

"You said you wanted to see it all, so I thought I'd let you see just how far my reach is. Negroes have been residing here since after the Civil War when they came to work in the ironworks and blast furnaces. It's a pocket-sized precinct, but it's a precinct and they all vote!"

Sarah then saw the other Negro wards, clustered together on the west and north sides of the city.

With each outing, her love for her husband deepened and her fondness for him grew: how high he held his head, how his eyes twinkled whenever he caught her eye, how his face still reddened when she smiled at him, how he cocked his hat almost imperceptibly to the side of his head. Sarah was fond of practically everything Jordan did.

Sarah longed to please him and began to thread an appearance here and there at a wake, vigil, or funeral. She did no more than act as Jordan's appendage, standing next to him as he consoled the bereaved when they entered and lent them his shoulder to lean or cry on as they exited. Myrtle would always accompany her son to the massive front double doors as the mourners arrived but had a standard packet of excuses for why she couldn't remain for long.

"I'm not feelin' right. Got the sniffles. Need to take some steam," she'd tell him as she covered her nose with a hankie.

"This blasted cough's come back. I need to fix me a toddy."

"Son, my stomach is actin' up. Gotta lie down."

Once, Sarah noted that Myrtle just looked up at Jordan until he nodded, and then took her leave.

Sarah rarely remained for the entire service but when she did, Jordan summoned Emma to accompany her to their bedroom afterward.

"I'll be right there. I have some unfinished business," he would explain and then head for his office.

She never questioned him, but once she regained her strength and her curiosity returned, she wondered what other matters needed his attention.

After one service, she shooed off Emma, hid at the top of the main staircase, and watched as, one by one, a dozen or so people filed out of Jordan's office like a rivulet: the men patting their chests and straightening their suit coats; others counting money; others with a fist balled up in their pockets; and the women, clutching their purses more tightly than normal.

After the last person left and she heard Jordan lock his door, she joined him in the corridor.

"Darlin', why are you still—" he started.

"Jordan, what is going on here? Who are those people?"

"They're mourners," Jordan answered.

"Well, I know that. I saw them inside the parlor, but it looks as if you are giving them money." She put her hands on her hips.

"Yes, that's what I do."

"But why?" she queried him.

"For what they *do*."

"Which is?"

"They're professionals." He paused. "Whenever it's clear that we won't have a full house, I call up enough of them, and they get paid to lament right along with all those who actually *knew* the deceased."

"To make the family and loved ones feel better?"

Jordan bobbed his head up and down. "And to make our business look good."

"Oh, I understand now."

"But there's one that I'm sure you've seen who doesn't have to be paid." He chuckled.

"The tall, brown-skinned woman with all the hats?" Sarah guessed.

"Yes, Imelda Tubbs. She speaks to no one and is the first to arrive and the last to leave. Her husband left her well fixed, but she's never been the same since he passed. She spends her time attending funerals now. Obsessed with them. Keeps him alive in some way...or not," Jordan surmised.

"It's so different here. In Sunset, everybody knew everybody. When anyone died, the whole community filled up every seat," Sarah explained.

"And it's a competitive business. That's why I pay more than any other funeral director. I bind these people to me, and they wait to hear from me."

Jordan held Sarah by her arm as he escorted her up the stairs. Once they reached the top step, Sarah stopped and turned to her husband.

"I've paid so little mind to all this. There's so much to learn here."

Jordan leaned over, picked her up, and carried her to their bedroom.

"And I have so much more to discover about you," he said, and kicked the door shut behind them.

As Sarah drifted off to sleep, she let go of worrying about getting pregnant, put her trust in God to bring her a child at the right moment, and vowed to embrace her new life. The morning after this threefold epiphany, she arose before Jordan stirred, pulled on her housecoat, and headed to the kitchen, lured by the delectable smells that wafted down the corridor.

"Why, Miss Sarah, I'm so glad to see ya gettin' up early and eatin' here instead of yo' room," Gwendolyn, the cook, said as she pulled out a chair from the table and motioned for Sarah to sit. "Miss Myrtle, Emma, and Douglas already finished, so ya my only customer for now."

"I've been so, well, you know why I've been scarce." Sarah hugged her stomach and looked downward for a moment and then back at Gwendolyn. "But I've turned a page and I'm ready. And there's no way I won't come here for breakfast so I can sniff up close."

She sat patiently as Gwendolyn walked to the stove, heaped cheese grits into a bowl, and put it in front of her mistress.

"Oh, thank you so much. And I want to get to know you and Emma and Douglas."

"That's mighty kind of ya. We all just simple folk."

"Nothing beats simple, my mama always said. I know Jordan's mother is still the lady of the house, but I want to help as much as I can."

"The way Mr. Jordan's been floatin' around here like he's walkin' on moonbeams ever since ya came, seems to me that ya doin' more than yo' share."

Sarah dipped her spoon into the creamy concoction and closed her eyes with each mouthful.

"I don't know if I've ever had any as good as these and we know a thing or two about grits in South Carolina," she said, and then scraped off the last bit that clung to the side of the bowl.

Gwendolyn smiled as she picked up the empty dish with one hand, and with the other, sat a small platter down, which was laden with pork sausage patties, over-easy eggs, and buttered toast.

"It's too much," Sarah declared.

"Ya may know 'bout grits, but St. Louis winters? This'll keep yo' innards warm all day."

Sarah wiped the corners of her mouth with a napkin when she finished. She picked up her plate, headed toward Gwendolyn at the sink, and handed it to her.

"No need, Miss Sarah. No need to do that."

"Oh yes, Gwendolyn, I do. Thank you again." Sarah pecked her on the cheek.

"Why, do tell," Gwendolyn sighed. "Ya so sweet."

"She's more than that," Jordan said as he stood in the doorway, until now, unnoticed. "She's one in a hundred million. And you're so radiant this morning. What's gotten into you?" He stepped toward Sarah and wrapped his arms around her.

"You," she whispered in his ear, and then backed away from him. "It's your turn now. You've got quite a meal in store for you."

"Oh, I know. Won't you stay here with me?"

"Not today. I've got a program for myself, I do. I want to do some wandering on my own. I have yet to take a studied look at the home."

"Glad to hear this," he answered. "Whatever you need from anybody, you just let them know."

Sarah stood on her tippy toes, kissed her husband, and sashayed toward the door, casting a sly look at him over her shoulder as she exited.

She returned to her bedroom and dressed hurriedly, eager to scrutinize the mansion. She slid past Myrtle's bedroom and the spare one for guests, but stopped as she came upon the fourth room, intended to become a nursery. She sighed and resisted the impulse to open the door and imagine how she would decorate it—if or when. She continued to the landing that led down to the grand foyer and admired the magnificent grandfather clock that crowned it, wondering why it never struck the hours.

Sarah then realized that she had been so enveloped by her sorrow that she had not ever considered looking at the help's quarters on the third floor. So she retraced her steps and climbed the narrow spiral stairwell next to the kitchen. She inspected the spotless bathroom and four bitty bedrooms, three inhabited and one vacant.

*I'll start with the hardest part first,* Sarah thought as she went down the stairs and arrived on the first floor. She braced herself for what awaited her and then proceeded to the steps that led to the basement. She raised her hem with one hand and gripped the railing as she descended. She stopped midway, let go of her dress, and squeezed her nostrils shut to lessen the acrid smell that permeated the underground embalming room. She continued and once her feet touched the concrete floor, she looked at the equipment and goose bumps popped out on her arms and legs.

Glass bottles, with intravenous tubes attached, hung from the ceiling. A half dozen foot-long metal needles sat on a tray atop a stainless steel rectangular table big enough for an adult. A similar table made of wood and folded in half stood against one wall. Numerous canisters, marked *formaldehyde, methanol,* and other names she couldn't pronounce, were grouped on a stand along another wall and a pleated church truck leaned against the third. Four small windows, just above ground level, dotted the far wall, allowing some light in. Each ledge held a rubber hose, neatly coiled, and a bucket. She followed a narrow corridor to the right and came upon the coal chute with a diagonal metal sheet that led from it to the floor. *Ingenious,* she thought. *Jordan's turned it into a method for receiving the deceased.* She shuddered again as she envisioned the bodies sliding down it and felt the blood draining from her face. She returned to the first floor and opened the back door of the house, stuck her head out to clear her nose, and inhaled the air that now contained a hint of springtime.

She lumbered up the back staircase and into the kitchen while Gwendolyn washed dishes.

"Been in the basement, have ya?" Gwendolyn asked without looking up from the sink.

"What a business this is," Sarah said as she stopped in the middle of the room.

"Well, ya seen the worst of the home."

"All those instruments." Sarah sat down at the table and rubbed her temples.

"Somebody's gotta do it." Gwendolyn dried her hands on a towel and approached Sarah. "And we, that is, *yo'* husband is the best in town. He's got the touch. Not that he does any of that touchin' anymore. Hires other embalmers for that, if ya didn't know. Drives some of 'em to drink."

"Bless their souls," Sarah sighed.

"But Mr. Jordan is so downright kind and sincere. People feel that and come here in droves."

"Yes, yes. I know. I've seen how he handles the mourners," Sarah said and looked up at Gwendolyn.

"And Mr. Jordan gives them more than just comfort."

"What do you mean?"

"Mr. Jordan never turns nobody away. If they can't pay in cash, he takes whatever they got to give, whether it works or not.

Like that big ol', broken clock at the top of the stairs." Gwendolyn laughed.

"Mystery solved," Sarah blurted out, and then chuckled as well.

"And I think Mr. Jordan put it at the top of the stairs so anybody who comes here will know that his funeral parlor is always open for business, no matter and no how."

"So you think that's why my husband has a drawer full of watches that would take him a month of Sundays to wear?"

"Probably."

"There's so much to learn here."

"Ya gonna catch on. Smart as ya are."

"I hope so. I have so many questions. Do you mind?" Sarah said as she motioned for Gwendolyn to sit next to her.

"No, not a bit."

"Downstairs." Sarah took a deep breath. "Those huge needles…"

"Trocar. That's the name. The embalmer punches it into the corpse so he can fill it with those liquids." Gwendolyn clasped her hands around a make-believe needle and thrust them downward.

Sarah clutched her throat.

"Yeah, Miss Sarah, I know it's gruesome, but like I said, somebody's gotta do it."

"And the pails and hoses along the windowsills?"

"They gotta get rid of the blood and what's all inside the body, so they drain it out that way, fill those buckets, and dump them into the gutters." This time, Gwendolyn pretended to pitch liquid.

"And the small wooden table up against the wall?"

"Oh! That's for house calls," Gwendolyn joked.

"What do you mean?" Sarah's face froze.

"Sorry, Miss Sarah. Don't mean to make no light of it. But ya see, some kin can't let go. They wanna keep the deceased home as long as possible. So, Mr. Jordan's gotta travelin' kit."

Sarah rubbed one arm and then the other to fend off the shivers.

"One last thing. I know we sell caskets in the building out back, but I understand that there are little ones, too." Sarah's eyes almost watered.

"Yeah."

"I want to see them."

"Don't ya wanna save that for another time?"

Sarah shook her head. "I want to see everything today."

Gwendolyn snapped a key from a large ring and offered it to Sarah but before letting it go, she said, "Take yo'self a minute before goin' there."

"Yes, yes, I will."

Sarah pulled an overcoat from the kitchen coatrack, descended the stairs, and meandered across the property toward the showroom, a nondescript, one-story structure.

She unlocked the door and saw four closed caskets mounted on pedestals, two hewn of wood and two of stainless steel. Another tiny one abutted the back wall.

"Little ones die, too," she reminded herself and sighed aloud.

Once composed, she returned to the main house and entered through the front door, walked through the impressive vestibule and into the majestic rectangular funeral parlor. It accommodated any type of service, be it a wake, a private family viewing, or the funeral itself, with or without a minister. She'd been in it, of course, but hadn't really absorbed its grandeur until now.

144

The wooden floor and walls shone; columns of folded chairs leaned against the spaces between the windows; and stacks of thick, rolled-up carpets filled the two front corners. A glistening wooden podium, sculpted with curlicues and floral wreaths, stood upon a platform at the head of the room with a Bible atop it. She bent her head upward, transfixed by the crystal chandelier with its countless lights.

The floor-length velvet brocade drapes stood like sentinels along the right and left walls, and when she pinched one, her fingernails disappeared inside the plush fabric. *I remember when I ordered something quite like this for the emporium*, she reminisced.

A stream of thoughts raced through her mind as she stroked the curtains—from her wanderings in the family emporium's storeroom as a child, to how her mother had groomed her to take over at some point, to how she had assumed that role when Big Sarah died, to how she dreamed of leaving Greenston, to how she had relinquished her role and dashed off with Jordan. She adored him, and the way he anticipated her every fancy, and she appreciated how Gwendolyn and Emma waited on her. Yet she missed running her family's store: ordering the goods and returning those that weren't up to snuff; balancing the books; enjoying the rapport she had with *her* staff; tending to the customers in *her* inimitable way; and above all, basking in the esteem the Sunset community lavished on her. She drank in the envious looks that the white folks in greater Greenston cast her way whenever she ventured downtown. They knew that Madame Sarah's Emporium rivaled their stores, and they deplored how her family had managed to hold on to acres of land no matter how many crafty whites had attempted to wrestle parcels away from them over the decades. Sarah pulled one of the chairs to the middle of the room, opened it, and sat down. She closed her eyes and envisioned her new role—as the home's doyenne. Her chest swelled as she draped this well-fitting mantle on her shoulders, like the sable cloak Jordan had gifted her.

With firm resolve, she strode to the windowless side room across from the lectern. It held an outdated sofa, a few chairs, and a locked wooden cabinet and matching table. *This must be where the family waits before the service begins*, she surmised, *but it's so drab. It needs to be more welcoming. A woman's touch. I wonder why Myrtle hasn't tended to that.*

Sarah continued down the corridor and passed the family living room, Jordan's office facing it, and Myrtle's minute sewing room. She heard the machine buzzing and her mother-in-law humming to herself, and decided to save a visit for later. *Don't want to intrude. I'll go after I've talked to Jordan about taking her place as lady of the house.*

After dinner, Sarah asked Jordan to snuggle with her on the front porch bench, their shoulders wrapped in a heavy quilt.

"Just love being out here with you after my duties are done and there's no service. Just the two of us," Jordan said as he kissed her hand.

"So do I," she responded. "But I'm worried about your mother."

Jordan started to laugh.

"But this is serious, darlin'," Sarah admonished him.

"Are you wondering why she's coughing and sneezing at all the services and then running off?"

"Of course I am."

"My mama's not social, that's all. We made a pact. She *has* to show up, otherwise folk will talk, but then she can go."

"Is that it?"

"Yes. That's the short of it," he answered.

"I'm relieved to know it's nothing serious."

Gwendolyn surprised them, carrying a thick, red, lit candle which she placed on the low-slung table in front of them.

"Just the way ya like it, Mr. Jordan, givin' that glow to yo' wife's face."

"You sure know me, Gwendolyn. Sleep well."

As soon as she left, Sarah dug a little deeper.

"Your mother doesn't have much interest in running the household, either," she said as she stroked Jordan's chest and she felt him melt into her touch.

"Yes, darlin', you've pegged her," he said and pulled her closer to him. "She's never been comfortable in this big place with staff to handle. That's why she sort of lets them run themselves, although I'd like a firmer hand. She preferred where we started out, but the business grew so fast that we had to move here."

"So, darlin', you think she wouldn't care if I got involved in…?"

"What? She'd be happier than happy to spend all her time stitching up shrouds."

"And you wouldn't mind if I did?"

"Whatever makes you content and I know how much you enjoy running things and filling the till. It'll keep your mind occupied, and off of…"

Sarah listened as Jordan's voice trailed off, and watched his eyes turn slightly red.

"I've turned it over to the Lord's bidding," she said and stroked his face. "Will you smooth the way with your mother?"

"Yes, I will, first thing tomorrow. You go visit her after lunch."

The next afternoon, Sarah tapped on Myrtle's sewing room door.

"C'mon in," Myrtle answered.

Sarah walked in and Myrtle looked up. She stopped pumping the treadle of her machine and let go of the handwheel.

"Why, Daughter, what a nice surprise! Don't think ya ever been inside here."

"Not really, Mother. Passed by but never stopped. Didn't want to disturb you."

"Never a bother. Never at all. Ya look around while I finish this up." Myrtle held up a pale purple funeral gown that only missed a collar. "And then we can have some tea."

Sarah surveyed the room. Myrtle sat behind a sturdy Singer sewing machine close to one wall. Bolts of fabric in white and varying shades of purple and blue spread lay on a table next to it. A built-in closet with no door revealed an assortment of funeral robes and a few men's suit coats.

She smiled when her eyes rested on the potbelly stove in the middle of the floor. She recalled how Clara kept their bulbous oven ablaze in the Franklin house, stocked with at least two irons, so she'd always have one at the ready as soon as the one she was using cooled off. Her mother's words rang in her ears. *Girls, I'm sure you will marry well and won't have to do much housework, but you must know how it's done correctly so you can instruct the help and make sure they are doing it right.* As a result, Sarah and her sisters, Mattie and Anna, could cook and sew and iron and scrub tubs and polish floors as well as anyone.

"There, there. All done," Myrtle said as she examined the robe. "I'll press it later 'cause it's teatime now, unless you want somethin' stronger?"

"Tea is more than fine, but I'm curious."

"About what?"

"Where's the door?" Sarah pointed to the closet.

"Oh, my memory's fading a bit and I like to see all the shrouds hangin' up just in case I'm missin' a size or a color. That's all. And I wanna make sure there are some spare jackets. Ya know, times are hard and the families of some of the men don't have anythin' to dress them in."

"Oh, I see." Sarah turned toward the stove. "And you still use flatirons? You don't want an electric one?"

"Heavens no! Especially since the handles are wooden now. I like heatin' the stove and workin' these irons. Keeps my arm muscles strong, too!"

"You are so organized," Sarah remarked.

"But not as good as you. Jordan told me how ya wanna start workin' again. Daughter, I'm relieved to know that."

"You wouldn't mind?" Sarah blurted out.

"Mind? I been hopin'. I know Douglas and Emma sneak off and nap when they should be workin', and Gwendolyn snitches some fatback and potatoes for some of her kin. But I just can't say nothin' to them. I'm no good at tellin' people what to do or checkin' up on them. But I just know ya could. Tellin' them how to act without makin' them feel bad."

"I can see they're like family. Don't want to step on their toes."

"Ya won't. I just know it."

Myrtle rose, interlaced her arm through Sarah's as they walked toward the kitchen.

"I think I *will* need a little something stronger," Sarah quipped.

When spring arrived, a raft of gardeners arrived to tend the flower beds, trim the evergreen bushes that defined the property's limits, and seed the lawn that carpeted the backyard and spilled from the front steps down to the sidewalk. A crew of masonry experts repointed the red bricks with an attentiveness Sarah had never seen before. *They could do this sleepwalking. Nothing for me to fix here*, she thought.

The household staff, however, was another matter.

One afternoon, Sarah entered the garage to the sound of snoring coming from the back room. She walked to the middle of the space, in between the Cadillac and the Buick.

"Achoo! Achoo! Achoo!" Sarah faked sneezing as loudly as she could and before long, Douglas appeared rubbing sleep from his eyes.

"Why, Miss Sarah. Ya got a cold, do ya?"

"Spring is in the air and it's in my nose as well." She laughed.

"Do ya want something?"

"I wanted to visit with you, Douglas. You eat so early in the morning and toil so hard keeping all these cars at the ready that we barely see each other."

"Yes, ma'am, don't rightly know that we do."

"But I'm going to change that." She smiled. "I'll just drift in and out of here every now and again. How's that?"

"Sure, Miss Sarah, whenever ya want."

"Love cars, I do. Want to watch you work, too. See you soon."

*One down and two to go*, Sarah thought as she strolled over to the home and entered the grand parlor. She headed toward the small room by the pulpit, drawn by snoring there as well. She barely turned the knob, found the door locked, and then jangled the ring of keys that she pulled from her pocket. Although each key was clearly marked, she patiently tried one bogus key after the other before opening the door. She found Emma half leaning on the table as she dusted it.

"Emma, my dear, good afternoon."

"Hello, Miss Sarah. How are ya?"

"I'm fine, but worried about you."

"Why's that?"

"You've locked yourself inside this tiny room while you're cleaning. Better to keep the door open and air it out, don't you think?"

"Uh, well. Yes, I guess so."

"Better for your lungs as well." Sarah glanced at the couch and the still evident imprint of Emma's body.

"Oh, and can you fluff up the sofa, please?"

"Yes, ma'am."

"Thank you, darlin'," Sarah said as she left, securing the door open with a sturdy wooden wedge that she pulled from her pocket.

She decided to overlook Gwendolyn's inclination to pilfer fatback and other tidbits for some of her relatives who were struggling. *It's food, after all, and we have more than enough.*

Now she had to further tackle Negro St. Louis.

"Jordan, darlin', do you mind letting me be the first to welcome each mourner now and again? I need to establish that we own this together, no?"

"Good tactic. Of course," he said.

"And maybe, just occasionally, you can have a cold or something and not come at all?"

"I feel one coming on now." He coughed and chuckled at the same time.

Before long, Black St. Louis recognized Sarah's sway over the parlor and especially over Jordan. The funeral business consumed her during the next two years. When she missed a period, she thought little of it because there were too many parties to attend or organize. When the second one didn't arrive, she knew and her emotions collided: elated one moment and fearful the next. The moment she told Jordan, he shouted.

"We're keeping this one. I just know it!"


On the third anniversary of their St. Louis wedding, Sarah presented her husband with a daughter.

"Sarah, you've given me the best gift any husband could want." Jordan sat next to her bedside in a single room at the People's Private Negro Hospital.

"Even though she's not a boy?" Sarah teased.

"Always wanted a girl. Less competition," he joked.

The nurse entered, cradling the infant.

"Vivian Graceful Sable has arrived. And how!" Jordan announced as a howling baby was laid in Sarah's arms.

"We chose a perfect name. Vivian means alive and she is vivacious," Sarah said as she calmed the infant by nursing her.

"And she gets her middle name from you, my darlin'. You are full of grace."

"I hope so."

"You've given me more joy than I ever dreamed of having. I only wish Papa was here to welcome his first grandchild," Jordan said.

"I'll do my best to fill that void with more love than I knew I had to give."

"And I give you mine 'til my last breath and beyond," he said and kissed her hand.

As Sarah further nestled Vivian, she felt her own heartbeat rise and fall in sync with her daughter's. She marveled at this miracle of love and life that God had delivered to her and Jordan and lost herself in the exquisite perfection of her infant. She drifted off and on over the next several days enraptured by the new love of her life.

Yet strangely enough, once Sarah returned home, another feeling crept over her. An emotion that she tried to ignore, but it kept nagging at her. As she walked the corridors and surveyed her domain, she envisioned all the work she had put into the funeral home in a few short years. She had increased business, so Jordan could concentrate on building his political clout. The staff now answered to her and her alone. She even had an idea to use the horse farm to help handicapped children learn to ride. How would an infant fit into her work? Sarah felt utter shame when she thought of how Vivian might interrupt her plans. What kind of a mother thought like this? But then she remembered her own mother, who ran a store, a farm, and raised four children. Sarah also wanted to provide the best example to her daughter of what a Negro woman could achieve. After she had regained her strength, Sarah rolled up her sleeves and set about organizing the household around its newest member.

"Emma, I want you to stroll her every day, and then bring her to me."

"And pretty as she is, I'll be the envy round the blocks." Emma puffed out her chest as she spoke.

"And once she is weaned, you'll be sleeping in the nursery with her."

Sarah noted Emma's startled look and ignored it.

"Yes." Sarah now addressed Douglas, Gwendolyn, and Emma. "I want you all to dote on her and fuss over her as much as your heart's desire. You hear?"

At the first dinner party Sarah threw after Vivian's birth, she felt more alive than ever. She ran up to Clara Darling, a woman she barely knew, and embraced her.

"Well, Mrs. Darlin', it seems like a lifetime since we've laid eyes on each other, what with me nursing Vivian and you keeping the books for your husband's business and then some." Sarah winked and threaded her arm through her friend's.

"I do declare, Sarah, you know just about—"

"Yes, I do. Everything in this community and I want Jordan to know what all the wives do. So tonight, you'll be sitting to his right."

"I will?"

"Indeed!"

Sarah had arranged these soirees before Vivian's birth, but she had followed Jordan's lead, inviting one after the other of his political cadres to keep a lock on their loyalty. But now it was she who dictated every detail.

"Now, let's see. Gwendolyn," she said as she laid out the place settings, "I want no possible bickering so we will keep Mr. Hill and Mr. Porter apart. And I want our guests with the deepest pockets closest to me and Jordan." She even directed the idle chitchat (that was anything but), and kept the parties intimate, no more than a dozen, so none of the guests felt commonplace. She held them in the main funeral parlor. And she cleverly only lit the chandelier above the table, so the rest of the expansive room disappeared, adding to the coziness of the space and obliterating its raison d'être.

# PART TWO

*Chapter 10*

# BIG WILL MOVES INTO A SABLE PARLOR

*St. Louis, Missouri, 1934*

Big Will set down his bag and stared up at the mansion he would soon inhabit. High atop a meandering driveway, it housed the most successful Negro undertaking establishment in St. Louis—the Jordan W. Sable Funeral Parlor and Mortuary Home. He bent over and grabbed his tattered grip, which he had bound with a thick rope. In any other man's hand, his suitcase would have appeared colossal but in Big Will's grasp, it looked puny. As he approached the house, he spotted the service entrance and headed toward it. He took a deep breath before he rang the bell.

His cousin, Sarah Franklin Sable, parted the white, opaque curtains that lined the inside of the door's glass windowpane. She threw open the door and let out a squeal.

"Oh, darlin', I'm so relieved you made it in one piece. Now come on in here." She looked up at him, hugged his chest, and laughed. "You're even taller than the last time I saw you. But there's not as much to hold on to." She stood back, beckoned him to bend down with her forefinger, and whispered, "But don't you worry. I know why." As Big Will righted himself, he saw her wipe away a tear from each eye.

"Cousin Sarah, I can't thank ya and yo' husband enough."

"No need for that. You're family."

She led him up the back staircase to the family kitchen where he saw a stout, middle-aged, caramel-colored woman sitting stringing green beans at a round, black walnut table, big enough to feed a baker's dozen.

"Gwendolyn, this is Big Will Anderson. He's from back home and he'll be driving for us."

Gwendolyn jumped to her feet. "Mighty glad to meet ya." She smiled broadly at him, shook his hand, and glanced Sarah's way. "Douglas know about this?" she asked.

"Never you mind about him. He can use another pair of hands to help out with the cars," Sarah answered.

"Douglas? Cousin, I don't wanna step on nobody's toes."

"And never *you* mind, either, Big Will. I'll tend to him," Sarah stated.

Big Will eyed the six-burner stove, ready to handle anything thrown its way. It was a well-stocked kitchen, he thought, everything spick 'n' span, filled with the smells of Southern cooking. He longed for the time when he could board as much as two men.

"Mr. Anderson, why ya must have an appetite," Gwendolyn said.

"Please call me Will or Big Will. Whichever suits ya better, ma'am."

"Well, you are a biggin, so I guess it'll be Big Will for me. And no ma'amin' me, ya hear? Now tell me what ya want?"

"Some bone broth and soft rice'd be fine."

"That's all? Ya mighty tall but ya need some meat on those bones. By the time I'm through with these string beans and salt pork, they'll be as sweet and juicy as cane sugar in mid-July."

"Fix him what he wants," Sarah snapped. "Big Will, you come with me. I want to show you where you'll be staying."

She led him up a stairwell to the third-floor attic. Bowing his head as he wound his way up the low-ceilinged passage, his broad shoulders brushed the walls, making him feel protected. As he followed her into a bedroom, the scent of fresh sheets and aired-out blankets reminded him of how the womenfolk in his family hung the washed linens on clotheslines to dry in the wind and beat the dust from the covers.

"You'll have to make do with this bed until I find one with a bigger frame and mattress..."

"Thank ya, Cousin Sarah. But ya got any room in the garage?"

"Why? Don't you like the room?"

"It's fine. Nice 'n tidy, but I'm gonna be driving for ya, so I might as well stay where I'm gonna be spendin' my time. And I snore somethin' fierce. Don't wanna bother nobody."

"Whichever way you want. We'll find that potbelly stove we haven't used in Lord knows when, so you won't freeze out there."

"Thank ya kindly."

"After you eat, you're staying up here until the garage is ready. Jordan's at one of his political meetings for the evening, but don't be surprised if he doesn't wake you when he gets home. He wants to meet you straightaway."

\* \* \*

Jordan stomped into Big Will's room just after midnight, chomping the daylights out of an unlit cigar. His dark skin glistened, he reeked of liquor, and his bloodshot eyes could have set off firecrackers. His new boss's attire, however, startled Big Will more than anything: cowboy boots, a shoestring necktie secured by the largest diamond stickpin Big Will had seen outside of a jewelry store window, and a white collarless shirt. His coat capped his knees, a sidearm peeked out at his waist, and he held a Stetson hat in his hand. *A cowboy sheriff sure 'nuff ready to go to meetin' or a funeral*, Big Will thought as he jumped up from his bed.

Jordan cleared his throat before speaking. "Sorry to wake you but I want you to know how happy I am to have you here."

The tenor of his voice also took Big Will aback. His words scratched against each other and sometimes cracked at the ends. The booming baritone he'd expected to come out instead was just above a raspy whisper.

Jordan tried to stifle a cough. "It's our home and it's a *home*, if you know what I mean." He smiled and uttered a faint laugh. "Sober business here but that doesn't mean we can't have some fun, now does it?" Jordan laid his hat down, dug inside his jacket, pulled out a silver flask, and took a swig. "I mean, not too much fun, given what folks are dealing with. But Depression or not, people get born and they die. Even more of the latter right in through here."

"Yessuh, Mr. Jordan."

"Anyway, welcome. This is *your* home now. Go on back to sleep. Take a day to get yourself together. Take a look around. You can start working tomorrow."

"I'll be ready in the mornin'."

"I said tomorrow." With that, he flung a lozenge in his mouth, picked up his hat, and left.

Big Will stretched his hands upward until they touched the ceiling and then sat on his bed. *Sure 'nuff a gentleman, but kinda frightful.* He laid down and drifted back to sleep. He awoke at daybreak, peeked out the door and, finding the corridor empty, went to the bathroom. Afterward, he opened his suitcase and the Mason jar almost jumped out at him. Two full nights and no ghoul, he realized. *Praise the Lord!* He patted it and buried it under his clothing. He selected a pair of trousers, his autumn-weight long johns, and a neatly pressed flannel shirt. Before he put them on, he sniffed each one. *Even a hot iron can't press the fresh scent away.* He descended the steps, bypassing the kitchen.

"Big Will?" Gwendolyn called out.

"Yes, ma'am," he answered from the bottom of the stairwell.

"Now, I told ya about ma'amin' me. Where ya off to without yo' breakfast?"

"Like to see the garage, the cars. Where I'm gonna be workin'. That's all."

"But ya need to eat. And I'm fixin' up some..."

"No offense, Miss Gwendolyn, but I wanna wait." He exited the house through the same door he'd entered the day before. As he strode toward the garage, he stopped short, mouth agape. *Well, I'll be. A yella poplar!* He dashed toward the tree that towered over the Sable house, pressed his chest and the side of his face against its bark, and wrapped his arms around its bole until his hands shook one another. *And yo' trunk's small enough for me to bear-hug! Glad to know I got somethin' bigger than me to hang on to.*

"Who's that?" a tiny voice rang out. He let go of the tree and turned around. Gwendolyn and a small girl, no more than seven, stood next to each other in the kitchen window.

Gwendolyn shouted, "C'mon in here and meet the young'un who runs this place!"

Big Will crossed the yard, wiped off his shoes on the back doormat, and bounded up the stairs and into the kitchen.

"Ever seen a prettier lil' angel?"

As Big Will approached the beige child with auburn banana curls cascading from a knot atop her head, he noticed how she trembled.

"Vivian, no need to be afraid. This is Big Will," Gwendolyn announced. "He's yo' mama's cousin. Guess that makes him yours, too. He just arrived from her hometown. Big Will, Vivian."

"Mighty pleased to meet ya," he said and knelt on one knee in front of her. She relaxed and giggled, and he broke into a grin, almost as wide as his shoulders.

"What are you going to do here?" she asked.

"Drivin', takin' care of the automobiles."

"And can I—"

"Vivian!" Gwendolyn interrupted. "Before ya start askin' all of yo' questions, ya gotta welcome Big Will to our household. Ya know, the way yo' mama taught ya."

"But he has to stand up," Vivian said.

Big Will rose and Vivian curtsied. He smiled even more broadly and responded with a deep bow from his waist.

"Can I ask him now?" Vivian said as she turned toward Gwendolyn.

"Yes, darlin'."

"Can I see as much as you can?"

"What ya mean, lil' lady?"

"Miss Gwendolyn, can Big Will pick me up? *Please.*"

She nodded. Vivian reached both arms upward and Big Will lifted her and sat her on one of his shoulders.

"Now ya can see even more than me."

She peered out the window. "I can almost see the top of the tree you were holding on to. Why did you do that?"

"Just reminds me of home."

"How?"

"Now, Vivian, ya gonna have plenty of time to get to know Big Will, but ya need to finish breakfast and get off to school," Gwendolyn said.

"Can you drive me to school?"

"I dunno. Gotta ask yo' pa," he answered.

"Papa!" Vivian began to run out of the kitchen, but Gwendolyn grabbed her by the shoulder straps of her dust-colored corduroy pinafore as she passed and swiveled her around.

"What did I say? First, finish yo' breakfast!"

Vivian returned to the table and scarfed down what remained on her plate.

"Papa," she called as she hurried out the door.

"And now—" Gwendolyn pointed her finger at Big Will.

"Just some warm milk if it's not any trouble?"

"That's it?" Gwendolyn wrinkled her nose. "All right, but I'm puttin' two of my biscuits alongside. Good for dunkin'."

Big Will let each sip of the milk rest in his mouth before swallowing and ended his meal with a pinch from one of the biscuits.

"There'll be sandwiches and soup here for lunch whenever ya feel the need," she told him when he finished.

"Thank ya, Miss Gwendolyn. I'll be moseyin' around the place, like Mr. Jordan told me to."

He began on the ground floor where the wakes and funerals took place. Instead of an expected gloom, he found that light filled every bit of the spacious parlor. A heavyset woman had just opened the last floor-to-ceiling drape and fastened it to the hook on the wall with a silk, braided pendulum tieback.

"Good mornin', Big Will. I'm Emma. I keep house around here. Heard all about ya."

"Nice to meet ya." He walked toward her, shielding his face from the sunbeam that struck him across his forehead. "Mighty bright in here." He glanced around the room.

"During the day, we like to keep it all cheery before we gotta close it up and fill it with chairs. And before the sobbin' starts."

"Yes, ma'am. Well, I'll be on my way."

"Glad to have ya. Once we sort out yo' room in the garage, I'll keep it straight."

"Miss Emma, no need for that. I can do it for myself."

"We'll see about that." She looked him up and down. "They told me ya were big."

"Guess I'll go where I'll be doin' my work. Ma'am." He gave her a slight bow and left.

When Big Will entered the garage, his eyes widened when confronted by the stable of vehicles: two Cadillacs, one a limousine, the other a half-coach hearse; two late-model Buicks, one a fresh-off-the-assembly-line Club Sedan, the other a more modest version; and a black, boxy, outsized motorized wagon.

Douglas emerged from the more nondescript Buick.

"Wondering about that one, are ya?" he said and pointed to the wagon.

Big Will nodded.

"It's a dead wagon. Use it to pick up remains and bring 'em here for embalmin'. I just got back from takin' the little one to school. I think she wants ya to do that from now on."

"Only if it suits ya."

"It's what she wants that matters. Boss says ya startin' tomorrow. We can talk then." Douglas slammed the car door shut, pulled out a dust rag from his pocket, wiped off the handle, and left.

Big Will surveyed the surroundings: extra tires fastened to the wall, a trolley and car jack, and a massive wooden rack laden with every kind of tool or accessory needed to assemble or dismantle a vehicle. He took a deep breath and smelled the oil in the air, tinged with an antiseptic sweetness wafting up from the glistening floor. *Got my work cut out for me, I do. Never seen a garage so neat and clean.*

He went back to his room, placed the Mason jar in the crook of his arm, and took a nap.

Just before five o'clock, Big Will went to the kitchen. He stood outside it and let the aromas fill his nostrils as he rocked back and forth on his heels.

"C'mon in here, Big Will," Gwendolyn called out from where she stood at the kitchen table, positioning the last knife for dinner.

Big Will remained a few steps back from the door.

"I know ya out there, so c'mon in, I said."

He put one foot across the threshold, then the other and stopped.

"Have a seat," she said.

"I'll wait for the rest. First time I'm havin' dinner with y'all. Don't wanna get ahead of myself," he answered.

"Go on and sit down now. Nothin's too formal here. Ya gonna see."

"But I'd rather." He stepped to the side of the door.

"Suit yo'self." Gwendolyn shook her head.

Big Will didn't move until the rest of the household, family and help alike, straggled in and took their places willy-nilly. Jordan pulled out a chair for Sarah to sit in and took a seat next to her. Vivian sat beside Emma, but once Big Will took his place, she sprang up and moved to be near to him.

"That's quite an honor she's giving you. She's usually more standoffish with newcomers or guests," Sarah commented.

"Not with Big Will, she's not," Gwendolyn chimed in. "Ya shoulda seen how she cozied up to him this morning."

"Is that so, Vivian?" Sarah asked. "Tell me why."

The little girl looked up at Big Will. "He's kind of like a big kid."

The table roared, and Vivian laughed as well and cupped her hands over her mouth, then beamed up at him as his face reddened.

"He's certainly big," Jordan added.

"And he's my little cousin, so I guess he qualifies as a youngster." Sarah laughed. "Glad you two are getting acquainted."

Jordan tapped a fork against his plate.

"Is Mama taking tonight's meal in her room again?" he asked Gwendolyn.

"Yeah, she is," she replied.

"Why doesn't Granma eat with us much anymore?" Vivian queried.

"She's been under the weather and Mama's a solitary soul. Always has been," Jordan answered. "Time to eat!"

Gwendolyn brought one dish at a time—fried chicken that still sizzled; mashed potatoes dolloped with chunks of butter and sprinkled with fresh parsley; pickled beet bulbs the size of a grown man's fist; and succotash that resembled a tented red, yellow, and green quilt. She passed each under Big Will's nose before setting them down.

"Stop it!" Sarah admonished her. "I told you that my cousin has a sour stomach. Leave him be!"

"My cookin' can cure whatever ails him."

"Miss Gwendolyn, I'm sorry. It all looks and smells so good but I just…"

Gwendolyn went to the stove and came back with an earthenware tureen brimming with rice and bone broth.

"I made it just like you asked for last night, in case I couldn't change yo' mind." She put it in front of him, dug into her apron pocket, and handed over a soup spoon wrapped in a linen napkin.

Big Will finished his meal after everyone else had left the table, except for Vivian.

"Why do you eat so slowly," she asked.

"Just my way."

"And not much?"

"Vivian, ya let him do what he needs to," Gwendolyn chimed in.

Big Will looked down at the child and smiled.

"I just don't have much of a hunger, that's all," he answered.

"But why wouldn't—" Vivian started.

"Go on, girl and do yo' homework. Big Will's not goin' anywhere. Plenty of time for all yo' questions."

"You'll be taking me to school. I asked Papa," she said matter-of-factly.

"If that's what Mr. Jordan said."

"Vivian, I said run along now," Gwendolyn insisted.

"Oh, all right," she said, and huffed out.

"Here ya go, Miss Gwendolyn." Big Will carried the half-full bowl to the sink and placed his napkin underneath it before setting it down.

"Nothin' at all. Ya the easiest of the bunch to please."

He descended the back staircase and walked into the looming night. He pointed his chin toward the heavens and searched for a bucketful of shining stars like the ones that showered the skies in Greenston. He sighed and his shoulders stooped when only a gauzy, covered half-moon returned his gaze. He shoved his hands in his pockets and walked toward the front of the mansion at the very moment the chandelier lit up the funeral parlor. Drawn to the dozens of starry lights, he entered the room to find Emma with a worried frown on her face as she stared up at them.

"Good evenin'," she said. "Guess ya wonderin' what I'm doin'."

He nodded.

"Gotta make sure not one of these bulbs is out. I do it every night, especially when nobody's here. Don't want Mr. Jordan to be embarrassed during a service, now do I?"

He nodded again.

"Can ya help me? Ya can probably see more of them than me," she said.

Big Will rose on the balls of his feet, circled the chandelier, and scanned it from every angle.

"There's one that's out," he said.

A tiny voice rang out. "I can help. I know I can."

Big Will and Emma pivoted toward it. Vivian had entered the parlor, dressed for bed in a full-length nightgown.

"What are you doing up?" Emma scolded. "Go on now. Off to yo' room, you little rascal—"

"But if Big Will puts me on his shoulders, I can change the light," Vivian interrupted. "You won't have to get the ladder, Miss Emma. *Please.*"

"Oh, all right." She handed Vivian a bulb, and Big Will hoisted the little girl. After she changed the light and Big Will set her down, Emma grabbed her hand.

"I'm puttin' ya in bed myself. No more runnin' around tonight. Say good night to the gentleman and off we go."

"Good night, sleep tight, and don't let the bedbugs bite," Vivian said. "Not that we have any, but you know what I mean, don't you?"

"Yes, lil' lady, I think I do. And the same to ya."

As Emma and Vivian turned and walked toward the light switch, Big Will glared at the teeny artificial torches. He squeezed his eyes shut and watched the spots of light dance inside his mind, just like the stars at home stood out against South Carolina's unsullied skies.

## Chapter 11

# BIG WILL SETTLES IN

*St. Louis, Missouri, 1934*

Within a week of Big Will's arrival, he had moved into the room that adjoined the garage. Emma and Sarah had roped two single beds together to accommodate his height and filled the crack between the mattresses with muslin so he could sleep on a diagonal without being bothered. They stacked so many quilts and covers at the foot of it that the potbelly stove they'd dredged up wouldn't be needed. He had discouraged them from decorating, but they insisted on hanging a framed drawing of a garden on one wall and set a vase of artificial flowers on his bed stand. Furthermore, they had Douglas install a chifforobe, outfitted with a full-length mirror on the closet door. Big Will placed the miraculous Mason jar, wrapped in a dish towel, deep inside one of the drawers and stuffed all his socks and underwear on top and around it.

He and Douglas divvied up the duties of maintaining the cars. Big Will, however, buffed and polished and oiled and scrubbed the lion's share, including, with Douglas's blessing, the ominous dead wagon.

Jordan's office suite took up the back third of the ground floor, and when Big Will passed by its open door the next Saturday afternoon, his boss called out to him.

"Come on in here. I want to show you where I take care of business."

Big Will entered the sizable office. A mahogany-colored, leather Chesterfield sofa and matching chairs, nestled on either side of it, faced Jordan's immense desk. His own chair looked identical to the other two, except its back dwarfed them. He stood up and rapped his knuckles on the desktop.

"Black oak. Missouri's finest. Just like the kitchen table. Look." He pointed to the bar behind Big Will, equipped with cut-glass crystal decanters, each ringed with a silver collar and gleaming plate, engraved with the name of the liquor the bottle contained.

"And if you need to relieve yourself?" He opened a door to a spotless bathroom, with fresh hand towels hung on stainless steel hardware.

"Nice office ya got here, Mr. Jordan."

"You come and visit whenever you like. Unless the door's shut. Don't even knock. If there's an emergency, just tell Sarah."

"Yes, suh, and thank ya mightily. I'll be goin' now. Yo' Club Sedan needs some tendin'."

"She's my latest buy and my favorite for now, so I guess I'll let you go."

Earlier that day, Big Will had washed the car and dried its white sidewalls, so it only needed a good dusting. Yanking a fresh chamois from the rack, he began. When he got to the driver's side door, Vivian popped up, grabbed the wheel, and pretended to steer it.

"Can't go very far without these, now can ya?" He swung a chain of keys back and forth around his massive hand, reached in the open window, and touched her freckled nose with the tip of one.

"Are you an Indian?" she blurted out.

He raised his eyebrows. "Why'd ya think that?"

"Well, you look like the one in my picture book. And that's what everybody here thinks. Is it true?" she continued.

"Don't know 'bout that."

"And you don't talk much. Indians are quiet, aren't they?" She continued to turn the wheel back and forth as she looked at Big Will.

"Ya better keep yo' eyes on the road," he quipped.

"If you aren't an Indian, why don't you talk much?" She stopped playing with the car.

"Just came out that way, I guess." He scratched his head.

"But you'll talk to me, won't you?" She knelt on the driver's seat and put her elbows on the window frame. "*Please*," she begged as she leaned her head out the window.

"Doin' that now," he answered.

"You're so funny and you don't even know it," she said and laughed.

"I know one thing." He smiled at her.

"What's that?"

"Ya a pretty lil' thing. Pretty as spring flowers back home."

"What do they look like?"

"I'll show ya some."

"When? Tomorrow?" She thrust her entire head and shoulders out the window.

"Tomorra's Sunday. We're all restin' and servin' the Lord," Big Will reminded her.

"Then Monday?"

"Awright. After school on Monday it'll be."

That evening Big Will asked Gwendolyn for some spare wire, string, and any leftover scraps of paper or newsprint. He rifled through the materials she gave him so he could fashion flowers the way his two sisters had taught him. He recalled how, at first, he struggled to fold the wee bits of colored paper with his huge hands. But anything for his sisters, and now anything for Vivian.

On Monday morning, he opened the front door of the car for her and she jumped in. Dozens of miniature flowers covered the dashboard.

"Big Will! You said after school!" she shouted and then gathered as many as she could scoop up. She buried her nose in the bunch and sniffed.

"I love them! And I love you, too!" Vivian climbed up to his shoulders and threw her arms around his oversize neck, scattering the buds.

"We gotta get ya to school," he said, placing her back on the seat next to him. As he backed out of the garage, a tear dropped in his lap.


Big Will kept the Club Sedan adorned with long-stemmed paper buds for Vivian's habitual visits to the garage. She'd follow him around the car while he slathered it with Simoniz car wax and rubbed it until it shone. She chatted about school and her friends, and he responded with no more than a nod or a fleeting grin. When he dusted the inside, she climbed onto the passenger seat and continued her monologue.

"Go on, now. Tell me what time it is," he said after he wound the clock and wiped it off.

"Four fifteen!" she shouted.

"Ya pretty and smart, too."

He let her play with all the newfangled accessories inside the Buick and listened to her call out the passing time on the timepiece. He even bent his head so she could style his hair with the comb and brush from the vanity case built into the glove compartment. When she pushed in the cigarette lighter and pretended to smoke, he drew the line.

"No good for yo' lungs, Miss Vivian. It'll stunt yo' growth, too."

Each day when he dropped her off at school, he waited until she crossed the threshold before driving off. Without turning around, she always waved her arm above her head to say goodbye. When he picked her up later, she usually had a few of her girlfriends in tow for a visit to her home. The first time he spied her stuffing a piece of clothing from her abundant wardrobe into a classmate's coat, he looked the other way, but not before throwing her a wink. Big Will got misty-eyed whenever he saw these kindnesses. She reminded him of when, as a youngster, he gave away half of what little he had to his friends who had even less. No one in his family could talk him out of it.

In spite of the embalming that went on in the basement, as well as the solemnity, eulogies, and sobbing during the services in the grand parlor, Big Will experienced a cheerful atmosphere in off-hours. Sarah invited her neighbors over for tea, biscuits, hand-shelled pecans, and gossip in the living room. Their laughter wafted throughout the house. Vivian scampered in and out of the rooms, secreting herself under tables and behind sofas, ready to surprise the staff by jumping out of her hideaways as they passed by.

One frigid December morning during Big Will's first winter in St. Louis, Jordan entered the garage.

"Big Will! Where are you?" he hollered.

Big Will rolled out from under the hearse. "Just checkin' that everythin's tight up under her belly."

"Douglas is sick, so you'll be driving for me today."

"And Miss Vivian?"

"Gwendolyn or Emma can fetch her. They need to do some walking," he said and laughed. "Warm up the family car. I'll be ready in half an hour."

"Yessuh."

Thirty minutes later to the second, Jordan breezed into the garage wearing a double-breasted camel-hair coat that capped his ankles. A fringed white silk scarf encircled his neck and a tan, wide-brimmed felt fedora topped his head. Before Big Will could grab it, Jordan lifted the raccoon-lined lap robe from its shelf as he passed the cupboard, got into the passenger seat, and covered his knees with it.

"Gotta tell ya, Mister Jordan. Ya lookin' mighty good, ya are."

"Why, thank you. And soon enough, you'll see why I'm dressed to the nines. We're going to city hall."

As Big Will drove up to the building, he slowed down in search of a parking space.

"Oh no. Put it right in front, where it says NO PARKING. And I want you to come in with me."

Big Will did as Jordan said and jumped out to open the door for his boss. He reached for the fur to store it in the trunk but Jordan stopped him.

"Only a fool would mess with this car or anything in it. Leave it on the front seat. And don't lock the door."

Jordan bounded toward the entrance as Big Will, even with his long stride, scrambled to keep up. A few Black men stood outside and opened the door for them while calling out Jordan's name.

"Nice to see you all," Jordan answered. "These ofays treating you right?"

"Sure enough," one replied. "But only because of *you!*"

Jordan smiled and continued his strut through the grand entrance hall. Before long, a white man caught up to them.

"Jordan. Why didn't you let us know you were coming?" He almost bowed. "I know the mayor would like to see you."

"Didn't come to see hizzoner," Jordan snapped. "Here to see my people."

He brushed the man aside and began talking to every Black person he came across. Big Will followed in his wake, mouth agape. Jordan shook their hands, listened to their woes, and even slipped some a buck or a few coins.

"Time to go, Big Will," he finally said.

They returned to the car and found it just as they had left it. Jordan waved off Big Will and opened the door himself.

He sat next to Big Will and stuck the lap robe between them.

"Now you've seen another part of my world. I led the exodus from the Republican side of the aisle to the Democrats, and we got something for it. We ousted those scumbags. I deliver votes to those crackers and keep them where they're sitting, and they help feed my people, *our people*, with jobs. That's the short of it. It's all about power. **Power.**"

When late summer arrived and the first anniversary of Big Will's deed as a posse member approached, his shoes turned leaden as he plodded around the grounds. One foot remained in place for a few seconds before he plunked the other ahead. He avoided looking anyone in the eye. Sarah finally pulled him aside.

"I've left you alone, but I need to know what's wrong, darlin'?"

"Need some time to myself. Just a few days, Cousin."

"You keep pretty much to yourself here in the middle of us all. But if you want to go off somewhere, you certainly deserve it, hard as you work."

That night Big Will walked away from the home with enough of his earnings stuffed inside his undershirt to buy liquor for a month. For the next two days, he holed up in a deserted alley and drank and passed out and drank and passed out until he awoke in the city's drunk tank.

"You got somebody who can come for you?" the policeman asked him.

"I don't want nobody to know," he answered.

"Yeah. Yeah. We just need a name."

Reluctantly, he gave him Sarah's and begged that he only speak with her. When she arrived, Big Will couldn't look her way.

"I'm so ashamed. Hope you didn't say nothin' to the boss." He spoke to his shoes.

"Darlin', that demon rum, or whatever you drank, will drill

a hole in what little of a stomach you have left. Don't do this to yourself." She patted his shoulder and raised his head.

"Year ago today, it was, Cousin. I took that bundle into the wood and...left it."

"I thought as much. But try to let this go. Find yourself a nice girl. We can always use more help at the home. You are part of my family and she will be, too."

"I gave up on that notion when I did the unforgivable. No girl'll have me."

"I said *let go*. You had no choice. Now come along. I drove myself, so no one else will know about this."

## Chapter 12

# SARAH CONDUCTS THE OVERGROUND RAILROAD

*St. Louis, Missouri, 1935*

M iss Sarah?"

Sarah heard Gwendolyn's voice along with her tap on the bedroom door. As she walked toward it, she basked in the afterglow of Jordan's surprise, predawn lovemaking before he left for his daily walk. She had tried to persuade him to stay with her and forgo his constitutional on such a frigid January morning but he was wedded to this ritual almost as much as he was to her. She threw on a housecoat and opened the door with a giddy grin.

"Good morning, darlin'."

"It's Miss Myrtle. She's..." Gwendolyn cast her eyes downward.

"Oh no," Sarah moaned as she ran to her mother-in-law's bedroom.

Sarah found her there, motionless. She touched her forehead.

"She's so cold." Sarah withdrew her hand and warmed it with her other. "Oh dear Lord. Take her into Your arms."

They stood frozen for a moment until both women began to weep in each other's arms. Sarah withdrew first.

"Gwendolyn, I have to go to my room. Tell the others, and then wait for me in the kitchen. I'll be with you all as soon as I can. If Jordan gets back before I join you, send him to me."

"Yes, ma'am."

Sarah returned to her bedroom and locked the door. She entered her bathroom, sat on the side of the tub, and squeezed out as many tears as she could, in order to put aside her grieving because of what lay ahead. She was sure Jordan would need to bolt himself in his office to drink, howl, or do whatever else was needed to assuage his pain. She would have to orchestrate Myrtle's wake, funeral, and burial on her own.

Once Sarah calmed down, she went to the kitchen and found Gwendolyn, Emma, Douglas, and Big Will.

"Such a kind woman," Emma said.

"One of us, she was," Douglas declared.

With a kerchief to her mouth, Gwendolyn stared at Sarah, and Big Will remained silent but looked distraught.

"My dears," Sarah began, holding in her own grief. "We will get through this together, as a family. We have work to do. And this work will keep us distracted from our sorrow."

They all agreed, then turned toward the staircase when they heard the downstairs door open and shut.

"It's Jordan!" Sarah exclaimed.

He bounded into the kitchen.

"You all look so glum," he remarked. "Did somebody die?" he joked.

"My love…" Sarah couldn't continue and covered her face.

He rushed toward her and held her tightly.

"What is it?" he asked her and the others.

"It's yo' mama," Gwendolyn answered.

"Mama? What are you saying?"

Sarah pulled away from him and looked him directly in his eyes.

"This morning. Gwendolyn found her."

Jordan dropped his arms and scanned the room.

"No, no. I don't believe you. She's just sleeping hard. She's been so tired lately." Jordan rubbed a knuckle into his forehead.

"Darlin', I'm so sorry," Sarah said as the others surrounded her and her husband.

"*No, no. I won't have this!*" he bellowed, as he pounded one fist into his other hand, and then bolted out of the kitchen.

Sarah trailed him to Myrtle's bedroom.

"This can't be true. She can't leave me. She *can't*," he said, kneeling next to her bed, holding his mother's hand.

Sarah patted his arm. "If only I could make it so. I know you need time alone. I'll handle everything. Grieve, my darlin'. Grieve."

He remained motionless under her touch.

"Without her love, I'm lost," he said.

"I can't replace a mother's love. I know that. But you have what I can give you. Forever."

Sarah remained seated beside him for a few minutes, then tiptoed out of the room and returned to the kitchen. She found Gwendolyn, Emma, Douglas, and Big Will huddled together at the dining table.

"He'll go to his office. I know he will. I'm afraid he will be for

183

a while. I don't know how many hours or how many days." She walked toward Gwendolyn. "Take his meals to him there. Set them outside the door and just knock."

Gwendolyn stood and nodded.

"All of you, follow me now."

Sarah led them to the main parlor. Before she spoke, she walked around the room, hands clasped behind her back, and inspected it from top to bottom and wall to wall to wall to wall. Emma, Gwendolyn, Douglas, and Big Will trailed her every step. She shook one of the drapes and motioned the others to follow her lead.

"We've got to make sure there's no dust hiding here. We've got to make sure that this room is perfect for the viewing. It's got to be worthy of her."

"Miss Sarah. We'll make sure. Ya can count on us," Emma said.

Sarah dropped her arms, rose to her full height, and began. "Emma, you take care of the floral arrangements. I only want a blanket of red roses from Jordan, Vivian, Jessica, and me on the coffin. All the rest go into the funeral cars to be taken to the burial plot."

"No bouquets at the wake or the repast?" Emma queried.

"Mother Myrtle detested the smells of flowers inside the home. She felt suffocated by them, that they reminded her of the dead. So, no."

"Yes, ma'am."

"Oh! And check on the shrouds to see which one is a fit and—" Sarah started.

"No need," Gwendolyn interrupted.

"Why so?"

"There was one hangin' on her bedpost when I found her. Probably stitched it up herself. Thought it might rankle ya and Mr. Jordan. Her knowin' she was leavin' and not sayin' nothin', so I took it down."

"All right," Sarah said, maintaining her aplomb. "You make sure Mr. Fennel gets it. I want him to do the embalming."

"Yes, Miss Sarah."

"Everyone! The wake will take place here in a week, but service will be at Grace Baptist since we'll need more room. The repast will be in this room after the burial. Gwendolyn, I don't need to tell you much about the meal. Just add a goose or two to the menu. Spare no expense and—"

"Have mercy! I ain't cooked a goose in Lord knows how long, but I got the recipe in my head," Gwendolyn explained.

"I know you will want to come to service so enlist some of your kin to set up the tables and chairs that morning. I'll leave money for that."

"Thank ya, Miss Sarah. My family needs any extra coins ya got."

"Listen up, all of you. We're expecting people from across the state and elsewhere, many coming by train. Jordan is one of the biggest Negro power brokers in the country. He's helped a lot of folk and they have to pay their respects and curry favor, if they know what's good for them. So Douglas and *you*, Big Will, will be picking them up from the station and shuttling them to homes all over town. The Overground Railroad will be in full operation!" Sarah said and the rest smiled and nodded at one another.

"Cousin? I don't understand," Big Will asked.

"That's what Jordan nicknamed it. It's how we beat ol' Jim

Crow with his own club. All the decent hotels are white-owned and segregated, so we, the community, house anyone who needs a place to stay."

"Well, I'll be," Big Will said.

"Most colored neighborhoods in the big cities do the same thing. But St. Louis has the Union Station, the most trafficked terminal *in the world*," she emphasized. "Anyone traveling across the country has to pass through it or change trains here. And, furthermore, you know what that gets us, darlin'—*all* year long?" Sarah drew out the last three words.

"What, Cousin?"

"Direct access to everybody: politicians, activists, attorneys, rabble rousers. They take the opportunity to stay with us locals. Jordan organizes meetings where these men explain how to kill Jim Crow. Local folk get connected to the cause in a personal way. They're *proud* to be contributing in whatever way they can, no matter how small." She paused for an instant. "And you, sugar, and all of us in this room, are a part of the network."

Big Will looked astonished and then turned toward the others whose chests stuck out as Sarah complimented them.

"I dunno what to say, Cousin."

"You're a part of this engine now! A part of using racism to end racism. You'll be proud of yourself soon enough." She patted him on the shoulder.

"Douglas, we're going to see Adelaide Tidewater. So warm up the town car in a half an hour or so and wait for me out front. Gwendolyn, I'll let you know when to call her housekeeper and tell her I'm coming."

"Indeed, Miss Sarah."

"Then I'll need to change into mourning, pin up my hair,

powder my face, but not too much..." Sarah muttered to herself as she walked toward the door. She regained her senses. "Oh! Forgive me. I don't know what got into me. I will see all of you later."

Sarah first went down the steps to the living room and dialed a number.

"Jeannette, I have some bad news"—Sarah took a deep breath—"Jordan's mama passed and—"

"Oh, I'm so, so sorry."

"Thank you." She paused. "You know what this means, don't you?"

"Of course. I'll get everyone on board. Once we start fanning out in the neighborhoods, we'll have more than enough rooms to house whoever comes to town for the funeral."

"We appreciate your help more than I can say."

"Pshaw, Sarah. We're always here for you and Jordan. I'll get back to you with names and addresses as soon as I can."

"And by the way, as you're spreading the word, tell everyone to come early to the funeral and fill up the church. I want the white politicians to have to search for seats in the back or lean up against a wall," she declared.

"No worry."

"Thank you so much. I can't talk now. I have to...have to run. Yes. That's what I have to do. I'm sorry. Bye, darlin'."

Sarah headed up the stairwell. She poked her head in the kitchen and found Gwendolyn alone, scouring the sink.

"You can phone the Tidewater residence now."

"Yes, ma'am," Gwendolyn responded. Sarah watched Gwendolyn drop her hands in the sink and hang her head.

"Gwendolyn?" Sarah said as she walked toward her.

"Oh, Miss Sarah. Myrtle…" Gwendolyn began without looking up.

"Tell me. What is it?"

"Ya know she let me call her Myrtle when nobody was around?"

"No, I didn't," Sarah replied.

"Yeah. She did. Her and me? We had a special bond. Somethin' glued us together."

"I'm so glad she had a friend in you. After Jessica got married and left town, she seemed to withdraw into her sewing and church. And of course, the sun rose and set over Jordan. But nothing else."

"She had me. And I had her."

Sarah gave Gwendolyn a hug.

"I know ya busy. Go on now. I'm fine. Just gave the lil' one her breakfast," Gwendolyn informed Sarah.

"Oh! My goodness. Vivian! I've got to tell her."

She stood before her daughter's door and collected her thoughts before entering. *Myrtle had distanced herself from almost everyone for the past year, even from Vivian, but that doesn't mean this will be any easier.*

Sarah found Vivian in bed, cuddling one of her dolls. She sat down next to her and stroked her daughter's hair.

"Vivian, I have to tell you something, sweetheart." Sarah looked at her child's inquisitive expression.

"Mama? What is it?"

"Your grandma has passed."

Vivian started to cry and let go of her toy when Sarah pulled her close and lifted her onto her lap.

"But, Mama—" Vivian began but couldn't finish her sentence.

"I know, my darlin'. This is difficult to understand. To accept. It's your first loss."

Vivian now clung to her mother with all her strength.

"She used to let me thread her needles but then she wouldn't," she whimpered.

"She was sick and didn't want us to know just how ill she was. Kept away from all of us."

"But she let Papa," Vivian explained.

"He was the only one."

"How is he, Mama?"

"He has to be alone for a while. He'll be with us when he can."

"Mama? Where do we go when we die?" Vivian asked and sat up.

"I really can't say. I hope there's a heaven. That we all go to…to rest and be together. That's what I wish. But there's really no telling." Sarah followed Vivian's eyes as her daughter looked upward.

"If there is that place, is it in the clouds?" Vivian asked.

"I just can't say…" Sarah hesitated. "But I can tell you that there will be no school for you until this is all over. You come with me while I change my clothes. Emma will stay with you until I get back from a visit I have to make. All right?"

"Yes, Mama," Vivian said, and then Sarah took her hand.

They went to Sarah's bedroom where she clothed herself in black: a floor-length, long-sleeved dress, laced-up boots, gloves that reached her elbows, and a hat with a veil.

"Where are you going?" Vivian asked.

"Before things get too hectic, I have to personally deliver the news to Mrs. Adelaide Tidewater. She's one of the grandes dames of Negro St. Louis."

"'Grandes dames'?" Vivian tried to mimic her mother's pronunciation. "Mama, what does that mean?"

"Oh, it's French for great ladies. Usually an older woman who stands out and has a lot of influence over others."

"Grandes dames?" Vivian repeated the words with more assurance.

"Yes, darlin', she is. Mrs. Tidewater is descended from Black people who came to St. Louis in the early 1800s. They established businesses and owned property. And above all…and Vivian, this is very important to know…they passed their wealth from generation to generation. They kept their money *in the family*, so to speak."

Vivian had kept her eyes glued to Sarah while she explained the sway that Adelaide had and Sarah was pleased. She wanted to school her daughter on what was expected of her.

As soon as Sarah assessed herself in the mirror, she escorted Vivian down the stairs and found Emma, tidying the foyer.

"Look after Vivian. I'll be back soon." She leaned over, kissed her daughter's cheek, and was off.

As Douglas drove Sarah to the Tidewater mansion, she reflected on the power this woman had. She and others in the same league still sit atop the Negro pecking order and could ruin one's reputation with a few words of well-placed gossip.

They soon arrived at the impressive house that sat on the highest point on the street. Sarah knocked on the front door and the maid led her into the parlor where the imperious woman sat. Before Sarah could open her mouth, Mrs. Tidewater stood and assessed Sarah's attire.

"And why are you in black?"

"Mother Myrtle passed this morning and I wanted to tell you in person," Sarah answered.

"Yes. You did well to come here. I certainly wouldn't want to hear word of this from all the hoi polloi that seem to be invading St. Louis these days, now would I?"

"No, of course not," Sarah assured her.

"Oh! Extend my condolences to Jordan." And almost as an afterthought, she added, "And of course, my dear, to you. I know this is difficult."

"I will and thank you. This *is* hard. She and I were close."

"Times have certainly changed since *my* great-great-grandparents came to live here and lent some refinement to this place. You know that they spoke French!" She patted her chest while speaking and ignoring Sarah's response.

Sarah bit her lip to keep from smirking and before nodding yes.

"I was hoping that you would inform the others in your circle," Sarah said.

"*Mais bien sûr!*"

"Thank you. I'll be going now. I have much to do. Funeral arrangements and all."

"Well, I will try to attend but I am not sure."

"I will hold places for you and your friends, just in case."

"You be sure to do that. *Au revoir,*" she said with a wave of her hankie as Sarah left the room.


Over the next few days, Sarah compiled the list of those coming from towns across the Midwest who'd called or sent messages. One telegram stood out.

DEEPEST CONDOLENCES STOP ARRIVING 5 PM
JANUARY 12 ON PCC&STL FOR TWO NIGHTS
STOP A. PHILIP

Sarah put her head against Jordan's office door as she knocked.

"Darlin'. I'm sorry to disturb you but I have to show you something," she said, and awaited a response.

She heard him unlock the door and kept from reacting when she saw how disheveled and groggy he looked. Bloodshot eyes. Days-old stubble on his chin. Overall weariness.

"He's coming," Sarah announced as she pressed the message into his hand. It took him a minute to focus on the paper in front of him.

"Well, I'll be," Jordan finally said. "The big man himself. He'll stay with us. Jessica and her family can go to her cousins."

Sarah did not see Jordan again until the day before the funeral, when he emerged in order to pick up A. Philip Randolph at the train station. Until that Friday, whenever she passed his office, she heard nothing but the sound of clinking ice cubes or him reciting a eulogy. And each time she paused to listen, the soliloquy was different. *He doesn't have to do this. No one expects him to. The Reverend Smith can take care of everything.* She worried about him and massaged her brow whenever she thought of how difficult it would be for him to stand at the podium and praise Myrtle's character. But she knew her husband. He'd be there all right.

Jordan drove the Master Six to Union Station with Sarah beside him. They easily located A. Philip on the platform because his presence overshadowed the other passengers. He carried his own luggage, although redcaps attempted to help him as he strode toward them. He put his bags down in order to shake Jordan's hand when they met, and Jordan deftly picked them up when A. Philip reached to hug Sarah.

"I'm just so sorry about this, Jordan. I know how much she meant to you."

"But you don't know how much *this* means to me. You coming here and all," Jordan responded.

"You're the man, Jordan. You started a union before I did."

"But mine was nothing compared to yours."

"Don't say that! Every cog in the wheel matters. Every chink in Jim Crow's armor has an impact."

At the wake that evening, forty to fifty mourners lined up for over an hour outside the funeral parlor in order to walk past Myrtle's open casket. Some wept, some bowed. Most remarked on what an excellent job the embalmer had done.

*"She just looks like she's sleeping." "Just as fresh as the day she was born." "I love the way he did her hair."* These were among the comments Sarah overheard.

Sarah admired how A. Philip sat in a back row, refusing to chat with anyone who approached him. She felt that he wanted everyone to know that this wasn't about him; it was about the grieving Sable household.

The next morning, the interior of Grace Baptist looked as if it would burst apart. The congregation filled every available space with some sitting on the pew ends. Scores packed the side aisles and vestibule. Adelaide and her cohorts had come in full force and Sarah had reserved seats for them in the second row, just behind Philip, knowing how much this would appease them.

The white politicians, the mayor included, sat sprinkled toward the back of the church, and Sarah smiled inwardly.

Only after everyone was seated did family enter.

Jordan carried Vivian in his arms as he walked down the aisle behind the coffin with Sarah and Jessica on either side of him. He looked straight ahead while the two women acknowledged the attendees.

Before they sat, Jordan put Vivian down and the four of them bowed deeply to the casket, which was adorned with a blanket of red roses.

Reverend Smith then led the full gospel choir into the church. He stopped at the first pew and placed his hands on each Sable family member as the singers assembled on the altar. They sang numerous spirituals and clapped and shouted, enthralling everyone except the immediate family who sat immobilized as if anchored to their seats.

After opening formalities, the pastor prayed for Myrtle and instructed the community to add their thoughts. Then Jordan took his place at the lectern.

"You all know that my mama was a simple woman, and she'd probably be embarrassed by all the fuss we have made here today. But it is my way of honoring the depth and breadth and height of this woman...my anchor, my sunshine. She warmed me every day, and her light gave me *my* life. Anything I have *ever* done, or *ever* accomplished is because of her reassurance and unwavering support from the day she brought me into this world."

Jordan continued in this vein for another fifteen minutes, while Sarah covered her eyes with her veil and Vivian sat still on her lap. She couldn't fathom how he could do this, knowing how deep his pain. But then again, she understood. He *had* to give his mother a fitting tribute. Sarah knew he was about to end when he took a gigantic breath.

"And dear Lord, thank You for giving me the parents I was blessed to have." His body collapsed around him with those last words and he stumbled to his seat.

A few in the congregation shouted *Amen* and *Praise God* and *Lord have mercy* when he finished. The proceedings, however, had been so formal and somber, strict almost, that the usual Baptist fervor was missing. Silence hung in the air between each lament.

The funeral cortege to the cemetery stretched for blocks with a police motorcade leading and ending it. The bereaved crowded around the Sable family plot as Myrtle's remains were interred next to her husband's.

When all returned for the repast, Jordan disappeared and Philip stepped in. He greeted each and every guest, giving words of support and an embrace where appropriate. And he replicated these gestures as the parlor emptied.

"Philip. How can I thank you?" Sarah asked after all had departed.

"Please, dear Sarah. Not another word."

*Chapter 13*

# THE MISSISSIPPI RIVER HAS ANOTHER SIDE

*East St. Louis, Illinois, 1934*

Nine-year-old Calvin Cahill waddled into the tepid Mississippi River on a scorching Sunday morning in August wearing an ankle-length white robe anchored to his body with two strips of fabric: one tied around his waist and the other loosely tied just above his knees to keep the garment from floating upward in the water. Two deacons steadied him as they all followed Reverend Wade toward the baptismal spot, marked by five towering stakes that formed an arc. Calvin knew that because of his small size, the waters would soon swallow him, so he stopped and let the grown men lift him by the armpits and carry him the last bit of the way.

He had been longing for this day so he could make his mother, Belle, proud and join her as a full-fledged member of the Liveliest Baptist Church of Christ. He glanced over his shoulder toward the riverbank and smiled at her and her best friend, Bertha Hayes, who had stitched up his gown.

"I baptize our little brother, Calvin Cahill, in the name of the Father and of the Son and of the Holy Ghost on the belief of his faith."

Calvin folded his hands in prayer, closed his eyes, and surrendered himself as the deacons leaned him backward and the waters engulfed him. When they stood him up, he looked to the sky, unbothered by the blazing rays of the summer sun or the muddy Mississippi's brown droplets that blurred his vision. He heard the congregation on the levee singing, *"Take me to the water, take me to the water, take me to the water, and baptize me."*

Once back on dry land, his mother and Bertha rushed toward him, stripped off his drenched robe, and covered him with towels. Belle carried paper-white trousers, shirt, socks, and underwear. He disappeared behind a clothesline draped with curtains and sheets and changed into his new garb. When Calvin emerged, the worshippers applauded and he bowed. He joined the flock, standing between his mother and Bertha, and squeezed their hands as the Lord accepted each successive child into His arms.

At the end of the service, Belle and Bertha picked him up and hugged him, nearly smothering him between the two of them. Breathing in deeply, he inhaled the talcum powder they had patted under their armpits and the geranium water they'd sprinkled on themselves for Sunday service.

The afternoon ended with a celebration for the newly inducted members of the congregation back at the storefront church. Turnip greens, ham hocks, and corn pone covered the picnic tables.

"We didn't need a Depression to make us poor," one of the men quipped with fork in hand.

"At least we know what to do with the parts what's left. But white folks?" Bertha laughed. "They sure don't!"

Calvin didn't care what he ate as long as he could stay in the bosom of his new family. Neither he nor his mother wanted to go home to their ramshackle clapboard house, located on a dead-end street, deep in the most dilapidated part of Negro East St. Louis. He clasped his mother's waist, and she kept one arm around his shoulder as they walked there. He had left his dazzling baptismal clothes with Bertha for safekeeping and once again wore the tattered shirt and pants he'd arrived in.

"Remember, darlin', to say that we were at Bertha's all day long."

When Belle opened the door, she found her husband, Maynard, sprawled on the sofa with a bottle of rye in one hand and a cigar in the other.

"So, where y'all been?"

Before they could answer, he jumped up, slapped his wife, and punched Calvin so hard his lip bled.

"That'll keep ya from tellin' whatever lie ya was thinkin' about," he growled. "Those jackleg preachers ain't nothin'. If I ever catch either one a ya near that broken-down, piss-poor shack they pass off for a church, ya gonna be sorrier than sorry."

Calvin watched Maynard drag his mother into their bedroom and slam the door. He sat on the front porch, covered his ears to block her screams, and prayed that he and she could escape together.

\*   \*   \*

By Calvin's tenth birthday, however, his mother had left, and he lived alone with his father. By the time he turned fourteen, he had a string of scars around his body to show for it.

"Almost a man but still a runt, now ain't ya?" Maynard said as he backhanded his son one fall Saturday morning. Calvin crumpled to the floor until his father reached down and picked him up by his collar.

"Stand up, ya scrawny lil' nigga and take it like the man ya outta be!"

"Mama!" Calvin cried out.

"Why ya callin' out for her? She's long gone. Run off with some no 'count."

He punched his son in the stomach this time and the boy doubled over.

"Stop hittin' me!" Calvin rose up and raised his arms in front of his face.

"Oh, ya don't want me to hit ya, pretty boy? That's 'bout the only thing ya got from me. That is, if ya got anythin' at all what with yo' mama screwin' everythin' that moved."

"That's a lie. Ya a liar and a drunk, and I don't blame her for runnin' off!" Calvin darted toward the door.

"Why ya bastard." Maynard started after his son, but Calvin sprinted ahead of his father. He ran four blocks to Bertha's house, hid under her porch, and sobbed. He folded himself into a small, barrel-like bundle, knees to chest, arms clasped around them.

"Who's that cryin'?" Calvin heard Bertha's voice and footsteps above him.

"Calvin? Ya Pa's been beatin' on ya agin?" she said as she peeked down on him. "C'mon outta here," she told him.

"Miss Bertha, I can't."

"I'm gonna beat ya worse than yo' daddy if ya don't." She laughed. "Now, c'mon, chile. Git outta the dirt." She stuck her hand under the porch and tugged at his arm. Calvin flinched at first, then tilted his head high enough so he could see her with one eye. "I said get outta the dirt. Ya already filthy enough," she said to him.

Calvin crawled toward her and stopped. He dried his eyes with his shirttail.

"No shame in cryin', boy, 'specially with a daddy like yourn."

Calvin stood up but cast his eyes downward. Miss Bertha lifted his chin.

"Ya always been a pretty, high yella thing, even when ya got two eyeballs all veined up." She took a hankie from her house-coat pocket, wrapped it around her index finger, and dug into the corners of his eyes to clean out the runny gunk.

"There. Least I swept that outta ya. C'mon in here," she ordered him, "but don't sit down on nothin'." She led him into her minute parlor.

"I'm gonna kill him one day. And then my mama'll come home. Come back to me."

"Well, befo' ya think 'bout how ya gonna do that, I'm gonna fix a hot tub a water out back, so ya can clean yo'self." She walked out.

Alone now, Calvin stared around the room and noticed how all the woodwork, no matter how worn or scratched, shone; how Miss Bertha had covered the sofa and chairs with identical fabric so they matched; how she'd arranged her bric-a-brac on a set of shelves, positioned to catch the sunlight; and how his mother's adage *a place for everythin' and everythin' in its place* rang in his ears. He remembered how each day when he returned from school, his mother had put their tiny house back together again after his father had done his darndest to tear it apart the night before. She'd have hot cocoa waiting for him during the colder months in a mug, more often chipped than not, and once spring sprang, a glass of something cool to drink. *Did she leave 'cause she got tired of doin' it over and over? Got tired of havin' to work so hard? Got tired of havin' to tend to me? It's so nice and quiet here. I could just stay put. Wonder if Miss Bertha would let me . . .*

"Ya can c'mon now."

He followed her voice to the back porch.

"Go on an' strip yo'self," she told him, but Calvin froze. "I seen plenty a Lord's children buck nekkid, honey. This water ain't stayin' hot for long."

Calvin unlaced his left shoe, pulled it off, and then rolled down his weatherworn sock with one hand while he tried to conceal the hole punched out by his big toe with the other. He did the same on his right foot. He unbuttoned his shirt, slipped it off, unzipped his pants and quickly stepped out of them. He hung onto the side of the tub and lifted his knee.

"Chile, take off yo' drawers."

"Miss Bertha, I'm fine like this," Calvin said as he placed one leg in the water.

"Whatcha hiding in there, boy?" Bertha yanked at his underwear. "Oh, I see. Ya packin' quite a bundle, now ain't ya?" She laughed. "I swear, ya short but ya don't need to worry 'bout gettin' no snatch, boy."

Calvin covered his genitals.

"Take those drawers all the way off so I can wash 'em. What with this Indian summer we got, yo' clothes'll be all dried out in no time."

He sat down in the water before handing her his underpants. Bertha threw him a bar of soap. "I wantcha even lighter by two shades by time I get back. Now scrub!"

Calvin closed his eyes and sank down in the tub until his body lay flat against the tin bottom. His mind drifted back to the last time he'd found solace covered in water, at the riverside. When his lungs screamed for air, he sat up and smiled for a moment. He lathered, washed himself clean, and then dried off with the well-used towel Miss Bertha had placed on the rail. As he wrapped it around himself, Bertha appeared from nowhere.

"Take a whiff of it," she instructed him.

Startled, he just stared at her.

"I said, take a whiff."

He pulled part of the cloth to his nose and smelled it.

"I hangs 'em over there for a touch a sweetness while the sun dries 'em," she said and pointed to the backyard where a sheet and some towels hung on a puny honeysuckle bush.

"Nice," he said.

She gave him a hug and patted him on his head. "Time to put somethin' in yo' belly. Put on this bathrobe and c'mon inside."

He changed into it, walked into the kitchen, and sat down on a wobbly wooden chair.

"I can fix this for ya," he offered.

"Ya a carpenter?"

"Naw, but I can put it right. I know I can."

"A pretty boy and handy, too?"

By the time the sun had set, his clothes were ready to wear, so

Calvin scoured the neighborhood for wood, found a piece, and returned to Miss Bertha's. He affixed it to the leg of the chair with the help of some putty and string.

"Can't sit on it now, but should be ready tomorrow," he told her. "Anything else ya need repairin'?"

"Listen, yo' pa's gonna be knockin' down this door soon enough to wrench ya by yo' ear and take ya outta here. Eat this." She put a bowl of thick soup on the table. "Ya best get ready to go on home with him or else he—"

"Can I stay here with ya? I'm small. Don't take up much space," he interrupted her.

"No, dahlin', ya can't." She turned away from him.

"Please, please. I'll do anythin'." He moved in front of her.

"No way that heathen daddy of yourn will let that happen."

Calvin hung his head.

"But"—Bertha pulled up his chin and winked—"ya can stay 'til Monday."

"Thank ya, Miss Bertha. Thank ya so much."

"But ya gotta promise me somethin'." She slightly squeezed the sides of his face with her thumb and forefinger.

"I said anythin'."

"Ya gotta go to school regular. I know ya been missin'."

"How ya know that?"

"I been keepin' a back-alley eye on ya. I made a promise, too!" She dropped her hand.

"Who to?"

"Never ya mind 'bout that. Ya gotta get some schoolin' so ya can get outta this rat's nest of a town."

"I promise."

Soon enough, they both heard heavy footsteps outside Bertha's front door. She pointed to the attic and Calvin hid in one of its cubbyholes and listened.

"I want that runt!" Maynard hollered and pushed open the door.

"Stop callin' 'em that! I'm no half pint myself and I can take ya on, Maynard Cahill, remember?"

"I was drunk that time."

"I can whup ya drunk or not. Go on, now. Git yo' dumb ass outta my house. Ya know this here broom got power. I sweep out demons what try to come in and yourn the nastiest one around." Calvin heard the broom swish across the floor.

"Ya ol' fool witch, that's what ya is."

"Nothin' more, nothin' less."

"He ain't stayin' here forever. I'm gettin' him back."

"And bein' the witch I is, I'm gonna put a spell on ya. Ya won't touch that chile agin."

"I'll see 'bout that," Maynard said and stomped out.

Calvin climbed down the stairs and hugged Miss Bertha.

"Are ya really a witch, Miss Bertha?"

"Everybody think so 'cause my mama came from bayou country and mixed-up roots, so I let 'em. C'mon, chile, ya gonna sleep and have some sweet dreams for a change." She fixed him a warm cup of milk and tucked him into a makeshift bed she had fashioned out of her sofa.

The next morning after breakfast, Bertha led Calvin into her bedroom to a carved wooden trunk that sat beneath the window.

"Help me with this. I ain't been in here for a month of Sundays."

They pried it open, and Bertha tossed aside a sheathing of

yellowed newspapers on top of a heap of men's clothing. After pulling out two pairs of trousers, a few shirts, a belt, and a jacket, she laid each one out on her bed.

"My ol' man Rupert was a tiny thing hisself but still bigger than ya," she said, and laughed.

"I can't fit any of these, Miss Bertha."

"I know ya can't. I'm gonna see what I can do, but I need some help."

She pulled out a bottle of moonshine from her dresser and took a swig.

"Ain't stitched up nothin' in a while. Let's start with the pants."

Calvin stepped into the first pair and held them up while Bertha pared them down to size. She did the same with a shirt.

"Can't do nothin' with this jacket. Too thick for me to cut and sew myself. Ya gonna have to grow into it."

Bertha worked all day and by the time she finished, Calvin had a made-to-order wardrobe.

"Geez," he said as he admired himself in Bertha's mirror.

"Now listen up. I know that yo' bastard father. If he sees ya dressed nice, he's gonna rip these clothes off ya. These are from my dear, departed husband. Ya comin' here each mornin' to get dressed, and 'fore ya go home, ya gonna pass back and leave everythin'. Can't do nothin' 'bout the shoes but I can punch some more holes into the belt."

"Don't know how to thank ya, Miss Bertha."

"Ya made a promise to git yo'self some schoolin'. That's enough thanks for me. Got somethin' else for ya." She pulled out a shaving kit, brush, and comb and handed them over.

"Never had anythin' like this." His eyes brightened as he marveled at the items.

"Ya leavin' these, too. Ya can clean up here in the mornin' before ya get dressed."

"Yes, ma'am."

"And, Calvin," she called as he headed for the bathroom. "Don't ya believe nothin' Maynard told ya 'bout yo' mama. She's a good woman."

"Then, why'd she leave me?"

"To save ya, boy. Maynard was gonna' kill the both of ya. That's all ya need to know."

From then on, Calvin attended school without fail and Miss Bertha's warning kept Maynard at bay. If he did try to attack his son after he'd been drinking, Calvin learned how to escape to Miss Bertha's out the back door before his father put a foot in the front one.

As classes adjourned one Monday afternoon, Calvin's teacher called him to the front of the room.

"Pull up that chair and sit down." He did so and plunked himself down. "You are probably the worst student I've ever taught, except in numbers. How do you know all the answers? I want you to tell me that."

Calvin shrugged.

"Have you figured out some way to cheat? Don't lie to me, Calvin."

"No, ma'am."

"You read like a ten-year-old. Your writing's no better than a scrawl, but you understand numbers in a way I've never seen in a fifteen-year-old youngster before." She wrinkled her brow and stared at him. "Why?"

"Dunno."

"Well, I'm going to stretch you as far as you can go and we'll see just how much you 'dunno.' As far as reading and writing? I *dunno*," she wisecracked.

As soon as he walked outside, he fielded another daily battle. Four of his classmates approached him, shouting "***Runt!***" and "***Dummy!***" Then the head of the pack snatched Calvin by the collar and ripped his shirt. Incensed by the thought of Miss Bertha's handiwork being touched and torn, he rammed his head into the leader's groin. While Calvin's nemesis screamed in pain, the rest of the group froze and Calvin lit into them, throwing punches like an out-of-control bantamweight boxer, above and below their belts.

"Ya crazy," one of them wailed, holding his privates.

"Now, that's a name I like. Y'all can call me that from now on," Calvin answered and strutted off.

A few of the girls trailed him.

"Ya showed 'em," Mary, the tallest one who looked down at him, said.

He turned toward her and stopped.

"Yeah, and I'd like to show ya somethin' else."

"What that mean?"

"Ya gonna like it." He laughed.

"Small as ya are? Ya can't have but so much."

Calvin balled his fists and clenched his teeth as he stared up at her. He felt like punching her, just like he wanted to beat his mother for having abandoned him.

"Only one way to find out. Follow me."

She giggled and said goodbye to her friends. He turned down an alley and went into an abandoned garage. Once she was inside, he slammed the door shut, wrestled her down to the floor, and jumped on top of her, tearing her panties.

"Ya too fast an' too rough." She wiggled out from under him, stood up, bent over, and smacked him across his face. "Ya lil' pipsqueak!"

"Don't call me that," he yelled, rose up, and forced her down again, surprising himself with his strength. He held her down, penetrated her, and finished in short order.

"Ya hurt me an' I'm gonna tell all my girlfriends to stay away from ya. Don't care how big yo' thing is." She straightened her dress, stuck her tattered underpants into her pocket, and strutted out.

After that, the neighborhood girls scattered whenever they saw him. Word that Calvin was an awful lay spread through the colored part of town like buckets of whitewash thrown up against every wall. So he turned his attention toward any type of game that involved numbers, especially poker and street craps, handily mastering them. His winnings provided him with money for a pair of well-fitting, brown-and-white Florsheim spectator shoes, which he added to the wardrobe he left at Miss Bertha's.

Calvin's gaming reputation grew and before long, a teenage hoodlum named Rocco Jones took note. After a poker game one night where they both came out on top, Rocco pulled him aside.

"I like the way you handle yourself. But I know where there's easier and bigger money to be made."

"Where's that?"

"Across the river in St. Louis. Some colored people over there got real money and stupid sons ready to lose it. You with that pretty face and me with some rounded dice and marked cards, we'll clean up. Plus, they're plenty of bored little daddy's girls looking for something more exciting than what their next door, sissy boys can give them. Since you won't be getting any pussy here"—he smirked—"you might as well go where nobody knows about you."

Calvin wanted to coldcock him, but knew he spoke the truth. "I'm in."

"But you have to stop sounding like a dummy."

"Don't ya call me that."

"Well, then stop talking like one. Listen to me and listen to the radio. Try to imitate those crackers."

Calvin spent the next year and a half catting around the upscale Negro neighborhoods in St. Louis. He and Rocco inveigled the boys into gambling after school let out. On any given day, Calvin would be shooting craps in one alley and Rocco would be playing cards in another. Afterward, they divided their winnings.

The gullible middle-class girls on the west side of the river fell for Calvin's phony gentility. He'd pick the most naive and willing girl in her clique to seduce and then move on to a different group.

One day Calvin caught sight of a diminutive girl with a head full of curly hair, skipping down a street. *The girls in my neighborhood stopped doin' that in kindergarten if they ever did at all.*

## Chapter 14

# VIVIAN FALLS IN LOVE

*St. Louis, Missouri, 1941*

By Vivian's fourteenth birthday, she had blossomed into a pubescent version of her mother: petite with a narrowing waist, dazzling eyes, an upright bearing, and an incipient charm she seemed unaware of.

She saw how her mother and father radiated pride whenever anyone remarked on her grace and composure. Vivian, however, disliked the attention because she found herself to be fundamentally nondescript. The Sable household doted on her, but outside this secure environment, she felt alone.

In early September she entered L'Ouverture Secondary School, the tonier of the two public high schools for colored children in town, as a sophomore, putting her a year ahead of her classmates. Her superior scholastic grade school performance warranted the placement, but further alienated her from her peers. Vivian intimidated the children of the Negro professional class, physicians, lawyers, and the like, since their parents didn't approach having the money or power of Jordan.

*"Do you see how she comes to school?"*
*"Chauffeur driven."*
*"And in a different car each day."*
*"She's so stuck up."*
*"Thinks she's better than us, she does."*

The students whispered these and other comments loudly enough for Vivian to hear them as she walked the halls.

After a few weeks of this torment, she insisted on walking to and from school, hoping to fit in. It worked and she now relished being able to chitchat with girlfriends along the way. With her head in the clouds after she and her classmates parted, she'd skip at times or sing out loud as she delighted in her newfound freedom.

One Wednesday afternoon in mid-October, as she scuttled along, focused on fending off the crisper temperatures, a teenage boy bumped into her and made her books tumble to the ground.

"Excuse me, miss. I'm so, so sorry. Please, let me get those for you." He scooped them up. "I'm clumsy. Forgive me. But I was rushing to the library."

"No, I should have seen you. No harm done, really." She reached for her books, but the boy held on to them and stood motionless, gazing into her eyes.

"Is there something wrong?" she asked, shifting from one foot to the other.

"Why would you say that?"

"You're looking at me so hard."

"Sorry but I just can't take my eyes off you. Like that song." He started to sing, *"Jeepers, Creepers, where'd you get those peepers?"*

"Stop. They're nothing special." Vivian looked downward.

"Oh, but they are! Mind if I walk with you a bit?"

"I don't know," Vivian said hesitantly.

"Didn't mean to be fresh. Maybe one day you'll let me."

"Maybe," Vivian said. She walked off, then looked over her shoulder and smiled back his way.

"Oh! My name's Calvin," he called out. "And yours?"

She turned around. "Vivian. I'm Vivian."

"Hope to see you next week. *Long live Vivian!*" he shouted, and waved goodbye.

Her sudden blush put the sugar maple tree's crimson leaves to shame. She fanned her cheeks and scurried off. *Ooh. He's so handsome and studious, too. And he dresses so well.* She counted the hours until the following Wednesday after school when Calvin tapped her on the shoulder. She pivoted and broke out in a giddy smile that matched his.

"Hello, Calvin. How are you?" She ran her fingers through her hair with her free hand.

"I'm fine, now that I'm laying eyes on you."

Calvin's intense gaze startled her and she turned away for a moment.

"You are too kind," she responded and stared at him.

"Kind? I'm just telling you the truth, Ruth!"

"But my name's Vivian. You don't remember?" Vivian's chest caved in and she dropped her head.

"Of course I know your name. How could I forget it, Vivian?" As he spoke, Calvin tipped her chin upward with one finger and then let go.

Vivian lost herself in his touch and finally stammered out, "Well, then how...I mean, why did you call me Ruth?"

"I was just joking. Making a little rhyme."

"Do you write poetry?"

"No, I'm just silly sometimes," he answered.

"I like silly."

"Gosh, I hope you do. I got a bunch of funny bones."

Vivian smiled and hugged her books to her chest as a gust of wind kicked up.

"Are you cold, Vivian?"

"Just a little bit. The weather's changing."

Calvin took off his jacket and wrapped it around her shoulders.

"Oh no, thank you. That's nice of you, but I have to go walk alone from here on."

"Not telling me where?"

"It's not a secret. It's just that..." Vivian glanced around.

"You don't know me. I'm a stranger and you're such a lady. Is that it?"

"My folks, well..."

"Wouldn't want to see you with someone they don't know. You being such a lady and all."

"But you *are* a gentleman, aren't you?"

"Maybe I am and maybe I'm not." He winked at her and licked his upper lip. "What do *you* think?"

Vivian's mind froze as she fixated on the underside of his tongue.

"I said 'what do you think I am?'"

"Oh, I don't know. I..."

"Well, you need to know. Listen. I go to the library each week around this time. I hope to see you again. I mean if you think I'm enough of a gentleman for you."

"Why, yes. Of course...I mean, if you really want to."

"Want to? It's all I've thought about since I met you. You and those peepers of yours."

Vivian took a deep breath. "Really?"

"Yeah, really." He smiled as he peered into her eyes.

"All right." She almost tripped as she strolled off.

The following Wednesday, Calvin showed up a bit early just as Vivian and her girlfriends parted company.

"Good afternoon, ladies," he said to the group. "Vivian? How are you?" He bowed his head up and down.

"Who's that?" one of the girls asked her.

"I've got to get home. See you tomorrow," Vivian answered.

"Well, whoever he is, he sure is cute," the girl announced, and the others all agreed.

Calvin laughed as they walked off. "Well, if that ever happens again, just tell them I'm your long lost cousin. From Atlanta. Yeah, I've always wanted to see that town."

"I've got an aunt who lives in Sweet Auburn. It's full of everything you could ever think of. And it's all owned by Negroes."

"Yeah. I hear there's no place like it. Maybe one day we can go there. When you're older."

"Oh, Calvin," she cooed.

They met the next two weeks and Vivian was smitten to the point that she couldn't think of much else besides Calvin. *He's short, the same as me. I like that. We can look straight into each other's eyes. I could just get lost inside the dimple in his chin. He's charming and funny and polite. And he's as good looking as one of the actors in those colored Hollywood films. When he grows up, I bet he could even* **be** *an actor. And he seems to understand me.*

After Vivian and Calvin's latest meeting, Vivian surprised Big Will in the garage as he pulled in the Club Sedan.

"Why, Miss Vivian, what ya doin' here? Ain't ya got school-work?" he said as he got out of the car.

"It can wait. I want to ask you something. I've met a boy I like."

"Oh yeah?"

"And I think he likes me, too. He shows up every Wednesday on his way to the library. He's so kind and he makes me laugh."

"What ya wanna know?"

"Everything! Please tell me," she pleaded. She then took a deep breath and continued. "About boys, and how to talk to them. I don't know anything about them. He's the only boy who really speaks to me. The others are afraid because of Papa. Or maybe they just don't like me. Even some of my girlfriends seem, I don't know, jealous. Sometimes they say things that aren't so nice. He's the only one who is *really* nice to me."

"Now calm down, lil' lady. Ya pantin' up a storm."

"I can't. I think about him all the time."

"Hold on, I said." Big Will rinsed out a glass, wiped it clean, and filled it with water. "Menfolk," he started as he handed her the glass, "well, a lotta them just can't be trusted."

"But Calvin can. I just know it."

"His name Calvin, is it?"

Vivian nodded and took a drink. "You won't say anything to Papa, will you?"

"I wanna see for myself."

"But you can't! I don't want him to know anything about us. About where we live, what we have."

"I can see without him knowin' a thing. Ya leave it to me."

That Saturday, as Vivian approached her father's office, she heard her parents arguing behind the closed door.

"You think I can't protect my own daughter?" Jordan bellowed.

"Hush!" Sarah barked back. "You want the dead downstairs to hear you? Not to mention Vivian herself?"

Vivian tiptoed up and stretched her neck up and over, flattening her ear against the door.

"She's a sweet girl. Always thinking the best of others, but I'm afraid for her," Sarah continued in a lower register.

"What are you so scared of?"

"This town and all the ruffians in it. I tell you she needs to go away to finish high school."

"I don't want to hear you say that again."

"Don't you *ever* tell me what I can and can't say. You know better than that!"

"You want to send our only child away? The love of your life?"

"It's because I love her just that much. And you know deep down inside that she doesn't want any part of this business. She doesn't need to stay around here and learn anything about it from us."

Vivian took a deep breath and shut her eyes. *If they send me away, I'll never see Calvin again. And he'll find someone else. I know he will. He can take his pick of any girl. I saw how my friends looked at him.*

"Don't know how she didn't get your mother wit or some of my pluck," Jordan said.

216

"What she did get from us is willfulness. If some sweet-talking, pretty-boy Floyd turns her head, she won't listen. She may already be smitten the way she's walking around with her head in the clouds lately."

"What?"

"Big Will. Go on. Tell him."

"She told me about a boy, and I did some snoopin'," Big Will explained.

Vivian stifled a gasp when she heard Big Will speak. *I told him not to say anything.*

"What boy?" Jordan yelled.

"Lower your voice, husband," Sarah said.

"Somebody who **says** he goes to the library on Wednesdays," Big Will said.

"And why didn't you tell me?"

"Just found out."

Vivian now fumed. *How could Big Will do that to me? I thought I could trust him!*

"And?" Jordan continued.

"One hundred percent no 'count is what I'd say. Struts around with his hindquarters on his shoulders. He's got a regular crap game goin' with some of the local boys."

"I'm calling Twigg," Jordan said.

Vivian heard her father pick up the phone and dial a number.

"Hello there, Lyda. My lawyer's just waiting to hear my voice, now isn't he? Put him on."

Vivian's heart started to thump.

"Twigg? I got a job for that flatfoot you got on your payroll. I want to know who the hell's been meeting Vivian after school." He explained the particulars and then slammed down the phone.

Vivian heard her father slide a bottle off the shelf, pour a drink, and bang the tumbler on his desk.

"Ah. I needed that."

Sarah continued. "She can go to Mattie. She's Vivian's favorite aunt and ever since her second husband died, she's been living alone in that big house in Cleveland. Mattie keeps herself busy, but Vivian will be good company for her, too. The world's changing and this town's not keeping up. You got me out of that backwater town in South Carolina for a better life here. Well, there's an even better life waiting out there for Vivian."

"Now just slow down a minute. Big Will!" Jordan shouted. "You'll be taking her to and from school just like before. I don't care what she says. I need some time to think this through. I can't imagine this house without her."

"Well, you obviously aren't paying much attention to her while she's *in* this house. You're still looking at her like she's a little girl. She's filling out quicker than a honeysuckle bush sprouts in spring. She's come into her womanliness," Sarah explained.

Vivian heard the gurgling sound of liquor being poured again. She looked down at her budding breasts and saw her nipples harden through her sweater. *Mama's never talked like this to him. She explained the change in my body to me, but now she's telling Papa?*

"But she's my little baby," Jordan said, and slammed down the glass again.

"Not anymore. She'll finish up the semester soon and I'll take her to Mattie's after the holidays," Sarah insisted.

"I said I need some time."

Whenever her father reiterated his position, Vivian knew

there would be no more words spoken. She also knew that her mother would win out. She always did. She slid away from the door and took the back staircase up to her room where she threw herself on the bed and buried her head in her pillow to muffle her tears.

The next day after church, Jordan and his daughter sat on the red velvet sofa in the family parlor, reading the comic strips together.

"Vivian, Big Will is going to be taking you to school again, just like before," he said and closed the paper.

"But *why*?"

"It's getting chilly now. The coal dust is back, thicker than I've ever seen it. Better for your health."

"But my friends will make fun of me and I won't be able—" she stopped herself short.

"If they do that, then they aren't your friends. And what won't you be able to do if you're in the car?"

She paused. "Skip and sing and feel like I'm like everybody else."

"Well, once it starts snowing, there'll be no skipping. You can sing all you want in this house. And let me tell you something, darlin' girl. You aren't like anybody else and you'll never be. Remember something. Each and every one of God's creatures is unique. No better, no worse. Just different, one from the other."

"But, Papa—" she started.

"My mind's made up." He snapped open the paper and returned to his reading.

Vivian stomped out of the room without a word and ran to the garage where she found Big Will standing next to the stove.

"Papa just told me."

He held out his hand. "Come on over here and warm yo'self."

Vivian stood her ground and shifted from one foot to the other to fend off the cold. Tears rimmed her eyes and she hugged herself. "You told him. *I know you did!* I asked you not to, but you did anyway."

"Miss Vivian, ya need to forget that boy."

"I can't! I won't. You ruined my life."

"Oh, lil' flower. Don't say that. I couldn't live with myself if I thought that."

"The only way I'll forgive you is if I can see Calvin one more time."

He looked down at her and nodded.


That Wednesday when Big Will picked up Vivian after school, he trailed her pack of girlfriends. She bounced up and down on the seat next to him.

"He'll be there soon, I know," she squealed.

Big Will kept his eyes on the road in front of him. As they approached the spot where Vivian and her classmates ordinarily parted ways, she spied Calvin.

"Look! There he is! Pull over and let me out. No, back up so he won't see the car." Big Will followed her instructions.

"Looks like he's talkin' to yo' friends," he said.

"I bet he's asking them where I am. He saw me with them once. They'll tell him about you and he'll know all about us." She sighed. "I don't care. I'll wait until they leave and surprise him."

"Ya ain't gettin' outta this car."

"You promised."

"Ya said ya wanted to see him. So take a look."

Vivian reached for the car handle, but Big Will slung his arm over her and held it shut. Vivian watched the girls go their way and then saw Calvin pull out a cigarette, light it, and finish it off in two drags. He puffed up his chest and walked, a willful strut, down the street and into an alley.

"I'm gonna show ya his library," Big Will commented and steered the car in Calvin's tracks.

Vivian sank down in her seat out of sight as Big Will entered the gangway. "I don't want him to see me."

Big Will slowed the car and watched as Calvin pulled out some dice and cackled at a group of teenage boys. "Ya been waiting for me to take yo' money, ya bunch of sissies. Well, I'm earlier than usual today. So, let 'em roll."

As the Buick came into full view, one of the boys yelled out.

"It's Undertaker Sable's car!" They all scattered except for Calvin, who put his hands on his hips and glared at Big Will as he drove by.

"Take me home," Vivian whimpered and curled herself into a ball next to him. At the end of the alleyway, Big Will turned right and then stopped the car. He cupped his hand around her chin with his fingertips touching one ear and his thumb cradling the other.

"Miss Vivian, he ain't nobody."

She looked up at him. "But he's somebody to me."

*Chapter 15*

# VIVIAN'S WORLD CAVES IN

*St. Louis, Missouri, 1941*

Vivian spent the rest of Sunday holed up in her bedroom. She sat in the window seat, stretched her legs, and glared out at the barren backyard. *I'll never meet anyone like Calvin again. I know he's a little rough around the edges, but he'll change for me. I just know he will.*

After she ate dinner with the household, she struggled with writing a note to Calvin. After numerous fits and starts, it read:

*Dear Calvin,*

*I won't be walking home from school anymore. But I have to see you. I'll try my best to stay home on a Sunday when everyone goes to church. Can you come and wait for my signal? I'll put an unlit, red candle in the front window. That's your sign to meet me in the garage. I'll try every Sunday until it works.*

*I miss you, Vivian*

On Monday morning, Vivian pulled one of her classmates aside.

"You've got to do something for me," she whispered.

"You've never asked me for anything." Dolly stepped back. "You're the one who's always giving."

"Here." Vivian pulled out a sealed envelope and stuffed it into her friend's coat pocket. "Take this to Calvin."

"That good-lookin' boy who's sweet on you?"

"You really think he is?" Vivian gushed.

Dolly rolled her eyes. "Of course he is and you know it. Don't play dumb."

"You'll do it for me? Please."

"Sure."

"He's on the corner where I leave you every Wednesday or down an alley with some of the boys from school."


Each Sunday, Vivian tried every excuse she could think of to stay home, but nothing worked. The Lord may have rested on the seventh day, but as far as her mother was concerned, the Lord's Day was not only sacred, but also an opportunity for the Sable clan to stir up some business. First, the entire household attended Grace Baptist together. Then Sarah, Gwendolyn, and Vivian, with Douglas behind the wheel, dropped in and out of several other after-church gatherings, handing out calling cards and chatting up the ministers and parishioners. Her father, Big Will, and Emma visited the Evangelical services with a different but standard funeral accoutrement—cardboard fans with the parlor's name, address, phone number, and logo. They always came in handy because, even on the coldest days of winter, fainting from the preacher's fervor was to be expected. When the Sunday between Christmas and New Year's Day came around, Vivian finally seized her chance. Vivian awoke early, stained the edges of her nostrils with some watered-down Mercurochrome, almost singed the inside of her mouth with hot water, and started coughing and sneezing. She rubbed her eyes until they burned.

"*Mama!*" she called out from her doorway and then jumped back into bed.

Sarah walked into the room. "Oh my! You look a sight." She returned quickly with a thermometer. "101.5. You're not going anywhere. I'll have Gwendolyn bring you some ice chips to pull that fever down and some dry toast. You just stay put."

After her mother left, Vivian pulled the blanket to eye level and stifled a laugh. *Today's the day! This drizzle will soon turn to sleet but that won't keep the churchgoers at home. And our Sunday ritual will even take longer: rain boots, umbrellas, and raincoats will have to be stored somewhere before the services and sorted out afterward. Calvin and I will have plenty of time.*

Vivian watched from her bedroom window as the entourage left for church. Big Will carefully steered the Cadillac down the slushy service driveway and Douglas followed behind in the bulky Buick. Emma stayed home to nurse Vivian.

Buttoning up a woolen dress under her bathrobe, she sauntered down the front staircase to find Emma half napping in Jordan's favorite living room chair.

"Miss Emma?" Vivian said.

Startled, Emma sat up straight. "Ya won't say anything to yo' ma about me nappin', will ya? She caught me once, and..."

"Of course not, but could you please make me something

warm? You know. Just some hot water and honey. My throat's beginning to scratch."

Emma smoothed out the seat and back cushions before going up the back stairs to the kitchen.

Vivian pulled out a red candle from her pocket, placed it on the middle windowsill, and drew the curtains back together. She waited until Miss Emma brought her the drink.

"Here. I added some cough syrup. It'll calm down yo' chest and help ya nap. Go on, now."

Emma handed her the cup and Vivian took a sip, smiling dreamily. She climbed the stairs to her room, and once inside, spat out the liquid in her bedpan, put on some knee socks and shoes, and fluffed her hair. When Emma began snoring again, she snuck down the back stairway and into the garage where Calvin awaited her. She ran toward him but stopped just short of throwing herself into his arms.

"Looks like you wanna see me as bad as I want to see you," he told her. He licked his lips as he looked her up and down.

"Yes, I've been waiting for so long, it seems."

"And I been hiding in the bushes every Sunday hoping to get a look at you." He winked and rubbed his gloveless hands together. "I miss seeing you every week. Had to be satisfied with seeing you in my dreams."

"You dream about me? Really? I dream about you all—" She stopped.

"You do?" he asked, cocked his right eyebrow, and smiled.

"Yes, yes. Tell me your dream, please."

"That we spent New Year's Eve together. That I got to dance with you and kiss you at midnight." He paused and looked into her eyes. "Now it's your turn. Tell me yours."

"No, no, it's too silly."

"Why not? It's just the two of us here."

"I know, but I feel like these walls have eyes and even ears." She bit her lip. "My parents love me so much, but sometimes, it's too much. Calvin. I miss you. I really do."

"Ya ever gonna start walking home again?"

Vivian looked at the floor and clasped her hands together.

"No—no. I don't think so," she stammered. Then she raised her head. "I'm leaving town. Going to live with my aunt in Cleveland."

"What? But why?" Calvin started, then fumed as he hollered. "Oh, I know why. I bet yo' folks found out ya was seein' me and don't want ya round no trash like me. That's it!"

"Calvin, lower your voice. Someone will hear you. And why are you talking like that?"

"Like the scum I is, that's why. They wanna keep ya from people like me."

"You're not scum. I know you aren't. Even though I saw you in the alley with…"

"Yeah." He laughed. "Maybe I ain't what ya think I am."

"Tell me who you are, Calvin. Please."

"Oh, 'tell me who you are, Calvin. *Please*,'" he derided her. "I'm ain't nobody. Ain't nothin' like ya and yo' folks. Y'all live in this fancy house, with all yo' airs and butlers and maids. Think ya better than me. I'ma *show* who I am, that's what. Ya gonna make my dream come true. Ya gonna dance with me, all right, girl." He jerked her toward him, pressed his body next to hers, and began to sway.

"Oh, Calvin, no. We can't dance like this. You're too close to me."

"Shut up!"

"I don't like it!" She squirmed free of him.

"Ya don't think I'm scum, so let me." Calvin pulled her close again and this time she felt a bulge in the front of his pants.

"Calvin! What's that?"

"Ya dumber than I thought."

"Let me go. You're hurting me."

She tried to push him away but the more she struggled, the more tightly he held on to her.

"I'm gonna show ya who I really am right now."

"Let me go, Calvin! Why are you doing this to me?" She started to cry.

"Ya stupid little daddy's girl!" he snarled. "Ya don't know nothin' 'bout nothin' but I'm gonna teach ya somethin' yo' Daddy can't."

He held on to her shoulder with one hand and slapped her with the back of his other, pitching her onto the cement floor. He yanked her up by the front of her dress until the buttons popped. He threw himself on top of her and covered her mouth with his palm while she writhed beneath him. She pounded on his back with her fists, pulled at his ears, and finally twisted her mouth away from his grip and bit the side of his hand.

"Why ya bitch." He punched her so hard that she blacked out.

As Vivian regained consciousness, she felt an ache across the back of her head. Confused, she rubbed her forehead in a misplaced attempt to ease the pain that attacked her from behind. She then rested her hands on her still-closed eyes. *"What happened to me?"* she whispered aloud as her mouth trembled and her teeth began to chatter from the cold. As she further awakened, she remembered that Calvin had slammed her to the floor and jumped on top of her. She recalled that she had fought back and tried to get away from him, but her recollection ended there.

Vivian then felt an odd sensation between her legs, as if a stick had been rammed inside her. She clasped her crotch, hoping to quell the feeling, and instead came upon a sticky, wet substance on her dress. She yanked her hand away as soon as she realized that, by holding on to herself in this way, the wool of her dress was scratching her genitals. *Where are my underpants?* She opened her eyes, looked down, and saw her disheveled clothing and her torn panties hanging off an ankle. She reached for them and was horrified when she saw bloodstains on her dress and inner thighs. *Did he make my period come on? How could he do that?* She lifted herself on her elbows and glanced around the garage. Calvin was gone.

Vivian clutched her knees to her chest to warm herself as a reality settled in. *When I had my first time of the month, Mama explained a little about how babies are made. How a husband and wife… Oh no!* she thought. *Did Calvin do that to me? I thought only married people could do that.*

She now only wished to disappear… to fold herself inside the dead wagon and have it carry her away to a place where no one would find her.

She pulled her panties off and tried to stand, but her throbbing head and smarting crotch made her collapse on the floor. She started to cry but thought better of it and stopped. *What if Emma hears me? No one can know about this. No one.* She got up and once again, she cupped her privates as she hobbled to the shelving in search of the lap robe. She wrapped it around herself, opened the gloomy dead wagon's rear door, and lay on its floor. She squeezed her eyes shut, clenched her chattering teeth around a piece of the robe, and prayed that she and the vehicle would vanish.

Vivian held her breath when she heard the garage doors open. One car after the other rolled in, and once Douglas harrumphed a "*See ya*" to Big Will and left, she could no longer hold back her desperation, and bawled.

"Lil' flower? What on earth ya doin' out here in the cold?" Big Will asked when he opened the door. He tugged at the lap robe, but she held on to it.

"Miss Vivian!"

"I can't let you or anyone see me."

"Why not?"

"I just can't. I want to die here."

"I have to get yo' folks."

"No!"

"Well then, yo' gonna have to tell me somethin'."

"Calvin...he hurt me."

"What?" Big Will shouted.

"Big Will, please! Please! No one can know." She looked up at him from under the blanket.

"He did that to ya?" pointing to the bruise spreading across her face and steadying himself against the doorjamb. "He did somethin' else to ya?"

"You have to make it all go away. I know you can. *Please.*"

"Afraid can't nobody. Now ya just close yo' eyes and let me pick ya up and take ya to yo' room. Cousin Sarah'll be there shortly."

"But you can't tell her."

"No way 'round it. Ya let me take care a' this. I'm gonna take ya upstairs."

Big Will picked her up like a box full of crystal, careful not to jiggle any piece of her as he carried her upstairs. He placed her on her bed.

"Don't ya worry 'bout nothing."

# Chapter 16

# BIG WILL STRIKES AGAIN

*St. Louis, Missouri, 1941*

Big Will found Sarah in the living room, sipping a glass of sherry.

"Cousin—" he started.

"Big Will, you look plumb shaken. What's the matter?"

Big Will knelt on one knee beside her.

"It's the lil' flower." He gulped and then whispered in her ear, "She's been messed with by that no 'count."

Sarah shot up straight, spilling the wine on her dress. She shook him by his shoulders.

"What are you saying? You can't mean…"

"I found her in the garage where he took her and…"

"Don't say it. Not another word. Where is she?" She moved to stand and Big Will helped her.

"In her room. I took her."

Sarah started to run from the room, but Big Will grabbed her by the arm.

"And Mr. Jordan?"

"Tell him what happened and have him call Ethan. He needs to get over here right now!" she screamed, wrenching herself from his grasp. "And keep Jordan away from us. I need some time with her alone," she added as she ran out the door.

Big Will staggered down the hall toward Jordan's office. The thought of seeing his boss's face when he told him about Vivian caused him to bump from one side of the corridor to the other like a drunken sailor.

Jordan's office door was ajar and Will rapped against it.

"Come on in. I'm always open for business, even on Sundays."

"Boss…"

"What's wrong with you? Looks like every drop of blood has drained out of your face. Seen a ghost?" He chuckled and got up. "Let me take a better look at you."

"Need to tell ya somethin'." He walked straight to the front of Jordan's desk and stared him in the eye.

As Big Will described what happened, Jordan's knees buckled until he found himself seated back in his chair. He chomped so hard on his unlit cigar that he bit it in two; one piece fell in his lap and he spat out the other. He ground his teeth and hammered both fists on his desk. "That two-bit punk. Came into my home and…" Jordan covered his face.

"Mister Jordan, suh. Cousin says ya need to call Dr. Cole," Big Will whispered.

Jordan flung his phone book at Big Will. "Here, you do it! I'm going upstairs!" As he stood, he dug his fingers into the armrests with such a force that the leather ripped, but he took no notice.

"Boss, Cousin says ya need to wait."

"Wait? **Wait?** For what? I have to see my daughter."

"Says the two of 'em need some time alone."

Jordan took a deep breath, but before he could speak, he crumpled into his chair and wept.

"Don't know what to say, what to do to help ya, Boss."

Big Will approached Jordan, but he waved him off, pulled out his handkerchief, and dried his eyes. "Go on, call Ethan."

"Yessuh, Boss." He dialed the number. "Dr. Cole, suh. The Sables need ya over here straightaway," he said, and then hung up.

"Now pour me a drink. And one for yourself," Jordan ordered and pointed to the bar.

"Ya know, Boss, I don't drink."

"Now Will, you've worked for me long enough to know that I know every damned thing that goes on here. I know you get shit-faced drunk once a year. This'll make it twice. I *ain't* drinking alone. Now pour for both of us!"

Big Will picked two glasses from the bar's shelf and half-filled them both with bourbon. Big Will sipped at his while Jordan swallowed the contents in one guzzle, then snarled.

"There will soon be one less little, good-for-nothin' bastard on these streets because I'm gonna kill him, you hear me? I am going to **kill** him with my bare hands if I have to."

"Mr. Jordan—"

He splashed more alcohol in his glass and swigged it down. "And I'll be driving myself. Don't want anyone involved in this but me."

"Mr. Jordan—" Big Will started again.

"Don't try to talk me out of it."

"Wasn't thinkin' 'bout doin' that."

"Well, what then?"

"I'm gonna take care of that for ya."

"What?"

"Like to do it myself," Big Will repeated as he scooped up a lone tear from his eye with his enormous knuckle.

"You did it once before and it almost killed you. Ripped your stomach to shreds."

"Didn't have no choice back then. This time, I do the decidin'."

"Sit down," Jordan told him.

"Mr. Jordan. I wanna stand if ya don't mind."

"I said sit down."

Big Will sat across from Jordan.

"I know how much she means to you, but this is for me to do. It's *my* duty, not yours," Jordan emphasized.

"Wouldn't be good for the Negro community if ya got caught, suh. Wouldn't be good at all. Everythin' ya built. Everythin' ya run."

"You think I care about any of that when it comes to my daughter?"

"No, suh. But I can do it and won't nobody know."

Jordan poured himself another glass of the liquor. "Are you sure?"

Will nodded.

Jordan unlocked the bottom drawer of his desk, pulled out a wad of tightly banded bills, and handed it to Big Will. He scribbled a note.

"This is where he lives. Across the river in a rathole."

Big Will took the paper but gave the money back to his boss. "Don't need yo' money, Mr. Jordan. I got my own. Hardly spend a penny of what ya pay me."

"I said take it. You're going to need it to get to wherever you're taking that heathen. Don't want his body showing up anywhere near us. Use the dead wagon. That's appropriate now, isn't it?"

Big Will kept his eyes on Jordan as he backed out of the office, slightly bowed his head, and hurried down the corridor.

As soon as the sun set, Big Will threw his suitcase on the passenger seat of the dead wagon and headed toward the Eads Bridge. After crossing the Mississippi, he soon found Calvin's house and parked within spitting distance of it. The frigid air permeated every crevice of the wagon, keeping him alert as he waited. Three hours later, he saw the boy rushing past him. Big Will jumped out and collared him from behind.

"Hey, nigga! What the hell..." Calvin shouted.

Big Will pulled a bludgeon from inside his coat and waved it in Calvin's face. "Who ya callin' what?"

"Hold up. Ya work for Undertaker Sable. I saw ya in the alley." Calvin's face turned white and he froze except for wrapping his arms around his chest.

"Got somethin' to hide, have ya?" Big Will put down the club and hung on to Calvin's neck. He turned him around, wrestled his arms open, and rooted inside his coat until he found an immense roll of bills.

"What'd ya do? Rob some ol' lady on her way to church?" He flung the money on the ground. "I don't need it and where ya goin', ya won't neither."

Calvin's feet barely grazed the sidewalk as Big Will hauled him to the back of the wagon, tied his arms behind him with some oily rags, and stuffed the rest of them in his mouth. He padlocked the door, crossed back into Missouri, and steered onto Route 66, heading southwest toward the Ozarks. *Plenty woods and wild animals there.*

Riding along the two-lane highway under a waxing moon, a long-ago image planted itself in his mind: the mammoth, writhing, chrysalis-like bundle that he'd left in the South Carolina woods years ago. Now he was riding into the night with another degenerate in the back of a wagon. A scoundrel whose neck he felt like crushing with the soles of his feet. But every time the urge came, his stomach turned inside out. Samuel had told him the weight of Maurice would lift. But all these years later, it hadn't.

When he drew near the bridge that led to Devil's Elbow in the Ozarks, he parked off to the side of the road and looked at the icy river below. Day wouldn't break for a few hours. He watched the swirling water as it rushed past. *If I went flyin' off a here, the wagon would break into smithereens and so would me and that bastard. They'd be pickin' us up in pieces downstream. Wouldn't have to think no more 'bout what I done back home. No more demon waitin' to holler names at me. And one less no 'count loose on the streets.* With this decision, Big Will felt like the carefree teenager he was before he joined the posse. The burden he'd been carrying since then drifted away, and he tilted his head against the seat back and sighed with relief.

"Hey, wake up!"

Big Will rubbed his eyes to find a white man pounding on the car window. The risen sun made him blink.

"If ya wanna cross this bridge, better do it now. We're shuttin' it down for the day. We got an emergency to fix. Work crew's already here."

"Yessuh. Thank ya."

"Looks like ya could use some more shut-eye. There's a truck stop up ahead. They serve colored in the back, so ya can get some grub, too."

Big Will slowly steered the wagon across the bridge and pulled over. The heaviness descended upon him again. The sun's frigid light filtered through the towering evergreens and onto the dense yet barren shrubbery. *Gotta wait 'til it's dark agin for whatever I do.* After driving to the roadside station, he gassed up, bought some water and biscuits, and returned to the road.

The squirrely package he had left in the South Carolina woods years ago now moved from his brain to his innards, roaming around like a tapeworm. He pulled off the road to calm himself, then ate a biscuit to the sound of Calvin's sniveling behind him.

Big Will unlocked the back of the dead wagon and a gigantic mouth, attached to floating, diaphanous wings, leapt out at him, howling **KILLER!** over and over again. The sight paralyzed him as he watched the beast hurl the Mason jar into the air. It crashed at his feet.

"I forgot to bring ya with me!" he hollered, fell to the ground, and vomited. He recovered quickly, ready to rip the lips of the phantom to shreds. Instead, he could only see the boy staring up at him. Calvin was crying like an infant and smelled like one whose diaper hadn't been changed. Big Will took the rags out of his mouth and almost smothered the boy as he cradled his head with his mighty hands. He watched the ghost drift off.

"Ya start makin' too much noise and these goin' right back where they was." He fed Calvin a biscuit, let him gulp some water, and then locked the door. He returned to the wagon and felt the grief and guilt of long ago grip him by the throat. He howled and collapsed over the steering wheel. *I can't do this agin. I can't. But I gotta make sure he's gone forever. I promised the boss, I promised.* He started the engine and headed due west, leaving the bridge, the freezing waters below it, and the forest behind. *I know where I'll take him.*

The weather got milder and milder until he hit Flagstaff, Arizona, at nightfall, and a chill set in. He then headed south, and eventually veered off the main highway onto a dirt road. The ride got bumpy and Calvin woke up and yelled, "Where the hell ya taking me, man?"

"Ya don't wanna know." He drove for hours.

The sun had just begun to interrupt the black horizon when he arrived at Fort Huachuca, Arizona, one of the outposts where colored troops trained before being shipped overseas. He stopped at the main gate and approached the guards on duty.

"My name's Will Anderson. Could'ya kindly let Captain Sammy Miller know I'm out here? We both from the same town in South Carolina. I know his daddy."

A guard lifted his walkie-talkie and a few minutes later an officer approached.

"Big Will! What in the world are you doing out here?" He pulled the huge man toward him. "You're a sight, you are."

"Sammy, don't have much time. Got somethin' serious to tell ya. Can we talk back of the wagon?"

After Big Will finished telling Sammy about the rape and his promise to Mr. Jordan, he said. "I thought I could do him in, but I can't."

"You did the right thing. I'll take care of it."

"I'm bindin' him to ya, Sammy. They don't want nobody to ever see this piece of trash again."

"Even colored troops will be called up for overseas duty soon enough. I'll do my best to make sure he never comes back."

"He's such a coward. Might try to run outta here."

"Anyone who goes AWOL doesn't get very far. Look around."

Big Will surveyed the flat, barren landscape and laughed. "Guess ya can see him for at least three days runnin' out here."

"That's exactly what we say. They can't get away." Sammy smiled.

"And can ya make sure all these fellas here know what he done? Many of 'em surely got sistahs of they own."

"Already thought about that. Calvin may not last until we get shipped out."

"Can I give ya these for takin' him off my hands?" Will handed Sammy the bills Jordan had given him.

"No, no. Don't want it."

When Big Will opened the back door, Calvin was asleep. He dragged him out by his heels until he could sit him upright. Seeing nothing but barren land and hearing only the wind blowing, the boy asked, "Where are we?"

"Ya stink, Calvin," Big Will told him.

"Ya did this to me. Not lettin' me—"

"Shut up. Here's yo' new home. They'll hose ya down soon enough."

"You mean ya ain't gonna—"

"Some things worse than death, ain't ya heard? But ya lookin' the wrong way, Calvin."

Big Will untied him and walked him to the front of the wagon.

They stood before row after row of one- and two-story army barracks.

"Get movin'. Ya got some papers to sign. And if ya don't, the thick end of my bludgeon goin' up the tight end of yo' ass and ya gonna get what ya was 'spectin."

Calvin puked.

"How old is he, Big Will?" Sammy asked.

"Don't rightly know. Don't rightly care."

"Well, he's supposed to be seventeen with parental consent," Sammy added.

"I'm only sixteen," Calvin blurted out as he wiped the spittle from his mouth.

"But yo' birthday's tomorrow, now ain't it? And I'm yo' daddy, right?" Will nudged the club into Calvin's buttocks. "Where do I sign?" He looked toward Sammy.

After the formalities were attended to in the administrative office, Big Will shook hands with Sammy and started to head toward the wagon.

"No, no, wait! Don't you want some breakfast?" Sammy asked.

"No, thanks. Gotta get back to work. Been gone awhile."

"Half an hour, more or less, won't matter. I'll take you to the officer's mess. C'mon."

As Big Will drove off later that morning, he patted his belly. It had been years since he'd been able to scarf down a pile of cheese grits, at least ten rashers of thickly cut bacon, a half dozen scrambled eggs, toast dripping butter, and a quart of coffee.

## Chapter 17

# MATTIE TAKES OVER

*Cleveland, Ohio, 1942*

When the phone rang on New Year's morning, Mattie jumped. She still wasn't accustomed to this contraption. She needed it for her catering business, but for some reason it put a fright into her. Before she could say hello, Sarah spoke.

"Mattie?"

"Yes, darlin', who else would it be?" She laughed.

"Happy New Year, big sister of mine."

"And the same to you. What a sweet surprise. You're usually too busy with preparing for that annual gathering of yours to call me so early in the day."

"We put it off this year," Sarah responded.

"Really? Why?"

"I'll explain when I see you."

"Lord knows when that will be. We haven't seen each other—"

"Vivian and I will be there tomorrow," Sarah stated matter-of-factly.

"What? Tomorrow?"

"I'll tell you everything then. And please keep this under your hat."

"But why? I don't understand you."

"I said I'll tell you when I get there. We'll take a taxi from the station. I have to run now. I love you, dearest one. Goodbye."

"Bye," Mattie said but her sister had already put down the receiver.

Although Mattie was puzzled, she jumped for another reason and squealed out loud. *Vivian is coming!* She wondered why Sarah chose to arrive on a Friday. The school year restarted on Monday, which meant their visit would be brief. She'd have only two days to spoil her favorite niece. *But now for more immediate business*, she thought.

She started pulling out pots and pans and ladles and stirring spoons and a flour sifter and some cake tins and another cast-iron skillet her mother had gifted her right before she left for Atlanta. The skillet she tried to kill Henry with beat out any she'd ever used, but lugging it along with her would have been like tugging a piece of him with her so she had tossed it. She had no inkling of what to whip up; she just knew that something would speak its name to her once she put her culinary palate on display.

**FRIED CHICKEN**, the pan almost screamed out; it was Vivian's favorite main dish. No matter that Gwendolyn most likely would include it in the shoebox lunch they would carry on board the train. It galled her every time she thought about how Negroes had to take their own food because they weren't allowed in the dining cars. Arthur, her second husband, had waited tables on damned near every route the New York Central

Railroad ran and even he couldn't sit down, have a proper meal, and rest his feet. *Without us, the trains wouldn't go anywhere. One nation, indivisible, with justice and liberty for all? Bollocks!* She then said a quick prayer for *that sainted Mr. Randolph, who started a union for Pullman car porters. Without his sweating and straining, we'd be even worse off!*

She then turned her attention toward making the crunchiest and most flavorful fried chicken north of the Mason-Dixon Line. She'd use the rest of her day to shop and would keep it simple. Only three sides: collard greens, candied sweet potatoes, and macaroni and cheese. The chicken, a big, fat yellow one, would come from the poultry shop. She might even cheat and buy a cake from the local bakery since the owner was a neighbor. Mattie liked her recipe and knew that all the ingredients were fresh.

The next morning, Mattie woke up earlier than usual, fixed herself an abbreviated breakfast of toast and coffee, and then put on her apron and hair net. She'd prepare the side dishes for now and save the frying for the end so the chicken would be piping hot when they arrived. The steps were in her head as were most of her elders' recipes. She pulled out an ordinary brown paper bag, filled it halfway with flour and added pepper, salt, and paprika. Then she squeezed the throat of the bag and shook the contents at an angle. She peered into the bag to check that the color of the flour and spices was a mild red, closed her eyes, took a whiff, and hoped she didn't sneeze. That was the telltale sign that she'd over peppered the mixture. She washed and dried each piece of chicken to the bone with an ironed, white kitchen towel, to ensure it wouldn't dampen the flour, weigh down the bag, and waste some of the ingredients. Then she added piece after piece of chicken.

*"A big part of it's in the shaking,"* her mother would say. *"You gotta make sure that every piece you put in the bag gets covered with flour. Don't forget to open the wings up a bit so you don't miss their crooks."*

Mattie clasped the bag shut with her right hand, cupped the bottom of it with her left, and started. She began with an up-and-down motion close to the center of her chest, then rocked it left and right, and finished by heaving it in front of her face for one last jiggle. By then, she was pretty much certain that she had accomplished her goal. She heated the oil until the moment before it bubbled, then pulled out the first piece of poultry, shook off any extra flour into the bag, and let the oil devour it without a drop of splattered grease. The rest of the first batch followed quickly. Now came the endurance test—standing at the stove and turning each piece again and again, so the chicken ended up with the same copper color all over and was cooked through and through.

At 9:00 p.m. sharp, she heard a car pull into her driveway and couldn't help but bolt out of the door. As she drew closer to her sister and niece, her heart sank. They looked drawn and tired and above all, worried. Their brows could have knitted an Afghan, as pinched and wrinkled as they were.

"Mattie! You'll catch your death out here with no coat on," Sarah admonished her sister.

"Hush! What on earth is wrong with you two? I've never seen you so—"

"Let's go inside," Sarah interrupted, and almost shoved her up the walkway.

"Vivian, go to your room, the one Aunt Mattie always keeps freshened up for you," Sarah said once they all crossed the threshold.

Vivian ran up the staircase.

"Why, what is going on?" Mattie started to follow Vivian but Sarah stopped her.

"Let her go."

"Okay. Well then, let me make some tea," Mattie turned toward the kitchen.

"That can wait." Sarah turned steely.

"No, it can't, *little* sister. I'm fixing it for myself, no matter what you say. You're sending a chill through me."

Mattie's silver tea service jangled, one piece against the other, when she returned to the parlor. Her hands shook even more as she placed the tray on her cocktail table.

"I can't beat around the bush on this. Vivian may be pregnant," Sarah said.

"But that can't be. She's too young. Too innocent. Too obedient. She would never let any boy get next to her."

"Yes, you're right and she didn't." Sarah eyed Mattie and said nothing.

"Who's the scoundrel? I'll take my skillet down to St. Louis and nothing will stop me this time!" Mattie shouted.

"He's been taken care of. Better not to ask any questions. That little hoodlum won't ever rape another unsuspecting somebody. That's all you need to know."

"Dear God. Why Vivian? So sweet and kind and loving." Mattie started to cry. Sarah moved next to her and hugged her.

"Never thought I'd be comforting you. You always cared for me, just like a mama. Kissing my bruises and binding my cuts and scrapes. Helping me with my numbers." Sarah poured her sister a cup of tea and handed it to her. "I'm now entrusting my only child to you."

"What if she's not?"

"Jordan and I had already decided she needed to leave St. Louis. And we already thought of sending her to you. Vivian didn't inherit any of our wiles, Mattie. She's too innocent for that town. She's meant for other places, bigger dreams. If she is, well, I want her with family. And if she's not, you and she can have some fun together. I've told everyone that you're ailing and that Vivian pleaded to come stay with you."

"Whichever way the wind blows, I'll school her myself, right here, so she'll be ready to pick up her studies in the fall."

"She's full of shame over this. Can barely look at herself in the mirror. Feels she brought it all on herself and on our family."

"Don't you worry. I'll shake it out of her. You'll see."

Mattie left her teacup, wiped her face dry, and walked up to the second floor and into the room that she'd prepared for Vivian. She found her niece huddled on the bed.

"Darlin', we'll get through this. Together," she said as she sat down next to her niece and stroked her head. "And no matter what happens, you and I are going to have a good time. I'll have it no other way and when I put my mind to something"—she tickled her niece's armpits—"you know it always comes to pass." Vivian didn't laugh, didn't move. "You're going to be fine and you're also going to get up and come downstairs and have dinner."

"I'm not hungry," Vivian whispered.

"Not even for *my* fried chicken? I bet Gwendolyn fixed some for the train ride, but you could never resist eating more once you got here."

"Oh, Auntie, I'm so ashamed."

"I know, Vivian, and you're here to get over that."

"But I can't. Please don't make me."

"You have to come with me, my darlin'." Mattie made her stand and led her down the stairs to dinner.

On Sunday Sarah left at daybreak and insisted on returning to the train station the way she came, by taxi. After a week of letting Vivian sleep as much as she wanted to in the morning, Mattie awakened her at dawn because she had planned her niece's days from sunup to sundown. She had dusted off her old lesson plans from her teaching years, believing that a focus on learning would help take Vivian's mind off what happened in the garage. They started in the kitchen with a proper breakfast, followed by morning classes, a luncheon pause for soup and a sandwich, a brief nap, and afternoon study. And then dinner and an hour or two of homework. In short order, Vivian eased into her new home like maple syrup slides across pancakes. Her appetite returned and Mattie was relieved as she saw Vivian enjoy her studies.

Mattie waited a full week, then another few days after Vivian missed her period before she brought up calling Sarah. She interrupted her niece as she studied at the dining room table.

"That's enough for now. I need to talk to you. I think it's time to call your folks. There's really no way to be sure just yet, darlin', but I think we should prepare them if you are."

"I am," Vivian responded. "I know it. I've never been late, and I can feel something stirring inside me."

Mattie knew it, too. She saw the flush in her niece's cheeks and a lustrous glow in her eyes. And then her own groin throbbed as she recalled the cavernous, barren space Henry left her with—one that would never be able to bear a child. She cradled her lower abdomen for a second and then sloughed off the memory.

"Auntie, I want to do everything I can to have a strong, healthy baby before I have to give it away."

"You've already thought about giving it up?"

"I know Mama and Papa would never let me keep it. But I want it to be the best baby in the world! A baby any woman would want."

"Now that's my Vivian. You've grown up overnight, you have."

"I just wish its father would have been nice and…" She stopped and started to cry.

"You just go ahead and let those tears roll out," Mattie said and held on to her, then picked up the telephone.


Mattie let a few more weeks pass and then decided to call Alberta Moore who, with her husband, Winston, lived down the street. She knew them from church but had never been to their home. *They may be the ones*, she thought. *God-fearing Christians. With plenty of assets. I hear she has more customers than she can stitch up garments for. Her white clients don't even mind coming right here to colored Cleveland to order and try on their clothes. That's how good she is. He owns the most prosperous Negro insurance company in town. And they're childless.*

First thing on Monday morning, she found their number in the phone book and dialed.

"Alberta? It's Mattie. How are you?"

"Why Mattie! I'm just fine, hearing your voice and all. How are *you*?"

"Doing well, I am. I'm sorry it's taken me so long to be neighborly, but there's no time like the present to get acquainted. I was hoping to drop by."

"Oh, I'd like that, I would. When can you come? Anytime is good for me. Anytime!"

"How about a week from tomorrow? After lunch."

"Oh! That's fine but you can't come sooner?"

"No, I'm sorry, but you'll see why. Okay?"

"All right, if I have to." Alberta sighed.

Mattie was delighted that Alberta sounded thrilled at the prospect of having her as a guest in her home. To further smooth the way, she'd bring a made-from-scratch mincemeat pie that would require a week and a day to make.

Mattie unlocked her piggy bank so she could splurge on top sirloin steak instead of cutting corners and using a round cut. A half day of cooking, a tableful of ingredients, and a week of letting the pie filling's flavors mingle in the refrigerator would be worth it. Once she came back from her butcher with the meat, she laid everything else on the kitchen table along with it: tart apples, candied orange and lemon peel, dark brown sugar, dried currants, pecans, raisins, an assortment of candied fruit, pitted sour cherries with their preserves, finely ground cinnamon, nutmeg, cloves, and mace butter.

"Aunt Mattie? Mincemeat! I can't wait," Vivian said when she saw what was up in the kitchen.

"This is for a client, but we can make a miniature version for you"—Mattie kissed her niece on her forehead—"if you help."

"Anything!"

"When the time comes, you can make the dough. But, darlin', can you study on your own today? I have to get this done. Last minute order."

"Who are they?"

"Someone referred to me. I don't even know them," she fibbed.

The morning of Mattie's meeting with Alberta, Vivian prepared the dough, rolling out two balls: a large one for her aunt's client and a teeny one for hers. She spread them into their respective pie tins and then Mattie helped her ladle the luscious mincemeat mixture in each.

As the pies baked, filling the kitchen with their delectable aromas, neither Mattie nor Vivian could think about anything else. When the pies had cooled, Vivian plunged her fork into hers and Mattie took a bite from it as well. They both swooned.

That afternoon, Mattie took out her straw picnic basket and lined it with a small flannel towel. She placed the weighty dessert inside and closed the lid.

"I'll be back in an hour or so. We can go over your homework then," she called out to Vivian as she exited her house without waiting for a reaction.

Alberta broke into a deep-dimpled smile when she swung open her door and greeted Mattie.

"I'm so glad we're finally getting together," she said. "C'mon in. It's freezing outside."

"The pleasure is really mine," Mattie responded as she placed the gift on the entry table and pointed at her overboots. "Can I put these somewhere? Don't want to dirty your sparkling floors," she remarked as she examined the hallway.

Alberta carefully placed them in a container by the door without taking her eyes off the bundle Mattie had put down.

"What's that?" Alberta asked and pointed to it.

"Just a little something for you and Winston," Mattie answered and handed it to her.

"Oh no. It can't be," she said as she pulled back the cover.

"Mincemeat pie! That takes a whole lotta fixing and at least a week."

"Alberta, I declare! You know something about baking pies."

"Know more about eating them," she said with a laugh.

"I hope you and Winston will enjoy it."

"If there's any left by the time he gets home," she joked and laughed again.

"I didn't rightly know if you drank, so I left out the brandy," Mattie added.

"We do, but I'll take it any way it comes. Let me have your coat and gloves. Please sit down." She led her to the parlor and left the pie on the cocktail table. "I'll be right back."

Alberta disappeared and returned with a silver tray holding a crystal decanter filled with a liqueur, two snifters, and two dessert plates with forks. "We can drink some or pour some on top." She laughed once more. "Or both!"

"No, no," Mattie said. "The pie is all for you and your husband."

"But you have to have a taste. I don't want to eat alone. *Please.*"

"Whatever you prefer," Mattie replied. "I've been meaning to be more neighborly, but it seems like time just flies by."

"I know what you mean."

Alberta gouged out two oversize pieces.

Mattie liked this woman more than she had even hoped. As they ate and small-talked, she noticed every detail about Alberta and her home. Not a strand of hair out of place, not a hint of lint on her dress, freshly buffed fingernails, recently polished shoes, and a corset that turned her portly frame into the semblance of an hourglass figure. A shiny, claw-foot, oak table already set for dinner with, for heaven's sake, chargers and enormous doilies separating them from the dinner plates. The glasses they drank from glistened, and the dessert plates sang each time the fork tines grazed them. And the smell of carnations intoxicated her—white ones in the living room and pink ones on the dining room table. Above all, Alberta's warmth permeated her home. *Yes, this will do.*

"This is so much fun," Alberta exclaimed. "Having somebody like you to chat with. You know, I'm a seamstress and I have my clients, Negro *and* white, but I try to be real businesslike with them so I'm alone here most of the time, stitching and sewing or out buying all my yard goods. Winston and I have our card games and parties, but we really wanted to fill this house up with children. They never came and now, well, it's too late." She glanced down at her empty plate and sighed.

"I wanted them, too, but God never sent me any," Mattie said.

"You, too?" Alberta didn't wait for an answer. "I was just sure yours were all up and grown."

"No, no. I've been married twice, and I almost had a child with my first husband..." Mattie's voice trailed off.

"Miscarried?"

"Yes, something like that."

"I'm so sorry. Didn't mean to meddle. I talk too much sometimes. Forgive me." Alberta reached for Mattie's hand but stopped just short of touching it.

"Oh no, Alberta. It was a long time ago. Over and done with."

"But can I ask who's that beautiful young girl who came to church with you for a while? She favors you a bit."

"My baby sister's daughter, Vivian."

"You and your family must be so proud of her. She's a sweet thing. It's written all over her."

"Yes, she is."

"But neither of you have been coming to service lately."

"No, we haven't. The weather's kept us in. My niece is sickly, so I've been schooling her at home."

"There I go again, poking my nose in your business. I mean, by asking about Sunday service."

"No, no. Not at all, but I do have to get on my way, Alberta. I just wanted to finally be a proper neighbor."

Mattie stood and Alberta accompanied her to the front door.

"I hope you'll come back some time," Alberta said.

"Don't you worry about that, my dear."

This time Mattie reached for Alberta's hand.

"I'd rather hug you, if you don't mind."

They both smiled and embraced.

That evening Mattie wrote an effusive letter to Sarah, telling her about Alberta. She ended by saying, *She makes good money as a seamstress and her husband has the most prosperous insurance company for colored in town. I know Jordan's heard of him. They're the best we could hope for. I'll wait for your go-ahead. Love, your big sis*


With Sarah's lickety-split blessing, Mattie planned her next visit to Alberta. This time she carried a lemon meringue pie.

"You're gonna spoil me to pieces. Won't be able to eat anybody else's food." Alberta closed her eyes and gushed after the first forkful.

"That's quite a compliment. Thank you."

"I can sew up a storm, but I'm not much of a cook," she admitted as she finished off the last morsel of the graham cracker crust from her fork. "Winston and I eat out a lot. But you know, there aren't many restaurants for colored in this town."

"Well, I'm not sure you know that I have a catering business. I used to teach school but stopped after my husband died.
Wanted more freedom with my time. I mostly do events, but I
have a few clients, too, and…" Mattie started.

"Would you? We're not fussy," Alberta declared.

"We can certainly think about it. But if you'll permit me, I
have something more important to discuss with you. I— I mean,
my family and I need to ask you something."

Alberta looked puzzled. "Of course. Tell me."

"First of all, my baby sister is married to Jordan Sable, the
undertaker."

"You're Jordan Sable's sister-in-law?"

"Yes, I guess that's what I am," Mattie affirmed.

"Oh my, my. Winston admires him so. He's a legend. Why, he
started a union for colored railroad cleaners, way before Mr. A.
Philip Randolph did for the Pullman car porters. And then put
together the biggest funeral home in Missouri. And I've read in
the newspapers, Black and white alike, that he's known as the
Negro mayor of St. Louis because he controls the Black vote.
I'm right, no?" By now, Alberta had run out of breath.

Mattie nodded. "Yes, he's quite a man."

Alberta then leaned forward. "And your niece is his daughter? But what could *we* possibly do for *your* family?"

"You're quite a couple yourselves. Jordan and my sister know
about your husband's business, too. Mr. Moore is making waves
here in Cleveland. And so generous. We know how he paid for
the burials of folk who missed payments during the Depression. Word travels both ways."

"We're just doing a job," Alberta demurred.

"And I know"—Mattie winked—"he couldn't have done all of that without a woman like you by his side."

By now, Alberta was blushing all over herself. She tried to talk but couldn't.

"Before I ask you, let's have another slice of this pie with some tea, Alberta. I know you've got a service to beat the band." Mattie laughed.

"Oh, silly me. I should've thought of that. Too anxious to devour that pie, I was."

Alberta went to her dining room, opened the oak breakfront that matched her table, and pulled out a silver teapot, creamer, and sugar bowl. She placed them all on a glistening tray and started toward the kitchen.

"I'll put on a kettle and be right with you," she called out.

Mattie moved to join her, but Alberta insisted that she sit back down in the parlor.

"I can handle all this myself."

Alberta arrived shortly with the tray and they settled into another piece of pie.

"Alberta, we have an unfortunate situation on our hands." Mattie cleared her throat. "My niece, Vivian, is in a family way. And let's just say that the boy doesn't figure into this at all."

"Oh dear." Alberta gasped. "I'm sorry. She's so young."

"Yes, she is. We, I mean, Vivian's parents, are looking for a home for the child. And I was hoping that you might consider…"

"Oh heavenly Father! You finally answered my prayers." Alberta stretched her hands upward and looked at the ceiling. "Thank you, Jesus!" She turned her gaze toward Mattie. "I never thought this would happen. I dreamed about it. Dreamed about raising a child together with Winston, who's the kindest man on this earth. And now it's going to happen after all these years."

"Are you sure you don't want to think about this? Talk with your husband first?" Mattie asked quizzically.

"I know my husband better than he knows himself. Winston will be as elated as I am. But are *you* sure? We aren't the youngest couple, you know."

"But you are the most righteous. I knew the good Lord would take care of this. We're just His instruments. He brought me to you and your husband," Mattie said.

"Indeed, He did."

*Chapter 18*

# VIVIAN MAKES A DEMAND

*Cleveland, Ohio, 1942*

As the weeks passed, Vivian's mind wandered and she had more and more difficulty concentrating on her studies. Her nostalgia grew along with her belly. She longed for Big Will's comfort and protection, Gwendolyn and Emma's warmth, and how they all indulged her whims. She also missed her friends, tried not to relive what happened to her, tried not to blame herself, tried to look forward to returning home and putting all this behind her. But she also felt a growing resentment toward her parents. They had made all her decisions. And now they were going to take her baby from her without even asking how she felt or what she wanted. She craved to turn back the clock to a day, any day, before the fateful one in the garage.

Above all, she couldn't stop thinking about Calvin. She had loved him and she had been certain that he loved her back. But he didn't. He had betrayed her and the pain of that realization gnawed at her, month after month.

Vivian remained inside as much as possible, embarrassed by her pregnancy. Fortunately, her aunt had arranged for Dr. Josephus Gray, the obstetrician, to examine her at home, leaving gossipers with one less tale to tell.

"You've just about another seven weeks," Dr. Gray told her in early August.

"Thank you so much for coming here to see me, so I don't have to…" Vivian paused and glanced at her aunt, who stood in the corner of the bedroom.

"It's a pleasure, my dear. I'll be visiting you every week from now on and—"

"Is there something wrong?" she interrupted.

"No, no. Because of your age, I will need to follow you more closely."

"Oh, I see. Can you please tell me again what will happen when it's my time?"

Dr. Gray explained what to expect: the various ways her water could break, the urgency of getting to the hospital immediately thereafter, and an idea of what contractions felt like.

"How much will they hurt, Dr. Gray?"

"I can't be any more precise. Every woman is different. Just be prepared for some amount of pain."

Mattie came forward, bent over, and hugged her niece tightly.

"It will be all right. Your mother and I will be with you," she assured her, and then stood up.

"Thank you again, Dr. Gray," Vivian said.

"I'm happy to do it. And of course, I'm always delighted to see your aunt. And taste a little pie, maybe?"

"Oh, you know I've got your favorite apple pie cooling in the kitchen. Vivian, darlin', get dressed. We'll be waiting for you downstairs," Mattie said as she and Dr. Gray left her bedroom.

Even before she finished putting on her clothes, Vivian heard them laughing in the parlor. Dr. Gray always seemed to have an excuse to linger after their appointments. When she joined them, she saw an ample cherry cobbler on the table.

"Your auntie fooled me this time."

"Couldn't resist the Bings, Josephus. They're about to finish up so I had to grab some," Mattie replied.

She cut three thick slices and Josephus devoured his. She started to serve him another but he stopped her.

"Wish I could stay longer, but I have to get to my office. Call me if you need anything. It's a waiting game now, Vivian. I'm always here for you, Mattie." He smiled. "And of course, for you, dear," he said and patted Vivian's shoulder.

"Such a nice man," Vivian commented as they waved him down the front walkway. "Is he married?"

"Vivian? Why would you ask that, child?"

"I think he's sweet on you, that's all."

"What he has is a sweet tooth. The man loves pies."

"And you make sure there's always one waiting for him."

"Yes, I do. He comes to us, after all. Might as well give him something for his time."

Vivian wriggled her nose at her aunt.

"Now, just what does that mean, young lady?" Mattie questioned her.

"I'm not convinced, that's all." Vivian paused to wash the plates and silverware. Then she got her history book and homework and set everything on the kitchen table.

"You are such a joy, my dear. What will I do with myself after you leave?" Mattie asked as they both sat down, side by side, and she opened her lesson plan.

Vivian didn't respond and instead began the class with questions about what she'd read. Before Mattie could answer, however, Vivian closed her schoolbook and her eyes, and began to knead her temples with the tips of her fingers.

"What is it, Vivian? Do you have a headache?"

"No!" she snapped and glared at her aunt.

"Oh my, my. Are you all right, dear?" Mattie looked taken aback by Vivian's response.

"Oh, Auntie, I'm so sorry. I didn't mean to . . ." Vivian looked down and cuddled her stomach. "Aunt Mattie?" She raised her head. "Will I be able to hold my baby before they take it away?"

"Of course, darlin'," Mattie replied and put her notes down.

"But what if I can't take my eyes off him . . . or her?"

"Vivian, you said from the beginning that . . ." Mattie reached for her hand but Vivian refused her touch.

"I know what I said. I know. But what if I can't let the baby go?" Vivian stared downward again.

They sat together in silence. She glanced around the kitchen, as if searching for her next words and then returned her aunt's gaze. "Aunt Mattie, can't you take my baby?" Vivian blurted out. "I could come and visit and see it grow up? I'm your niece and he or she could be my . . . Oh, I don't know. Maybe I could stay here with you, for a little while. Then I can see her first steps. Or hear his first word. We can tell folks it's your baby. Or that you decided to adopt. You're so smart. You can figure it out, can't you?"

"Why Vivian, dear, you know that can't be."

"We could be a family. We *are* a family." Vivian wrapped her arms around Mattie's waist and rested her head on her shoulder as she spoke. "I could stay here and finish school and be with you. You're my favorite aunt. You know that, don't you?" Vivian stared at her aunt, but Mattie turned away.

"Child"—Mattie untangled herself from her niece's hold and stood—"as much as I love you and want you here with me, the Lord has other plans for you. You're young and it may be hard for you to see the wisdom in what your parents have decided. But it's what's best for you."

"They've always figured out everything for me and I've always done whatever they've said. But what's best for my child? A child needs its mother's love!"

"Of course, it does, and Alberta is brimming with love to give a child. She's waited so long for this."

"But I'm the mother!" Vivian shouted. "*Not* Mrs. Moore."

"Please try to calm down," Mattie said as she patted Vivian's hand.

"It isn't supposed to be this way. You get pregnant when you're married. When you are going to build a family with someone you love and who loves you…not from what happened to me. But I'm now so attached to what's growing inside me that even thinking about having to give the baby away and never seeing it again makes me go crazy."

"No, you won't go mad!"

Vivian now clasped Mattie's hands. "Does that mean that you'll…?"

"That means that I'm going to tell you a story. A true story about my life and my baby."

"Aunt Mattie! I didn't know you had a—"

"I did and then I didn't. And then I did and then I didn't."

Vivian sat speechless as Mattie put on the teakettle, cleared the table, and pulled out two cups and saucers from the cupboard.

"You're old enough to hear this. It's a tale of caution, my dear—about love, life, and men. And about being with the right kind of man. If you keep this child, you'll be headed down a different path. Not every man with the right breeding will be anxious to accept another man's child."

"I don't care about finding a man. I just want to be with my baby."

"You say that now, darlin'. You've been sullied and stained by that—" Mattie picked up a dish towel from the rack and twisted it into a knot as she spoke to her niece. "I can't even call his name." She threw it into the sink. "But as you mature and put this behind you, you will want someone's arms around you. Someone to have other children with."

"I told you—I don't care about that."

"And I'm telling you that you will. We all got nature. Sometimes we want to deny it, but we all have it and answer to it. You'll see."

When the water boiled, Mattie made the tea, then sat down.

"Vivian, did you ever wonder why I carry so many last names?"

"Yes, I did but didn't want to ask."

"Mattie Franklin Cornwall Hughes! That's my full legal name. You've grown up faster than most girls, so you need to hear this and know what happened to me when I was just a few years older than you."

"Were you…"

Mattie looked into her lap, then raised her head.

"Well, I was born a Franklin, just like your mother." Mattie lightly tapped Vivian's head with her teaspoon and smiled.

Vivian beamed at her aunt.

"And my mama and papa, your grandparents, taught me a lot about how to be in this world, especially as a colored woman. How to carry myself and stand up for myself and be proud of who I was no matter how whites or anyone else, for that matter, treated me. So I've always kept their name as a reminder of all they instilled in me."

"I've seen their pictures."

"It's too bad they died before you were born. Fine, strong, elegant, intelligent people. There just aren't enough words to describe them. They were heads above most people you'll ever come across. You've been to Sunset and have seen what they left us: some of the most fertile land in the area, an emporium that surpasses what the whites have in downtown Greenston, and a sense of what a Negro community can achieve when it sticks together and spends its money with its own. Sunset may be small but it's strong and prosperous and welcoming to anyone, including whites who behave right. You've seen how your Uncle Nathan has honored and tended to what they built."

"Yes, yes. The farmland is beautiful and so big."

"And it would've been bigger if only..." Mattie stopped, slapped her thigh, and sighed.

"What happened, Auntie?"

"Well, my first husband, Henry Cornwall, ended up squandering the land that Papa gave us when we got married. You see, he was my childhood sweetheart and the man I thought I couldn't live without. My parents warned me that he came from different stock. Against their better instincts, Papa and Mama allowed us to marry. In the beginning, Henry proved them wrong."

Vivian watched her aunt close her eyes and pat her forehead.

"Aunt Mattie? Are you all right?" she asked.

"Oh yes, dear. I was just remembering the good part of our union…his soft touch and his adoring manner. He was the best husband a girl could dream of. We worked our land like nobody's business. Sometimes I still dream about all the colors." Mattie stopped and smiled.

"What do you mean?"

"We grew all kinds of greens and each one has a distinct shade. Mustards got a tinge of yellow. Collards are kind of, I don't know, dull, like they could use a good dusting. And turnips! Girl! Now that's a true green for you." She laughed.

"I thought you always taught school. You were a farmer, too?"

"Yes, I was, and very happy being one. Then I got pregnant but couldn't hold on to it. It flowed right out of me one morning in bed. And Henry washed me so gently and cleaned up everything. That's just how devoted he was. After that happened, Henry insisted that I just cook and sew."

"Oh my, Auntie, that's so dear."

"Yes, he was. But then the war came along and it seems like the minute he became eligible, the army drafted him. He wrote to me of how he suffered as a stevedore in a place called Brest. In France. How the white American soldiers mistreated him and the other colored he worked with." Mattie held back a tear.

"How sad," Vivian said.

"He returned injured, in body and mind and spirit. He became angry and violent. Like the devil jumped into his skin over there and never left. Poor soul. And as much as I tried to help him—and he would change and repent at times—but he stayed that way. And then he raped me…more than once."

"But how? You were married," Vivian gasped.

"You listen to me. Just because you're a wife doesn't mean your husband can have his way with you if you don't want to, or don't feel like it, or for whatever reason you aren't moved to. You understand me?"

"Yes, ma'am," Vivian responded, startled.

"And I conceived again. And lost it, too."

"I'm sorry."

"Don't be. I couldn't imagine raising a child with a father like that. I think the good Lord took my child in His arms and carried it away so He could care for it. That's what I think." Mattie pointed her finger straight at Vivian. "Darlin', I saw the bad side of love through Mr. Henry Cornwall, and by keeping his name, as painful as it can be at times, it keeps me aware of steering clear from any man who feels wrong. Any man you feel is damaged in some way."

"I see," Vivian reflected. "I think that Calvin was damaged, too. I think I knew it, but I thought he loved me and that he'd change for me and that…" She started to cry again and Mattie embraced her.

"Yes, my dear, I know. Love can blind you but experience will open your eyes," Mattie whispered in her ear.

"I'm so sorry for you, Auntie," Vivian whimpered.

Mattie then let go and took Vivian by the shoulders.

"But darlin', don't be! I was redeemed by my dear, sweet Arthur Hughes. I got to know a love that was rock solid and soft as a teddy bear. I met him in Atlanta when I went there to live with Aunt Anna to get away from Henry. Arthur was a Pullman car porter just like Northrup. But he was based out of Cleveland, so we married and I moved here. He had a bad heart and didn't even know it. He passed away a few years later, before you were born."

Vivian grew still.

"Aren't you happy for me, sweetheart? It all turned out well. Yes, I lost Arthur, but—"

"Calvin wanted to go with me to Atlanta. We talked about it," Vivian interrupted.

Mattie scooted next to her niece again. "You'll get over this. I promise you. And your Arthur is out there waiting for you. Mark my words."

Vivian rubbed her forehead with both hands.

"Aunt Mattie, I'm so confused."

"*Jesus is the way, the truth, and the light.* If you want your confusion to lift, ask Him for guidance. We're going to skip our lesson for today, get in the car, and go take a stroll in the woods. We can get some relief from this blasted summer heat and there's no better place to do some praying."

They rode outside the city in near silence. Once they began their walk, Mattie pulled Vivian close to her, and rested her arm on her shoulder.

"Aunt Mattie, can we talk about—" Vivian began.

"Hush, child. Empty your mind and fill it with what the Lord has bestowed on us—the trees, the ground under our feet, the air that keeps us alive. And thank Him for His grace."

Vivian slowed her gait and breathed deeply while she gazed at the greenery. She felt a twinge in her back and sat down on the nearest tree stump. And then she broke out in tears, and in between her sobs, she howled out.

"I should never have let this happen. I should have killed myself. That's what I should have done and I wouldn't have to go through any of this."

"Vivian! Don't say such things. This wasn't your fault."

Vivian buried her face in her hands and wept so violently that her shoulders heaved and her legs trembled. Mattie began stroking her niece's arms from behind, but Vivian shook her off.

"Let me be! I just want to die!" she screamed.

Mattie tiptoed in front of her niece, knelt down, and cupped Vivian's hands.

"I'm not letting go of you, Vivian, so don't even try to push me away. You are going to have this child and you're going to live a full life and I'm going to keep you sane."

Vivian now clasped Mattie's hands. "Does that mean that you'll…?"

"I don't yet know what it means." Mattie held on to Vivian's knees, patted them, and stopped their quivering.

"You're thinking about doing it?" Vivian asked.

Mattie stood and brushed the dirt and dust off her skirt. She took Vivian's hands and helped her up.

"Let's go home now." Mattie turned on her heel and began walking toward where she had parked the car, but Vivian didn't follow.

"Aunt Mattie. Will you help me? I can't do it all alone. *Please*. This will be our baby. *Ours. Yours and mine!*"

Mattie stopped in her tracks and turned toward Vivian.

"Child, you just don't know what you're asking."

"I'm asking for your help. You are the only one who can do this for me."

"Vivian, if we keep this baby, you'll be going down another

road altogether with your life. As I told you, there may be a decent man out there who might not mind raising another man's child, but he may not be acceptable. Your parents might not…"

"No matter what you say, I don't care about finding a man. And I don't care about what Mama and Papa have to say!"

"I never thought I'd have a child to rear at my age."

"Then, you'll do it? Oh, please say you will." Vivian walked up to her aunt and hugged her.

"I still need to rest with this. Still need to consider the consequences."

"You will. I know you will."

"Hush. I need to think."

On the way home, Vivian closed her eyes and listened to her aunt hum one spiritual after the other. *I can keep this baby, keep it in the family. I really don't care about anything else.* She leaned her head back and envisioned her child's face and every inch of its perfect, little body until Mattie's melodic voice turned into a gasp for air.

Vivian's eyes shot open and she turned toward her aunt.

"Aunt Mattie? What's wrong?"

"No, no, nothing. Let me pull over for a moment." She slowed the car to a crawl and stopped on the graveled side of the road. Vivian saw her flushed and sweaty face and started to fan her.

"Auntie! What is it?"

"Just the thought of raising a child is filling my heart with such joy. Feels like fresh blood is swishing through my whole body." She opened her bag and took a handkerchief out to wipe her brow.

"Oh, I knew you would figure this out for the two of us," Vivian squealed.

"Your folks will not like this. We'll keep it to ourselves for now."

"You've made me the happiest girl in the world. I'll keep my baby and live with you." She threw her arms around her aunt.


Throughout the next week, Vivian awoke to a different song each morning. Mattie sang spirituals, standards, jazz classics, anything she knew by heart when she entered Vivian's room with a breakfast tray. She even pulled out Arthur's banjo and strummed a few chords now and then, in between preparing meals for her clients. Mattie's buoyancy infected Vivian although she noticed her aunt seemed to tire more easily.

"Auntie, are you sure you're all right? You won't change your mind, will you?"

"Not on your life, my dear. No, no. It's the heat, that's all."

The following Saturday morning, Vivian found Mattie seated at the kitchen table gasping for air with both fists jammed into her chest.

"Aunt Mattie?"

"Call Henry," Mattie whispered as she gulped air.

"I don't understand! Henry?"

"No, no. I mean Josephus."

Vivian rushed to the phone. She dialed Dr. Gray's home number and once he answered, screamed, "It's Aunt Mattie! I don't know what's wrong with her."

"Calm down, Vivian," he said. "You need to tell me what you are talking about."

"She's not well. Oh, please help me."

"Listen to me, Vivian." He paused and then continued, "Take a long, slow breath, you hear me?"

"Yessir," she responded, then inhaled deeply.

"Now, describe her state to me as accurately as you can," Dr. Gray stated.

"She's out of breath and she's holding her chest. Right in the middle."

"You'll need to get her to the hospital as quickly as possible. Can you get a neighbor to drive her there? I'm afraid an ambulance will take too long to get to you."

"Oh yes. Yes, I can."

"Cleveland General. I'll meet you."

Vivian slammed the phone down and returned to her aunt. She helped her stand, threw Mattie's right arm over her own shoulder, and maneuvered her to the car. She guided her carefully into the passenger seat and got behind the wheel.

"But darlin', you can't drive," Mattie said.

"Oh yes I can. Papa taught me how to handle cars, tractors, anything with four wheels down on the stock farm. You're safe with me." Vivian turned on the ignition and spun out of the driveway.

"But the baby—"

"Fine. Everything's going to be just fine."

Vivian swerved around anything in her way and broke the speed limit. When the path was clear at stop signs or red lights, she blasted through them. She pulled into the emergency lane at the hospital with two police cars trailing, sirens wailing. When Vivian got out of the car, the officers dropped their pads and pencils.

"Miss, are you all right? I mean, is it your time? Is that why you were moving like lightning? Why are you driving yourself? How old are you?" One question after the other rang out.

"Oh no, no. It's my aunt. She's so sick."

A gurney appeared and the orderlies rolled Mattie inside with Vivian following. The cops scratched their heads and left.

"Mrs. Hughes, you've had a mild heart attack. I expect you will recover in due time, but you will need complete bed rest," the doctor on duty told her. Josephus appeared in the doorway but remained quiet.

Vivian stood at Mattie's bedside, holding one of her ice-cold hands. Josephus walked over and clasped the other.

"I'll take care of you, Auntie. Don't worry about a thing."

"Darlin', call your mother. She needs to come. You need care and—" Dr. Gray started.

"Anna told me to grieve Henry, but I didn't listen. I just kept him all tucked up inside my heart until it exploded," Mattie murmured.

Vivian bent over her aunt.

"I asked too much from you. I'm sorry."

Mattie smiled and drifted off.

"She's going to be all right, isn't she, Dr. Gray?" Vivian said to him under her breath.

Josephus pulled up a chair, sat down, and watched Mattie sleep.

"Oh yes, my dear. I'll see to it."

# Chapter 19

# VIVIAN DELIVERS

*Cleveland, Ohio, 1942*

Initially, Vivian was happy when her mother arrived. The two of them spent most of their days together at the hospital with Mattie until she was discharged. Once Mattie returned home, however, Vivian grew despondent.

"Vivian? You're so distant. Is something wrong?" Sarah asked one day as they sat in the parlor.

"No, Mama, just watching my dreams float off." She looked up to the ceiling.

"What do you mean? What dreams?" her mother asked.

"Nothing, nothing at all. Just wondering what's next for me after—"

"The whole world awaits you, my dear."

"What if I don't want the whole world? What if all I want is to raise my baby in our own little world? *Just the two of us! Without you and Papa deciding everything for me.*" Vivian's voice boomed and Sarah jumped in her seat, but quickly settled herself.

"Now, my dear, I want you to listen to me and listen well."

A chill descended on Vivian as she observed how steely *and* calm her mother had become.

Sarah placed Vivian's chin between her thumb and forefinger. "Are you paying attention *to me* . . . now?"

"Yes, ma'am," Vivian said and stared downward.

"I want you looking at me, missy." Sarah lifted Vivian's head back up, then dropped her hand. "There is no place in the world that your father and I have built for a bastard child."

"Mama! I made a mistake, but I can make it right. I just know I can."

"Yes, you made a mistake, my dear. And that boy made an even bigger one. But our family is not going to pay for it. My parents and Jordan's parents were not too far from slavery. You know how far we've come. Nothing will jeopardize that, young lady. Nothing will besmirch our name, our reputation."

"I can go away, I can—"

"No, you can't. Stop talking foolishness. Your father and I have taken care of this situation. Because that's what this family does—that's what we've always done, and that's what we will always do."

A lone tear rolled down Vivian's face, followed by a torrent. Her mother softened and reached for her.

"I'm so, so sorry about this," Sarah said as she squeezed Vivian. "I wish I could make this all go away. Wish I could carry this burden for you. I love you with all my heart, and someday I hope you'll realize the wisdom in what we've decided."

\* \* \*

A week later, as Vivian brushed her teeth, her water broke and she panicked. She wasn't due for another two weeks or so and she imagined her baby suffering. She put a towel between her legs and wobbled to the second-floor landing, where she called out.

"Mama! Auntie!"

"Not unusual," Josephus said as he stroked Vivian's hand in the hospital room. "This sort of thing happens to young mothers. You and your baby are going to be fine. You've got my word. Just stay calm and I'll be back to check on you." Josephus left, Sarah took his place, and Mattie stood across from her. They both patted Vivian and smoothed the covers.

"It will be all right, won't it?" Vivian asked.

"Of course," Sarah answered. "I need to call your father. He'll be on the next train."

"He's coming to take care of this, I know."

"Vivian, he **does** want to see his grandchild."

"Before he makes it all go away," Vivian said before another contraction started and she winced. "Oh, Mama," she cried out. "It hurts so bad."

"Mattie. Find a phone and call Jordan. He needs to come now."

Vivian labored until just past midnight. She waved goodbye to Sarah and Mattie as the orderly rolled her into the delivery room. As the doors closed, a clap of thunder rang out so loudly that the hospital seemed to shake. And then the rain poured down.

"Little lady, you just leave everything to us. You've got some work to do, but we're here to guide you," Josephus assured her. He positioned his hands between her legs and told her to push but tilted his head upward toward the ceiling when the lights flickered from the growing storm. When he looked down, there she was, squiggling in his hands.

"Well, I'll be a son of a gun. Vivian, she slid out of you without a peep, she did. And with only one heave-ho."

"It's a girl?" Vivian asked.

"Yes! Just listen to her." He slapped her backside and she gurgled. A nurse took the newborn to bathe, measure, weigh, and swath.

"She's a placid baby, Vivian," Josephus declared. "I've delivered a boatload and you don't normally see one of these. And, I don't know, she's kind of nonchalant. Yes, that's the word. She's different as hell. That's what she is." He barely contained his excitement.

The nurse returned and laid her in Vivian's arms. Vivian was lost in her baby's every pore, every hair, every fold of her skin. She watched her eyeballs move back and forth under closed lids, saw how she clenched her fists when she yawned, and smiled when her minute mouth puckered.

"Miss, I need to take her now," the nurse said. "She needs to be fed."

"I can do that! She's not going anywhere."

"Miss, your milk isn't ready," the nurse said. "She needs some formula."

"You're going to take her and I'll never see her again. Can't I feed her just once?" she said and clung to the infant.

The medical staff looked from one to the other and then scrutinized Vivian.

"Vivian, it's best that you don't," Josephus said. "I explained this to you. It creates a bond that's not healthy for either of you," he emphasized.

Vivian's eyes began to tear up. She remembered his warning and she had agreed. But this stirring in her chest? This feeling she had deep inside her soul? No one could have ever prepared her for this. As Vivian bawled, she stroked the baby's face. She cuddled her chin, bent over, kissed her forehead, letting her lips linger. When she pulled away, she saw how her tears had come to spread across her baby's face.

"With my tears of happiness and sorrow, I baptize you, Eva Mathilda. I will love you more than you'll ever know. God bless and protect you."

Vivian's arms dropped to her side as the nurse took her baby away.

## Chapter 20

# SARAH TAKES CHARGE AGAIN

*Cleveland, Ohio, 1942*

The night after Vivian gave birth, Sarah stood on the platform for Jordan to detrain the New York Central. When he descended the stairs, they barely embraced. They walked toward the hall, hands by their sides, with Jordan carrying an overnight grip.

"Dr. Josephus Gray delivered the baby, and he has everything ready at the hospital. He's a fine man and has helped Mattie and Vivian so."

"What's she like?" Jordan asked without looking at his wife.

"She's Monday's child…fair of face, just like the nursery rhyme says. And she's, I don't know, the most self-possessed little baby I've ever seen. Josephus called her placid. Says there aren't many like her." She watched for her husband's reaction, but there was none. He continued to look ahead as Sarah threaded her arm through his.

They took a taxi to the hospital, went to the basement, and

walked down a barely lit corridor to an office, outfitted with a long table where the baby lay in a bassinet. Josephus had been sitting with Alberta and Winston Moore, but all three stood the moment Sarah and Jordan entered the room. Sarah rushed over to her granddaughter, who was clothed in a salmon-colored singlet, with a cap and booties to match.

"My, my. What a beautiful outfit, Alberta," Sarah said, breaking the silence. The room grew quiet again.

"Her name is Eva," Alberta said. "That's what Vivian named her."

"Darlin', this is Dr. Gray and the Moores." Sarah saw how Jordan's lifeless arms hung by his sides and was thankful when no one attempted to shake hands with him.

Jordan fixed his eyes on the infant and the corners of his mouth turned upward. Sarah sighed heavily, relieved that he was allowing himself some emotion. He continued to look at Eva as he backed away and almost tripped.

"Jordan? Are you all right?" Sarah asked.

"Yes, yes. Of course I am." He straightened out his feet.

"Director Sable, why it's a pleasure—" Winston began.

"It's Jordan, please."

"Oh, why thank you, Jordan."

"It is— I—I mean, it's Sarah and I who are grateful." He reached inside his jacket and pulled out a roll of greenbacks thick enough to choke a rhinoceros.

"Jordan, put that money away," Sarah admonished him, horrified.

"I *have* to make sure that this child gets everything she wants." He kept his eyes steadfast on the Moores. "I don't want you to have to strain. I'm prepared to pay for everything the child wants. I mean— I mean everything *you* decide she should have."

"Darlin', you know all about Alberta and Winston. I told you money is not necessary."

"Excuse me, Sarah, but Jordan," Winston interrupted, "you gotta understand something yourself. We don't need your money, don't want your money. You've just given us all we need— your trust. We've prayed for this for so long. Anything little Eva wants, anything. A wardrobe full of dresses, summer vacations wherever she pleases, piano lessons, ballet lessons. She'll get them all. I give you my word."

"Just one moment. There is one thing that *I* wanna add." All heads turned toward Alberta, who had moved away from her husband's side. "We are willing to do everything for Eva. But I want to make sure that she never knows the truth. She has to be all ours. Don't want any confusion . . . never and no matter."

Sarah yanked on Jordan's sleeve and nodded at him.

"Yes," they both said.

Josephus now spoke and pulled Eva's birth certificate and a carbon copy from his satchel. "There's the final matter."

Jordan began to unroll one bill after the other from his wad.

"I've already taken care of this," Sarah said to her husband. "Alberta and Winston. You only need to sign here." She pointed to the lines marked father and mother.

"Take her now, please, and go," Sarah said and they did.

"Before I see my daughter, I need a drink," Jordan said as soon as they left the room.

"I thought we all might." Josephus pulled out a pint of bourbon from his medical bag along with three shot glasses.

*Chapter 21*

# CALVIN GETS SHIPPED OUT

*Bougainville Island, South Pacific, 1943*

Colored troops finally got shipped out from Fort Huachuca. The heat and steam of Bougainville Island in the South Pacific beat any Calvin had endured in East St. Louis. He marveled at the impossibly tall trees. The terrain's underbrush, which ranged from a tangle of roots and branches to forests of twelve-foot, razor-sharp elephant grass and bamboo shoots, not only entrapped the soldiers' feet, but also caused the platoon to lose sight of one another. And then came the mud: knee deep and ubiquitous.

In some ways, he was grateful. Fort Huachuca was no walk in the park. His commanding officers confronted him constantly about the rape in front of the other men, and he was dragged out of bed in the middle of the night and beaten by a faceless gang on countless nights, kicked continuously in his genitals. During the days, they made him double the boot camp exercises. He was set up and provoked into fights, land-ing in solitary confinement more than once, often without food and water for hours on end. But through everything, he would not buckle. He would not cry out. Just as he did when his father beat him, he floated to another place in his head so he did not have to feel the pain. The other soldiers could not break him, despite the bruises, deep cuts, and agonizing pain. At some point, befuddled, they gave up taunting and torturing him, and instead pretended he did not exist. He was not spoken to or regarded, other than to convey orders.

Now, in the jungle, he had only just gotten accustomed to the way sweat streamed from his forehead, stinging his eyes and lips. Assigned to the Graves Registration Service, his job was to search for dead GIs and dig holes to bury them. He'd stopped puking at the sight of mangled men, their open wounds filled with coagulated blood. However, he never got used to the corpses' heft. *Never understood what that meant—"dead weight's heavier"—until now.* And he'd almost forgotten what sleep felt like. Day after day, he and his squad waited until the shooting, firing, and bombing stopped in order to pick through battle areas like vultures scavenging for carrion. Two men shared each four-handled litter to transport the bodies.

Calvin grew thinner each day, although he stuffed all his allotted rations down his throat and even picked the pock-ets of the dead for leftover scraps, like most of the troops did. As he and his partner, Frankie, secreted themselves in the dense vegetation awaiting the call to action, Calvin hugged his knees to keep them from trembling. He imagined himself under Miss Bertha's porch, but now he was hiding from the war rather than from his father. *Why didn't my mama take me with her? My daddy beat me twice as hard after she left and cursed her name long after she was gone. It's all her fault. I wouldn't be here about to die. I would—*

"Double time," the sergeant shouted.

Calvin cuddled himself more tightly and felt his body grow numb. *If I move, I'm gonna die.*

"C'mon, we gotta go," Frankie said, slid his boot under Calvin's buttocks, and nudged him upward. Calvin unwrapped himself and stood as straight and rigid as a tree trunk.

"Pick up those handles, ya jackass!" Frankie screamed as he grabbed the front two.

Calvin did so, but then froze in place and dropped them. Frankie almost fell backward from the full heft of the stretcher behind him. He turned toward Calvin.

"Shoot me!" Calvin yelled. "I want ya to kill me, ya hear?" He started to run toward the sound of gunfire in the distance, but Frankie stopped him, swung him around, and slapped him across the face.

"Ya ain't goin' crazy on me. We gotta job to do."

Another colored soldier joined them, took one of Calvin's handgrips, forced Calvin to take the other, and pushed him along. They all started moving as fast as they could along a pencil-thin trail. When they reached the combat area, they began their rummaging, and immediately found a motionless soldier. Frankie felt for a pulse, found none, and on count, the three of them lifted the lifeless body and placed it on the cot that lay open on the ground. Before they stood, Calvin gaped at the dead boy's face. *He's small like me. Can't be more than eighteen. Same as me.* As they hustled along, a land mine exploded ahead of them, pitching them into the air. Calvin landed on top of the corpse, face-to-face.

"Ah," the boy sighed. Calvin jumped up and eyed the body.

"Are you—" he started.

"Ah," came out of the boy's mouth again.

"Help!" Calvin screamed. "This one's alive." He looked around. A full-fledged skirmish had started up and the noise blotted out his call. He bent down over the boy.

"I'm dying," the voice rattled.

"No, no. We'll get ya—"

"Just a prayer?"

"I don't know—"

"Please..."

Calvin struggled. "The Lord is my shepherd. Our Father in heaven. I'm sorry, but I don't know nothin' else."


When Calvin opened his eyes, he saw a low-hanging black ceiling fan above him. He found his left arm attached to an IV drip and his right leg in traction. His chest was bandaged, and pains shot through him every time he took a breath. And then he started to shake. "What happened to me?" he coughed out, and then looked side to side and found cots filled with Negro soldiers.

A colored nurse approached him. "You have to rest," she said.

"Where's my squad?"

The nurse looked away and then back down at him. "They didn't make it. Only you survived."

"And that lil' white boy?"

"White boy?"

"The one I landed on top of, that one. He was still alive, I tell ya," Calvin insisted.

"You need to calm down. Just be thankful that you're the lucky one who made it."

"No, no. I gotta know. Tell me."

"They found you in a foxhole. You either landed there or someone dragged you to it. That's all I know. You must be quiet now. Sleep." He watched as she added a liquid to his IV.

The next time Calvin opened his eyes, a colored man with a cross around his neck stood next to his bed.

"I'm Chaplain Charles Foster. But just call me Bud. I hope I can become your buddy. What do you think?" The man leaned closer to Calvin.

"I don't know nothin' right now, suh."

"It's Bud. Call me Bud, okay?"

"Okay."

"And you're Calvin Cahill, right?"

"Ya gotta help me," Calvin pleaded.

"That's why I'm here."

"I think I'm losin' my mind. I landed on top of a dead white boy when that mine went off and he woke up and talked to me. Made me pray for him. And then I passed out, but they're saying they found me in a ditch. That can't be." Calvin squirmed on his cot.

"Now, I'm going to help you figure all this out," the chaplain said. "But you have to be still; you have to heal."

The next day the chaplain returned and prayed over him.

"I'm leaving you this for comfort." He put a psalm book in his palm.

"I don't read too good."

"By the time I'm finished with you, you will be reading as well as I do. I've helped a lot of our colored troops improve."

"Don't just confine yourself to preachin', huh?"

"This is a way to preach, Calvin. Our people must be educated. It's power, and we need all we can get in this white man's world. Don't forget that when you leave here."

"When I get outta here…" Calvin began.

"Yes? What are you going to do? Do you know?"

Calvin started to cry.

"What is making you sad? Tell me," Bud encouraged him.

"I can't."

"Well, you rest now. I hope one day you'll confide in me. Or you can take your troubles directly to the Lord. He always listens."

Over the next week, the chaplain visited Calvin daily.

"Bud? Do ya think I talked to a dead man?"

"I don't know what you saw, but whatever happened, you prayed."

"I learned from my church. I got baptized in the Mississippi when I was nine years old."

"Glad to know that, son."

"Never had a man call me son before." He closed his eyes and smiled.

"Your father never…"

Calvin turned his head away. "No. All my daddy did was call me a runt and beat the livin' daylights outta me whenever he could get his hands on me. He fell down the stairs trying to catch me once." Calvin attempted to laugh but his aching ribs stopped him. He looked back at the chaplain. "Say it again, please. Call me that."

"Son."

"Sounds so nice. Ya got one?"

"A son? Yes, I do."

"He's lucky. Wonder if that dead white boy had a father. Dead, then alive. He was young like me. He talked to me. I know he did."

"The Lord comes in all shapes, and he may have talked to you through that boy. I don't know. But count it as a blessing."

Calvin's recovery continued in a makeshift rehabilitation center, packed with other colored soldiers. The chaplain prayed over all the men each day and spent individual time with several of them. He'd always save Calvin for last, encouraging him to reveal more of himself during each visit.

"Well, I'm good with numbers, and my mama's best friend, Miss Bertha, kept me lookin' sharp, and I can fix stuff, too. Helped her around the house."

As his health improved, he became more prepared to unload his sins on the chaplain.

"Bud?" he called out as the chaplain approached. "I'm ready to tell ya, even if ya end up hatin' me."

"Nothing to fear there, my son."

"But, Bud. It's bad and I like ya so much. I want ya to like me, too," Calvin started.

"But I already do, Calvin. You can go straight to the Lord if it's too hard for you."

"But I gotta tell somebody. It's too heavy for me."

"Tell me when you're ready."

"I can't hold it back no more. I been with a lot of girls. They mostly gave in, but this one. She didn't and I made her. I knocked her out and left her on a stone-cold floor."

Bud made Calvin clasp his hands and repeat each phrase of Psalm 51 after him.

*Be merciful to me, O God,*
*because of your constant love.*
*Because of your great mercy*
*wipe away my sins!*
*Wash away all my evil*
*and make me clean from my sin!*

"Repeat these words every day until you know them by heart. But they alone aren't enough to absolve you."

"I'll do anythin'. Just tell me," Calvin pleaded.

"You must face the one you harmed." Bud paused. "And beg her pardon. Do you understand?"

Calvin nodded and hugged the chaplain.

Calvin attacked his rehabilitation as feverishly as the Japanese tried to obliterate the Allies just a few miles away. He began each morning by reciting the psalm on his knees, although it caused him great pain since his leg had yet to heal. He ended his day the same way.

"Calvin, you got religion now?" the head nurse from the field hospital asked him one evening as he struggled to pull himself onto his cot.

"I want to be like the chaplain."

"A minister?"

"No, but a good man. I want to walk out of here cleansed."

On one of Chaplain Foster's daily visits with Calvin, the chief physician arrived.

"Bud, I'm glad you're here." He turned toward Calvin. "I've got some news for you. Mind if the chaplain hears it, too?"

"Course not. He's like a father—"

"Yes"—the chaplain looked at the doctor—"he's like a son to me."

The doctor pulled up a chair and sat close to Calvin.

"Calvin, you've worked hard here. Done everything possible and more to strengthen your leg. But no matter what you do, your leg will never be the same. I was there when they brought you in. We had so many casualties that day. Your leg wasn't bleeding so the medic hardly looked at the bones when he set it. No more field duty for you. You'll be working in scullery. Take care, soldier," the doctor said, then left.

Calvin turned toward the chaplain.

"It's all right. The Lord will provide. You've taught me that. Guess I was just meant to be small, smaller even now."

"You're still heads taller than many. You're turning yourself inside out for the Lord, son," the chaplain told him.

"Can ya baptize me again?"

"No need."

"Ya sure? I sinned somethin' terrible."

"You've made up for it. No need."

Calvin hung his head. "Still haven't done enough. Still haven't asked her to forgive me."

"But you will, won't you?"

"As soon as I get back. That's the first thing I'll do. I swear."

Calvin started his shift in the officers' mess as soon as he was able; it began at daybreak and ended just after lunch. After a week of sitting at a table, cleaning, peeling, and slicing vegetables, he craved more strenuous work. He wanted to *feel* his remorse. So he buried himself into the platoon assigned with restocking the field with munitions as they were organizing their next foray. He located a boy just about his height and skin tone.

"Hey," he called to him.

"Yeah, what ya want?"

"Wanna take yo' place."

"Ya nuts?"

"I don't care. I gotta do more."

"Each time I go out there, I know it's my last. And ya got a limp." The boy pointed at Calvin's bum leg. "This'll hurt ya."

"I told ya. I don't care. I gotta do more. Let's trade dog tags in case the sergeant says something."

"He won't. Tryin' to save his own ass. Just shouts orders and barely knows us. Are ya sure?"

Calvin nodded and they switched identities that day and every day thereafter.

No one paid him any mind and he always managed to escape the sergeant's command. He hobbled along, without a complaint. Each painful step a self-imposed addition to his penance, he thought. He came to welcome the physical torment at night as he tried to sleep.

The war ended in September 1945, but the armed services' demobilization process was protracted and colored troops were some of the last soldiers to be brought home. By mid-1946,

Calvin received an honorable discharge and headed to East St. Louis. As he walked from the train station, carrying everything he owned stuffed into his backpack, Black men tipped their hats and Black women beamed his way. For the first time in his life, he felt appreciated. He headed straight to Miss Bertha's and before he mounted the stairs, he peeked under her porch. *Don't have to hide anymore because I got the Lord on my side.* Calvin eased up the front steps of her house and knocked.

"Miss Bertha? It's me. Calvin." He heard footsteps.

The door flew open, and Miss Bertha hiked him up in her arms, and backed into her living room. She put him down and almost burst at her seams.

"Why bless yo' heart, Calvin. Thought ya was dead by now. But look at ya! All growed up and wearin' a uniform. Did ya enlist? Never a figured ya for that. Why looks like ya might even got a wee bit taller."

Calvin pointed to his right leg. "Other way around, Miss Bertha. But the army is going to make it right. Give me some shoes to even things out. Maybe even another operation."

She looked him over. "Well, ya bigger in my eyes." She hugged him again and kissed the side of his face. "Now let me fix ya somethin' to eat. I wanna hear all 'bout wherever ya was."

He followed her to the kitchen.

"Ya never wrote me," Bertha admonished.

"Couldn't. Didn't know how, but now I do. Chaplain Foster helped me. With reading, too."

"A white man did all that?"

"No, a colored chaplain. He schooled us. Made us understand that we got to get educated. And made a Christian out of me."

"Yo' mama would be so proud. Sounds like a nice man."

"He let me call him Bud and he called me son." Calvin looked at the floor and went silent.

"What ya thinkin' 'bout?"

"My daddy still around?"

"Ain't seen hide nor hair. Heard he finally got run outta town for foolin' with somebody's wife. Don't think he's comin' back. Could even be dead."

"Don't feel much for him but pity."

"Ya sure is a Christian, now ain't ya?" She laughed and Calvin smiled at her.

"Guess I am. And my mama?"

"Sugar. I don't know nothin'. But she loved ya, remember that."

"And I forgave her, too. Know she did what she had to."

"But that Rocco. He's an even bigger hoodlum now and he's gunnin' for ya. Says ya run off with his money. Brings up yo' name whenever he sees me. Always askin' if I heard from ya, where ya at."

"I don't fear him, either, Miss Bertha."

"I believe in Jesus, too. Ya know that, but Satan's pretty powerful and I'd get outta here quick."


Everything at the Jordan W. Sable Funeral Parlor and Mortuary Home looked more or less the same as it had the last time Calvin saw it, except grass covered the sprawling front lawn. He hid in the bushes just as he had when he awaited Vivian's signal four years earlier. But now he waited for nothingness to cover the building's facade instead of an unlit candle in the window.

Waited for complete silence, total darkness, and the absence of a living soul.

Chaplain Foster had addressed the envelope to Vivian in cursive and added his name and return address in the upper left-hand corner. He and Calvin reasoned it was the only way she would open it. With the chaplain's help, Calvin had crafted the letter in proper English.

*Dear Miss Vivian Sable,*

*I know there is nothing I can do to repair the damage I did to you. You were so kind to me, so innocent and pure, and I robbed you of something precious. I only hope that you have been able to go forward with your life and that you have found, or will find, sacred love with a man who deserves you.*

*Please know how truly sorry I am, how much I have suffered, and how, if possible, I would undo the wrong I did you. I know there is no way I can receive your forgiveness but I ask it of you all the same.*

*You were the best person I have ever known in my life.*

*Thanks to Chaplain Foster and the military, I believe I have become a better person and I have found Christ.*

*With my deepest regret,*
*Calvin Cahill*

When the last light in the funeral home went off, he crossed the street and started up the driveway, clutching his apology with both hands. He stopped suddenly when someone grabbed him by the neck, jerked him backward, and almost cut off his windpipe.

"You stole my money and then skipped town. Well, you won't be skipping ever again."

Calvin didn't need to turn around. He knew the voice and the threat remained fresh in his mind.

Rocco stuck his knee in the crook of Calvin's back and bent him back even more to immobilize him.

"Wanna make sure I got ya just where I want ya."

Calvin felt the knife enter his back just below his left shoulder blade. Rocco jabbed it in farther and gave it a full turn before pulling it out. Calvin dropped to his knees and fell on his back. He looked up and saw Rocco's upside-down face hovering above him.

"Shoulda never come back here." Rocco leaned down and cleaned his blade as he ran it back and forth across Calvin's overcoat. He watched as blood filled Calvin's mouth. "Well, all done here." He slipped the weapon into his pocket and disappeared from Calvin's view.

Calvin's mind ran back to the soothing waters of his baptism, his mother's prideful hug, Miss Bertha's refuge, and how Bud had called him son. Vivian's face hovered above him, wrapped in a pink aura.

He offered her the letter, but she refused it.

"I don't have to read it. I know what it says." Her face faded as quickly as it had appeared. Calvin closed his eyes and relished the moment, but then he felt someone jiggle his shoulder. He looked upward and saw Big Will towering over him. He spit out as much blood as he could.

"Big Will," he whispered, and held up the letter with both hands. "She has to read it. *Please.*"

Big Will stared down at Calvin's body. "How dare ya come back here? I let ya off the hook once. But you'll be dead for real now."

Big Will took the envelope and put it in his pocket as Calvin choked and stopped breathing.

# Epilogue

Eva Mathilda Moore felt giddy as she walked the corridors of Northwestern University's economics department. It was her first choice among all the schools that had accepted her into their PhD programs, and the only place she really wanted to go. She arrived early for her first appointment with her graduate student adviser, and paused outside his office, counting the minutes on her watch. She closed her eyes and took a deep breath, inhaling the scent of the seasoned wood and the mustiness of time-worn books. She smoothed out her gray pleated, calf-length wool skirt and tugged slightly on the Peter Pan collar of her white blouse. She plucked a lone piece of lint off the long, thick sweater that she'd added to her standard outfit in preparation for the September winds from Lake Michigan.

Her mother had always preferred her to wear frilly, pastel frocks, but Eva often balked, finding them impractical and too eye-catching. She'd only succumbed to her mother's taste on two occasions. Her parents had died within six months of each other and for both funerals, she dug out one of the many flouncy pink dresses her mother had made for the parties Eva never attended. She ignored the chuckles as she followed the coffins in and out of the church. Eva sighed out loud as she pondered the sad fact that neither parent had lived to see her enter graduate school. The appointed hour arrived, so she knocked enthusiastically on her adviser's door.

"Come in."

A blond man rifled through a stack of papers on his desk without looking up.

"Excuse me, sir," Eva said.

He raised his head and squinched his pea-green eyes at her.

"I don't need any cleaning right now. You're supposed to come after hours."

"I beg your pardon," Eva replied.

"There's no need for you now. Come back later, I said." He waved her off.

"I am Eva Moore. We have an appointment."

"What? **You** are Eva Moore? But you're a Negro." He gulped.

"Well, that's apparent." She took a step closer to his desk.

"And an uppity one at that!" he huffed.

"I only affirmed what you said." Eva's eyes began to burn.

"Well, I wasn't expecting someone such as yourself. There's nothing in your documents that says anything about your race. And you went to Western Reserve! They have an excellent undergraduate program in econ." He scratched his head and frowned as he stared at her.

"Yes, *I know*," she answered crisply.

"Well, I still need to speak with the department chair and get back to you." He again motioned for her to leave but Eva didn't move.

"Why is that?" she asked.

"This is a very challenging program—"

"I could have gone to a number of other demanding schools, but I wanted Northwestern," she interrupted.

The man looked befuddled, opened his mouth, but remained silent.

"Others?" he finally blurted out.

"Yes, many others. I was admitted to Columbia, Princeton, and even the University of Chicago." Eva walked up to his desk as she spoke.

"Well, I will still need to consult with, with, with someone."

"And I still need to know why?"

When he didn't answer her, she leaned over, and put her fists on his desk. "I didn't hear your answer, sir," she insisted.

Startled, he pushed his chair back from his desk.

"I have no time for this, girl. Please." He pointed his hand toward the door.

"Girl? I will not spend my inheritance to be insulted!"

"*Your inheritance?* You are surely joking," he said with a smirk.

She turned her back to him and walked out.

Eva fumed as she rushed away from the adviser's office. A weight settled down on her shoulders. In all of Eva's twenty-two years, she had never realized how fiercely her parents had shielded her from the world. She had lived in a warm, welcoming neighborhood where everyone knew her name, even before she did. The Negro teachers at the schools she had attended expected and accepted nothing less than her best, and they had encouraged all the youngsters to pursue their dreams, no matter how lofty. Western Reserve's student body was largely Caucasian, but she had glided through its rigorous program as a day student, almost unnoticed, and had never reflected on her white classmates.

And now, here she was. She had inherited more money than she knew what to do with from her parents. She certainly wasn't going to throw it into the coffers of an institution that didn't need it and that would, in all likelihood, treat her as an underprivileged student with remedial needs. She knew she was going to withdraw, but she also knew she'd have to wait a year to begin another graduate program. And now she doubted that she even wanted to continue down this PhD path. Eva always had a plan but, for the first time in her life, she felt adrift.

She pushed open the double doors at the end of the hall and filled her lungs with fresh air. Then she began to systematically assess her skills. She enjoyed and excelled at theorems, equations, formulas, logic, statistics, probability—mathematics in general. She had little use for or competency in social interactions. Her parents were so adept at dealing with people. Her mother, Alberta, as a seamstress, delighted in chatting mindlessly with her customers as she fitted them and served them tea and sweets. Her father held on to a stream of clients for his insurance company with charm and banter. All this bewildered Eva, and when confronted with having to make decisions about how to handle his business after her father died, she eagerly passed the reins over to the family attorney.

She also liked geography; the world outside Midwestern America seemed worth investigating. And she loved to eat, although never had the knack for cooking nor any interest in becoming a chef. *Perhaps a stop by the university's counseling office might further spark some more ideas*, she thought. Eva headed there and looked at the job announcements on the bulletin board, tidily arranged according to academic major. Under **Economics**, her eyes locked on an ad for the United States Foreign Service that, besides explaining the application process, read:

> The U.S. State Department encourages applicants with economics degrees to apply due to a current shortage of officers in this specialty.

*Hmm,* she thought. *Economics, travel, and foreign cuisines.*

Eva unpinned one copy from the bunch affixed to the board and shoved it into her purse. She now knew her next step. She needed to go home to Miss Mattie, her mother's best friend, who had a solution for any dilemma. For as long as she could remember, Eva had spent part of every Saturday in her kitchen, soaking up her wisdom and watching her cook up a storm. Eva took a train leaving for Cleveland from Chicago's Union Station that afternoon and arrived at Mattie's door the next morning.

"You did what, Eva?" Mattie exclaimed as soon as Eva explained what had happened. They both sat down at the kitchen table.

"I just couldn't stay there." Eva turned away.

"And I'm so proud of you." Mattie swung her around and hugged her, but Eva pulled back.

"You are? I mean you aren't disappointed that I didn't face the adversity and stick with my plan?" Eva asked quizzically.

"Oh no, my darlin'. This is *your* life. You've never been mistreated and there's no reason to start now. You did the right thing!"

"It seems like I did, but now I feel so lost. Without a map to follow and cling to." Eva finally let the tears flow, the ones she had been holding on to ever since she'd left the adviser's office. She sobbed, harder and louder than she ever had in her life.

"Oh, my darlin', come here," Mattie said and embraced Eva.

"Without you, Miss Mattie, I'd have no one. That's all I know. You'll help me figure out what to do, won't you?"

"Of course, I will."

"I do have one idea." Eva pulled back, dug into her pocketbook, and pulled out the job offering. "But it might be too rash. Or even impossible."

"Nothing is impossible. You remember that I've said it to you a thousand times. What are you thinking of doing?"

"Look! They want economics grads," Eva said as she gave the slip of paper to Mattie.

"My, my," Mattie said as she looked at the paper. "This would be quite a step." She chuckled. "They could send you anywhere on this planet."

"I've wanted to travel ever since you showed me all your geography books." Eva sat up straighter, buoyed by the idea.

"Darlin', from what I know of this State Department, here, it's full of white men, most of them just like the one at Northwestern." Mattie stared deeply into Eva's eyes. "Are you sure you want to take this on?"

"That's why I came to you. To talk about it, think it through." Eva took the sheet and flattened it on the table.

"It's an exciting opportunity, that's for sure. And I'm sure as sure can be that you would get in, smart as you are, but..." Mattie hesitated.

"But what, Miss Mattie?"

Mattie now looked straight at Eva. "You'll be out there, some-where in this whole, wide world, all alone. Doesn't that worry you?"

"Not really." Eva put a forefinger to her temple, rested her elbow on the table, and then continued. "No, no, not at all, in fact. I've always enjoyed my own company and never had much of a need to socialize. Mama and Papa are gone now, so I wouldn't feel as if I'd be abandoning them. You'd be the only one I'd be leaving."

"And I'd miss you terribly."

"But you could travel to see me." Eva got more excited at the thought of Miss Mattie visiting her. "If Dr. Josephus wouldn't mind, that is," she added.

"My husband loves you almost as much as I do. And I still make my own decisions. So, of course. He may even join me. But no matter what you say, I'm concerned about you being so far away, all by yourself."

Mattie bit her lip.

"Miss Mattie? What is it? Is there something bothering you? Something else you want to tell me?" Eva probed.

"Yes, Eva, I do." Mattie spoke deliberately.

"More reservations? Another warning of some sort about this position?" Eva queried.

"It's nothing like that." Mattie now clutched the tabletop's edge with her fingers.

"Tell me, please. You know how much I value your advice."

"Eva, on her deathbed, your mother and my dear, dear friend, Alberta, wanted me to tell you the truth when the time came. She even made me swear. And I believe that time has come." Mattie clasped her hands together.

"They weren't my parents," Eva said with certainty.

"How did you know?" Mattie leaned closer to Eva.

"Well, first of all, we didn't look anything alike. Mama and Papa were dark, squat, and roly-poly, sort of like the chestnuts you roast for the holidays." She grinned. "I'm light-skinned and more like a bean pole. I've even got a few freckles that pop out in the sunshine. Mama pressed her hair, but I don't have to. I can tame mine with a few strokes of a brush and a bobby pin or two. And her hair was so dark. Look at mine. It's almost auburn, wouldn't you say?" She pulled a lock of hair in front of her face.

At this point, Eva watched as Mattie took a hankie from her apron pocket and started fanning herself. "You are really something, girl. All this thinking and reasoning."

"I even asked them once about our differences."

"You *did*?" Mattie's eyes widened as she spoke. "*And?*"

"They told me there were some Scots-Irish and full-blooded Indians in our family tree. But there weren't any photos of anybody in the house, so why should I have believed them?" She waited. "Miss Mattie, was I adopted?"

Mattie cleared her throat before responding. "Yes, darlin'."

"I knew it. I knew I was right!" Eva almost jumped up from her seat. "Do you know anything about my real parents?"

"About one of them, I do. Your mother."

"Tell me! Tell me! I want to know all about her. What did she look like? What does she do? Where does she live?"

The questions tumbled out of Eva with glee, but when Mattie backed away a bit, Eva paused and said, "She's still alive, isn't she? She *has* to be."

"Yes, darlin', very much so." Mattie stood up. "I'll be right back."

Eva heard Mattie walk up to the second floor. In the meantime, she gazed around the kitchen, a place that had brought her so much joy. She'd spent hours here as a child, watching Mattie prepare food when she had her catering business, licking spoons, and tasting samples of new recipes. She always felt safe and sound, as if she belonged in this woman's home. Mattie returned quickly, holding an ornate, medium-sized picture frame.

"This, my dear, is your mother." She placed the black-and-white photo in front of Eva on the table and sat next to her. "When she was just a few years younger than you are now."

Eva lifted it and peered at it in silence. She noticed how the shape of her mother's jaw mirrored her own, how a few freckles were sprinkled across her nose and cheeks, and how the texture of her hair was the same as hers. She couldn't identify the color of her eyes, but their shape seemed exactly like hers.

"We favor one another, don't we?" Eva said as she glanced at Mattie.

"Yes, very much so," Mattie answered.

"But why do you have this?" Eva asked while continuing to inspect the image in the frame.

"Let me boil some water. I need a cup of tea." Mattie walked to the stove. She put on the kettle, sat back down, and took Eva's hands in hers. "You are my niece's child."

Disbelief spread across Eva's face, and then settled into a relaxed smile.

"Oh, Miss Mattie, I've always felt a kind of kinship with you, but I didn't dream of this. You are my great-aunt!"

Eva grabbed Mattie and squeezed her so tightly that their chairs almost tipped toward each other.

"Yes, that's what I am to you," Mattie said when they let go of one another.

"And my mother? I want to know more."

"Well, her name is Vivian. She stayed here with me throughout her pregnancy and we all got to know the Moores. They wanted children so badly, but never had any. And we had to ensure that your upbringing would be safe and secure, so we decided…"

"Who did?" Eva asked.

"It was done as a family, even though your mother didn't…"

"Want me?"

"Oh no, no! She wanted you more than anything in the world. I write to her and tell her about you all the time. I even sent her your graduation picture, with you in your cap and gown, looking so radiant!"

"But I can meet her now, can't I? The Moores are gone and…"

"Eva, when you were born, your mother was so very young. When she had to give you up she lost a piece of herself. She doesn't know about the promise I made to Alberta, and it's been a secret for so long, that we just have to be…thoughtful. Or careful." Mattie paused before continuing. "You should know that she does have another family now."

"Another family?" Eva whispered.

"Yes, you have a brother and a sister. And I don't know if they know about you." Mattie pulled Eva into her arms. "Just as this was the right time for you to know the truth of your birth, the day will come for you to meet your mother…and your siblings."

"I understand," Eva said slowly. "I've waited all this time without knowing. I will be patient. But I want to know everything. Everything!"

"Well, my love, to know your mother, you have to go back a little bit further and know about her mother, and her father. You are descended from a truly amazing family. From people who have always had their own, fought for their own, protected their own. And I will tell you everything. From the start."

They hung on to each other until the teakettle that they'd both forgotten started to sing.

# *Why I Wrote This Book*

I was born at the cusp of the modern civil rights movement in St. Louis, Missouri, a Jim Crow town that was beginning a problematic tug-of-war with desegregating its public facilities. My parents threw their hat in this ring by taking an unheard-of step: they moved into an all-white neighborhood that would remain so for decades. It befuddled their friends and gave me daunting challenges growing up there. And it was a far cry from the segregated Black community that had nurtured them as youngsters and had turned them into successful and coura- geous adults in spite of the blatant racism they confronted.

Their stories of growing up in its bosom fascinated me: daz- zling formals in a Black-owned penthouse or someone's man- sion; smaller parties and gatherings where anyone, including Cab Calloway, Lena Horne, Thurgood Marshall, and Leontyne Price, might show up; and solid institutions (restaurants, news- papers, mortuaries, shops of every stripe) that Blacks owned where there was never a question of being "refused service." They spent their time with and money on each other. My mother always said that the only white people she encountered were life insurance peddlers, grocers at the farmer's market downtown, and the tire salesmen who kept her parents' funeral home's stable of cars rolling.

Yet this type of pre-1950s Black community, tightly knit and largely upwardly mobile, with a common mission to defeat Jim Crow, had scarcely been documented or celebrated. So I wrote my family memoir, *At the Elbows of My Elders: One Family's Journey Toward Civil Rights*, in homage to them and their ignored history.

*The Sable Cloak* was born from this book. When my friend Ramona Harper recounted a grisly story about how a colored community dealt with crime in her grandmother's day, I had a compelling starting point for my novel. But where was the rest? It turned out that the *rest* resided in my memoir. People I had written about began popping into my head. Among them, there was Jordan Chambers, a prosperous undertaker and, above all, political boss who controlled the Black vote in my hometown for decades; my grandmother, who not only ran her own funeral establishment but also powdered, dressed, and embalmed many a corpse; her numerous sisters, one funnier and more determined than the next, and all wizards in the kitchen; and my mother's imposing yet taciturn nanny named Big Will. "Who better to serve as my characters?"

Since leaving my day jobs (university teaching and diplomacy), my mission has been to reveal the accomplishments of overlooked Black Americans, who succeeded in the face of prodigious odds, served as examples for their progeny, and set in motion a social movement without end.

*The Sable Cloak* is my latest effort. I hope I have done them justice.

—Gail Milissa Grant
Fall 2022

# Acknowledgments

*The Sable Cloak* displays Gail Milissa Grant's dedication to work, passion, and creativity. Sadly, after a battle with metastatic cancer, my sister Gail passed away in May 2024 at her home in Rome, Italy. Her final achievement was to deliver into the hands of her publisher the final draft of her first and only novel. Fortunately, she also was able to approve the colorful book cover she had envisioned. While she is no longer with us to personally express her gratitude, I would like to acknowledge, as her brother on her behalf, the individuals and organizations who played pivotal roles in bringing her work to life.

First and foremost, thanks go to Gail's husband Gaetano Castelli, her nieces Amara and Dana Stuehling, and her stepchildren Chiara and Cristiano Castelli. Their continuous love inspired and fortified her literary dreams. Gail would especially want to call out our parents, Mildred and David M. Grant, and all her ancestors whose spirits whispered softly as she endeavored to write this book.

Gail would certainly want to acknowledge her closest sister-friends, Angelique Electra and June Baldwin. They provided a cloister of unwavering love and essential support especially as Gail lived so far away. Gail would also acknowledge the Vision Board Group in Rome, which fueled her determination to accomplish this lifelong goal.

Gail had many friends in the US, Italy, and around the world. They enriched her life as she powered not only through the years of writing *The Sable Cloak* but also, with grace and tenacity, through her recurring illness.

Appreciation goes to Gail's literary agent and friend, Cherise Fisher. Her commitment and belief in Gail's talent and efforts were instrumental in navigating the journey from manuscript to publication. Further, the Wendy Sherman Associates literary agency early on recognized the promise of this novel and steadfastly supported its publication.

A heartfelt thanks goes to Karen Kosztolnyik, Mari C. Okuda, Shasta Clinch, Kamrun Nesa, and the entire team at Grand Central Publishing. Their expertise, excitement, and commitment to the book have ensured that Gail's vision was brought to the readers with the care it deserves.

Finally, Gail would laud you, the readers, for bringing to fruition, by your own imaginations, the world she has placed before us. Thanks to you, you keep her spirit alive.

—David W. Grant
February 2025

# About the Author

**Gail Milissa Grant**, author, public speaker, and former US Foreign Service officer, was born on May 5, 1949, in St. Louis, Missouri, to civil rights activist and lawyer David M. Grant and Mildred Grant. She dedicated her life to cultural understanding and civil rights advocacy.

Graduating from Washington University and Howard University, and after teaching art and architectural history at Howard, she embarked on a diplomatic career in 1980. As a Foreign Service officer with the US Information Agency and the US State Department, she was assigned to Norway, France, West Africa, and Brazil, and did extensive press advance work for three US presidents on four continents. Retiring in 2001, she pursued writing full-time, publishing the acclaimed memoir *At the Elbows of My Elders: One Family's Journey Toward Civil Rights* in 2008, showcasing the civil rights advocacy and history of her accomplished family. Ms. Grant presented her book and lectured on civil rights history at more than eighty venues, including Oxford University, Columbia University, New York University, Mohammed V University in Morocco, the Smithsonian Institution, and numerous US embassies throughout

Europe. The book won the Benjamin Franklin Book of the Year 2009 for autobiography/memoir and also received an Award of Merit from the American Association for State and Local History.

In 2006, she married Gaetano Castelli, a renowned stage designer, and lived the remainder of her life with him in Rome, Italy.